TOUCHING EVIL

ALSO BY KYLIE BRANT

TOUCHING EVIL

THE CIRCLE OF EVIL TRILOGY, BOOK 2

KYLIE BRANT

THOMAS & MERCER

Published by Thomas & Mercer, Seattle

www.apub.com

Amazon, the Amazon logo, and Thomas & Mercer are trademarks of Amazon.com, Inc., or its affiliates.

ISBN-13: 9781477829806
ISBN-10: 1477829806

Cover design by Marc J. Cohen

Printed in the United States of America

For John—the one I live with, laugh with, and love.

Prologue

I'm sorry, Mommy. I'm really, really sorry."

He stared at her in the darkened room, his heart thudding hard enough to jump right out of his chest. Mommy didn't say anything. Just stared and stared, with mean on her face. In her eyes.

Dread prickled over his skin. The words tumbled from his lips. "I didn't leave my baseball glove at the park on purpose. But I could go find it now, I bet. Can I, Mommy? Can I ride my bike to the park and get it? I'll be right back. Promise."

But Mommy didn't answer. And his stomach sank down to his toes. He was only five, but he already knew what it meant when she looked at him like that.

Other mommies gave hugs and kisses. He saw them in the park sometimes with their kids. They smiled and laughed, and if they got mad, their voices got high and sharp. Mommy's quiet was worse. Way worse. Quiet meant Mommy was going to open his bedroom door and let a monster into his room again. A monster that was big and smelled bad. A monster that was going to hurt him in his private places and make him scream and scream and scream.

He ran to hide in his bedroom closet, but Mommy got there first. She stood in front of the door and folded her arms, still staring.

So he turned and ran toward his bed. Crawled under it, quick as a bunny. Curled up in a little ball and continued to shake.

He could no longer see Mommy's face. Only her feet and part of her jeans. "Hey, Curt!" she called out. "Come meet my son."

His shorts got wet, and pee trickled down his legs to puddle on the cracked linoleum floor beneath him. Heavy footsteps clomped down the hallway. Paused at his door.

The monster.

As the door began to creak open, Mommy walked to the bed. Crouched way down to smile at him. An awful, terrible smile. And in that instant he realized that Mommy was a monster, too.

And someday she was going to have to die.

Chapter 1

C'mon, Jonah. Don't be such a wimp."

"You try carrying a pony keg on your shoulder. Through the woods. At night." Jonah Davis puffed as he stumbled on the winding path. Branches of scrub bushes scratched at his arms and snagged on his jeans. How the hell had he gotten stuck doing all the work while Spencer Pals got to help Trina Adams over every fallen branch and around each tangle of brambles?

'Cuz Jonah had been a dumbass. He'd figured to impress Trina by being all macho and shit. Yeah, she was going to be real impressed about the time he fell over of a heart attack and the keg knocked her on her fine little ass.

She turned, flashlight in her hand, to give him a melting look. "Are you sure you're okay, Jonah? You should make Spencer take a turn. That's so heavy."

His chest swelled. "I've got it. You just watch out for Spence. He thinks these woods are haunted. He's liable to piss himself if he hears a noise."

"Fuck you," Spence said.

She gave a tinkling laugh, and the sound of it went straight to Jonah's groin. Before today Trina Adams had never so much as glanced his way in the hallways of Valley High, but there was nothing like the promise of a kegger to help people make friends. He'd looked at her, though. He'd looked plenty. She was Jennifer Lawrence hot with a smokin' body that would look even finer under his.

Before the night was over, he was going to know that from personal experience. Sometime after this keg was gone and she was feeling awfully friendly toward the guy who'd carried the damn thing the whole way.

"Sh-h." Spence threw out an arm to stop Trina from going any farther. Probably copped a feel while he was at it, too. He was that type of guy. "I think I heard something."

"Here we go." But Jonah was none too sorry to put the pony keg down. Even if they hadn't yet reached their usual party spot. "Is it a ghost, Spence? Or maybe a zombie." In an aside to Trina, he said, "You should see Spence in the morning. He looks like an extra from the cast of *The Walking Dead*."

She laughed again, and his dick took a bow. Thank God she couldn't see how damn happy she made his pants.

"Listen, Hulk—there's someone up ahead."

Jonah shot Spence a glare. He hated that nickname. But then he heard the noise, too. Voices too distant to really make out.

"You think the others beat us here?" he asked doubtfully. The spot next to the Raccoon River had always been his favorite spot for keggers. But not everyone coming tonight knew where it was. He'd had to send out maps.

"I don't see how."

Trina handed the flashlight to Spence. "Whoever it is, let's sneak up and scare them."

"Okay. Be vewy, vewy quiet."

She muffled a laugh at Spence's stupid cartoon character imitation, and the two of them went off. Neither waited for Jonah to wrestle the keg to his shoulder again and nearly have cardiac arrest doing it.

Somehow this wasn't going at all like he'd planned.

By the time he caught up with them, the sweat was snaking down his back. Even the back of his shorts was wet beneath the jeans. He made a grimace of distaste. Butt sweat was really the worst.

Twin shushing sounds came from Spence and Trina. Since they were crouched behind a rock, he set the damn keg down. Again. His muscles quivered with relief. But they could have picked a better spot. The place reeked. Like an animal had died nearby.

His flare of annoyance vanished when Trina reached up to grab his hand and yanked him down beside her behind the huge boulder. "You won't believe this. There's a couple down there making out. And the guy's like . . . old."

"Not old-old," Spencer said in a whisper. "But like Halston's age."

Trina smothered a giggle with one hand clapped over her mouth. "What if it *is* Mr. Halston?" She and Spence snorted with laughter.

Jonah craned his neck to see. Halston was one of the gym teachers and an okay guy. And he wasn't old. Not really. Maybe Jonah's mom's age. Forty or so. But Halston was married. And Jonah couldn't see any married guy boning on the banks of the Raccoon River. What would be the point when a couple had a house and a bedroom where they could bump uglies?

The place Trina and Spence had chosen wasn't the greatest vantage point. They were well hidden behind the jutting rock from the people yards below them. But they also couldn't see shit. Jonah moved away from Trina so that he could peer around the edge of the rock.

They could hear just fine, though. Not so much from the woman, but the guy. He seemed to be doing most of the talking.

5

"This will have to be the last time together like this. I know, I know. I feel it, too. Shush. Darling, are you crying? Don't cry." The guy touched the woman's face, but Jonah couldn't see her well in the darkness. It didn't really matter, though. The stars were bright enough that he could occasionally get a glimpse of bare skin.

It was enough to have his stiffie standing at attention.

"Don't cry. We still have tonight. One more time. Our favorite way."

Jonah's eyes about bugged out of his head when the man turned the woman over. Was the guy going to do her up the ass? Oh, man, this was better than a porno flick. Far better than *Cracked Rear Entry*, the DVD Spence had filched from his dad's collection.

"Get ready."

Jonah pulled his head back to protest. "No, man. Let them finish. I hate to interrupt a guy in the middle of getting some." That should be written in the man rules or something. It just seemed wrong. Unless it was that creepy Roland Ott, who'd been trying to get in Jonah's mom's pants for weeks. Jonah would interrupt *that* as much as possible.

But there was no talking to Spence and Trina. "On three, okay? One, two . . ." The two stood up, shining the flashlight down on the couple, screeching, "Get a room, already! Zip it back up, Daddy Long Leg!"

That last was from Spence, because, well, he was an idiot. But not to miss out, Jonah rose, too, hoping for a better glimpse of the naked woman.

The man jumped, yanking his pants up, grabbing at something on the ground. "Fucking little bastards! I'll kill you!" He started for the rocky incline toward them, and Spence screeched like a girl.

"Gun!"

Trina caught the woman in the flashlight beam then and shrieked as if she'd seen an ax murderer. Jonah grabbed the light to steady it, because the woman was just lying there. Maybe the guy had drugged her or something.

But then he screamed, too, every bit as high and girlishly as Spence had.

Because the female on the ground was more zombie than woman. She was all bloated and leathery-looking, and he had a sudden flash of comprehension about the source of the smell.

The woman was dead.

"Run!" Dropping the flashlight, he grabbed Trina by the arm and yanked her along. Back into the woods. Crashing through the brush. Leaping over downed limbs. Brushing aside branches. They ran until they got to the road. Where Spence already had the car running and ready.

Jonah pulled open the back door and shoved Trina inside. There was the sound of a gunshot. Then another. The guy was screaming something, but Jonah wasn't waiting around to listen. He leaped into the car, sprawling on top of Trina. "Go!" Spence took off, leaving the maniac behind.

And leaving the zombie woman lying on the banks of the Raccoon River.

o o o

Division of Criminal Investigation agent Cam Prescott watched the activity silently. After being alerted by the Dallas County sheriff, he'd dispatched a crime scene team and had arrived only moments before they did. Generators had been hauled through the woods and down the embankment to power spotlights illuminating the area. Criminalists and evidence technicians dotted the inner perimeter, and medical examiner personnel surrounded the body.

Foreboding cloaked him, dark and suffocating. Given the jurisdiction, the Dallas County medical examiner's office had first been called to the scene. This victim was likely completely unrelated to the six female bodies they'd discovered buried in rural cemeteries around Des Moines three weeks ago. He badly wanted to believe that. But after they found the box this corpse had been kept in and the cave where it had been hidden, he'd alerted the state medical examiner's office, just in case. Cam had been unsurprised to see Lucy Benally arrive.

Cases were assigned at the Iowa Office of the State Medical Examiner on a rotating basis. But Lucy had autopsied the victims in his last case. Cam knew she monitored every call that came into the state ME's office and would insist on being at the scene. She wasn't the most senior pathologist on staff. Just the most practiced at throwing her diminutive weight around. Right now that suited him fine. He might have quibbles with her personality, but she was the best suited to quickly determine whether this victim was connected to the others they'd found.

Dallas County sheriff Mort Feinstein detached himself from a cluster of law enforcement personnel and ambled over to him. "I might have broken protocol by calling you personally," he told Cam, "but the Polk County sheriff, Dusten Jackson, is a good friend of mine. Kept me abreast of the details regarding the Vance arrest a few days ago. From what he said, Vance had an accomplice." He jerked his head toward the scene. "Maybe I'm overreacting, but this seemed like a helluva coincidence. Thought you'd want a look."

Cam waved away Feinstein's concern. The call might not have followed the usual channels, but he was glad the sheriff had contacted him. Special Agent in Charge Maria Gonzalez had given him the green light to respond. "Under the circumstances, protocol is the last of my worries."

Mason Vance was a sadistic sexual deviant he'd arrested just days earlier on eight counts of kidnapping, seven counts of rape, and six counts of murder. Dr. Sophia Channing, the forensic psychologist consulting on the case, had been Vance's latest kidnap victim. And as Cam watched Benally's assistants zipping up the body bag, he couldn't shake the thought that Sophie had escaped a similar fate only through sheer guts and cunning. The thought had his insides twisting.

Feinstein slipped his hands in his uniform pants pockets. "This one wasn't found in a rural cemetery buried on top of a burial vault, but do you think . . . Is it possible she was one of Vance's victims?"

"I'll let you know after I talk to the ME." He looked around. "Where are the kids who reported this?"

"Back at the road, out of the way. The parents are anxious to get them home. I told them to hang around until one of your agents interviewed them. They're pretty shaken up, but hey, it was a gruesome scene. And they're kids. The big one, Jonah Davis, seems to be the steadiest." The sheriff grimaced. "Turned away about fifty cars after we secured the outer perimeter. Must have had a helluva party planned."

"I'll get to them in a few minutes," Cam promised. First, though, he needed to speak to Benally.

"Prescott," she said without preamble as he approached her. "Somehow it's not surprising to find you where it's damp and dark."

"Ah, the famed Benally wit," he shot back mildly. "Immature, and yet . . . not funny."

"I'm hilarious." She stood then and nodded to her assistants, who lifted the body bag onto a stretcher and began the careful transfer through the woods to the ME vehicle on the road above. "I do stand-up comedy in my free time." She watched the progress of the stretcher until it entered the woods and then switched her focus to Cam. "You want to know if there's a chance this one is related to the first six victims."

The fact that she'd taken charge of the body already gave him that answer. "Dammit to hell." He tracked the stretcher's progress with his gaze until the woods engulfed it. "There were no other missing persons reports matching Vance's MO." The offender had targeted wealthy single women primarily for their looks and bank accounts, and he'd cast a wide net, hunting both in and out of state. Each victim had last been seen alive withdrawing a large amount of cash from her bank.

The next time the women had been seen was when Benally extracted them from shallow graves.

"Then this body can't possibly be related to the others." Lucy tossed her long, dark braid over her shoulder and peeled off her gloves.

Cam gave a mental sigh. "Quit toying with me, Benally. What'd you find?"

She looked up at him. Way up. What the woman lacked in stature she made up for in attitude. Way overcompensated in that area, to Cam's way of thinking, but she was usually worth the aggravation she caused him.

"I'm going to have to get her in the lab and take a better look," she began.

Cam was used to the hedging. To the ME, perfectionism wasn't a character trait; it was an art.

"This body differs from the other six in one significant way." The woman waited a beat for impact. "It was embalmed."

The news rocked him. "Embalmed? Are you sure?"

It was the wrong question to ask. Benally's gaze narrowed. "I'd have to be a moron to miss it. Is that what you're suggesting, Prescott?"

Suddenly his tie felt too tight. It was a common reaction in the woman's presence. "It's just a surprise. None of the other bodies were. So maybe this one isn't related at all."

The ME's face was grim. "That's what I thought until I turned her over. There are injuries visible on her shoulder that may turn out to be consistent with cigar burns."

He reached up to rub the back of his neck. "Shit."

"Yeah, shit. No way could I make out a wound pattern, but maybe when I get her back to the autopsy suite. The only thing I can say with any certainty is that she's been dead for months."

Vance had numbered his victims, branding them with lit cigars. Cam had recently discovered the man's first victim, a woman named Rhonda Klaussen, still alive. She claimed to have been kept chained in the offender's basement. They were still checking out her story, but Sophie thought Vance might have practiced his atrocities on Klaussen as he evolved. The six bodies in the cemeteries had borne numbers ranging from ten to fifteen. Klaussen bore similar wounds in the shape of a one.

Which left a lot of numbers unaccounted for. And explained the nasty tangle of nerves in his belly.

"Sophia was the one who figured out Vance's system. I'll invite her to the lab when I'm ready with this one."

"No." Cam ignored the warning signs in Lucy's darkening expression. The woman didn't take kindly to the word, but he didn't particularly care at the moment. "Dr. Channing is no longer a consultant on this case."

Benally braced her fists on her hips. "Well, shit, Cam, she wrote the damn victimology report. I think if this victim turns out to be related to the others, Sophia's the best equipped to figure out how she links to this case."

"We'll see." His answer was noncommittal. But his objection wasn't. Sophie was still healing from the trauma she'd been through. He wasn't going to compound that trauma by yanking her back into the center of this case again. "Keep me posted."

With the aid of his Maglite, he walked across the clearing and made his way up the steep embankment and into the woods. When he exited them, he played the light over the people and cars still gathered there. Right away he picked out the kid Feinstein had mentioned.

Jonah Davis was sitting facing the road in the open back passenger door of a car. After a few words to the kid's father, Cam approached Jonah and led him through the story he'd already told a half-dozen times tonight.

Listening without interruption, Cam waited until Jonah had run down. "See that red-haired agent over there?" Cam pointed to where Jenna Turner was questioning another teenage boy, who looked considerably more shaken up.

"Yeah, I've noticed her." Jonah gave Cam a wink, man to man. "Walking hard-on material, am I right?"

Cam fixed him with a steely look. Waited for the kid to visibly quail before continuing. "She's a DCI agent. She's also a forensic artist. If you got a good look at the guy, she'll be able to use your descriptions to draw a sketch." He took a folded-up piece of paper from the inside breast pocket of his suit coat.

Shaking it open, he passed it to Jonah. "Agent Turner did this one a couple weeks ago with a witness we interviewed up in Edina."

The kid stared at the composite drawing, mouth hanging open. "But . . . but . . . that's him! The zombie-lover guy!" Mr. Davis swiveled in the front seat, a concerned look on his face.

"Settle down, Jonah. It's okay."

"No, Dad, this is the guy we saw." Jonah stabbed his index finger at the sketch. "I got a really good look at him. Not so much the woman, at least not until the end. But this is the guy—I swear it."

With a sense of bleak resolve, Cam took the sketch back and tucked it away. Gave the kid's father the okay to take Jonah home after eliciting a promise to bring him in for a formal interview the next day. Jenna could individually interview the other two kids tomorrow to do sketches, which could then be compared with the one he'd shown Jonah.

But given the boy's response, there was little doubt what the outcome would be.

He walked a few feet away and called Micki Loring, the DCI agent he had stationed with Sophie in his absence. "We've got reason to believe that the man identified by the Edina chief of police as Vance's accessory was seen revisiting another victim tonight," he told her tersely. "How is Dr. Channing?" A little of the tension seeped from his body at Loring's response. "Good. She doesn't have to know about this." Maybe Loring would stand up better to Sophie's gentle probing than he did. He could hope.

Not for the first time, he wondered if he should have arranged Sophie's protective custody to be overseen by another agent. But Cam knew he'd never entrust her safety to anyone else. Not when they'd discovered Vance hadn't been working alone.

Not while Vance's partner was still free. When the man had every reason to go after the only surviving victim who could provide the testimony that would put Vance away for good.

o o o

Sonny clung to the branch he was perched on, peering through the leaves at the scene below through night vision binoculars. Once he'd chased off those kids he'd wasted no time. He'd left his Janice—sweet, quiet Janice—and run for the car he'd hidden half a mile down the road. After circling around, he'd stashed it a couple of miles away and hiked back into the woods. But he hadn't dared get too close because he knew those damn kids would never keep their mouths shut. And he'd been right.

A sheriff's car had been on the scene when he returned, and within an hour the woods were lit up with LED bars, flashlights, and spotlights, with at least two dozen people milling around. And all of them interested in Janice. Lovely, lovely Janice.

Good-bye, my love.

The thought of losing her wrenched something inside his chest, made it go tight and hot, like an iron vise that wouldn't let him breathe or feel or think. It was better this way. The thought punched through the tension. Better cops than if those fucking kids had gotten more kids to come and look . . . At least the cops would treat Janice with respect.

They'd take her away forever.

His breathing went ragged and fast, the way it did before he got light-headed and dizzy. Once he'd even fallen and hit his head when he breathed like that, and he didn't want that now. Not when he was sitting in a damn tree. He'd break his neck. And wouldn't Vance be pissed then?

He giggled, muffling the sound against his shoulder. Vance could go fuck himself. Or maybe someone was doing that for him, since the man was currently sitting in jail while Sonny was free as a bird. Who was the brains now?

Sobering, he studied the sight below with renewed interest. He hadn't intended to see Janice after tonight in any case. It'd been too long, and it was past the time he should have allowed himself with her. He ignored the pang that accompanied the thought. He'd been weak where she was concerned, but she'd been his favorite. So gentle and *quiet*. And she'd pleaded so sweetly at the end. No screams or struggles that would have only delayed the inevitable.

If he had a wife, Sonny imagined she'd be a lot like Janice, unassuming and giving. Always soft-spoken.

At that moment he was tempted to forget all about Vance, forget the plan, and slip out of the state. He could start over by himself. Choose a real wife and take her away somewhere secluded to live where it would be just the two of them. No muscle-bound Vance calling the shots. No Mommy whispering in his ear, telling him what to do. He could hear her voice now, as clear as if she were sitting on the branch beside him.

Get the woman. Do it now.

"Shut up, Mommy," he murmured, staring hard through the night vision binoculars. But her voice never shut up, at least not for long. Except for the time Sonny had wrapped his fingers around her throat and squeezed and squeezed and squeezed, until her eyes bugged and her lips turned blue. She'd gone very still. She'd been quiet for a long, long time then. Years.

But she hadn't stayed gone. She hadn't stayed quiet.

A bat launched out of the tree next to his, did a slow, lazy loop before zooming off to hunt for dinner. Mommy's voice sounded more insistent this time. *Get Channing. Do it now.*

Channing was Vance's problem. The kids were Sonny's. It had been dark on the banks of the river, but they'd had a flashlight. How close a look had they gotten at him? Good enough to describe him to one of the cops below? He had to be cautious. First thing tomorrow he'd get his hair cut and then buy one of those do-it-yourself dye kits. Grow facial hair, wear some clear-lens glasses and a ball cap . . . he was practiced at the art of deception. The kids wouldn't be a problem. But the cops . . .

He'd stuffed the condom in his pocket while chasing those fucking kids. He checked, discovered it was still there. He hadn't worn gloves with Janice, but what could they get prints from?

He craned his neck to focus on the female in the center of the activity around Janice. She'd fascinated him since first arriving on the scene. Too often cops and other workers in the area had concealed her crouched form. She seemed to be directing things, gesturing to nearby helpers to bring her items or to bend down beside her for a moment.

But mostly she worked alone, her activities sometimes hidden by the constant movement of cops in the perimeter around Janice. Something about the small female drew his attention. Demanded it.

She wore a long, dark braid that she nudged impatiently over her shoulder whenever it fell forward. But it wasn't her appearance he noted. It was her manner as she tended Janice.

Respectful. As tender as she would have been with a newborn. Watching her, it was easy to forget the cops, forget the kids who were surely somewhere in the area spilling their story. All his attention was zeroed in on the dark-haired woman below. And the longer he watched her, the more Sonny became certain that she *got* it.

To most people—Vance, for instance—dead was dead. Get rid of a woman and move on to a new one. But Sonny knew. Dead was dead only after they were buried. Deep in the ground, where daylight wouldn't penetrate, or weighted down in cold, dark waters. He chose all the women's graves himself, and his favorites—like Janice—got special treatment. Sonny knew that the reason Mommy had come back was because he hadn't buried her. He'd left her body on the floor and run away, and that was the reason she was in his head now. Sometimes even standing at his shoulder, or talking from across the room, the mean still in her eyes even when she kept it from her voice.

But there was something about the woman in the blue coveralls below. There were two other overall-clad workers, and they deferred to the tiny female. She didn't spend much time talking; all her focus was concentrated on Janice. And Sonny knew—he could feel—that the woman understood death as well as he did. Maybe even better.

He watched while his poor Janice was zipped away in a bag and hoisted on a stretcher. Then the woman started to talk to a man who, even from this distance, Sonny could tell was a cop.

But the man didn't interest him. Now that Janice was being taken away, the woman would leave, too, and Sonny wouldn't see her again. The thought had his head buzzing the way it did when he got upset. His heart galloped, and his mind raced for a way to make sure that didn't happen. He needed to learn everything he could about the dark-haired woman with *IOSME* emblazoned across the back of her navy overalls. And then he and that particular female were going to get better acquainted.

A sense of urgency nudged at him, and he sighed inwardly. But first he had to do as Vance had ordered. Sophia Channing was a threat, so Sonny had to eliminate her.

Get the woman. Mommy's whisper was louder this time. *Do it now.*

He let his binoculars hang from the strap around his neck and began to climb down from the tree. There was only one way to silence that voice.

And that was to obey it.

Chapter 2

Sonny hummed along to the radio as he drove. He'd made a quick stop at home to get the things he needed and then headed for Channing's condo. He'd been watching it ever since Vance had gotten word to him. Yesterday all the state-issued vehicles had left the address, one by one. Sonny hadn't been inside before, but Vance was thorough, in spite of being a complete maniac. The man had left information about the security system and crude maps detailing the layout of the condo's interior and the approach from the rear.

Getting rid of the women had always been left to him before, but this time Vance had been specific. Use a gun. At least three shots. Maybe Vance knew something Sonny didn't. Maybe guns were different and the woman wouldn't need to be buried to be really dead. Maybe three shots to the head and dead was dead.

He smiled at the rhyme, repeating it a few more times as he turned into the development that housed Channing's condo. There was a cul-de-sac to the back and right of the condo, across her backyard and another. Sonny preferred to park farther away and approach from the rear on foot.

First he donned gloves and slipped a small penlight into the pocket of his hoodie before fitting night vision goggles over his eyes.

Vance had laughed at his fascination with military and police equipment, but since Vance was sitting in a cell under round-the-clock guard, Sonny could be pretty sure the man was no longer laughing.

Taking his time, he crossed yards, avoiding houses with kennels in the back. He paused occasionally, looking around carefully, but all was still. It was after three. Most would be asleep.

The cul-de-sac was ahead, and a single street lamp bathed the circular space with a soft glow. He jumped the fence in the next yard and veered to the other side so he wouldn't be spotlighted in it.

An urgency was building inside him, ignited by the whispers in the back of his mind. But he didn't need to listen to them. He knew what he had to do. And the sooner the deed was done, the sooner he could concentrate on the other woman he'd seen tonight. The one who had taken such care of Janice.

He needed to find that woman. Needed to be sure she was exactly what he thought she was.

But he was already certain. They were kindred spirits.

Which meant she might even understand what he was about to do.

o o o

"We've got activity."

Cell phone in hand, Cam strode toward the back of the inside perimeter that had been established around the crime scene, dodging Seth Dietz as the criminalist wrestled one of the massive strobes into a different position. "Where?"

Agent Tommy Franks's voice held a note of suppressed excitement. "Back corner of Channing's lot. He's headed for the rear door."

Adrenaline spurted through Cam's veins. The covert operation at Sophie's condo had been a gamble, especially since they'd had no indication—until a few hours ago—that Vance's accomplice was still in the area. Maybe the unknown subject was tying up loose ends before he fled the state.

Which meant this might be their one and only chance to capture the man.

"Do you have a visual of his vehicle?"

"Negative," came Franks's laconic reply. "Might have parked on the street a block in back of hers."

"I'll be there in twenty," Cam promised, heading toward the steep embankment beneath the tree line. And that was going to push it, even running with lights. "Call for backup. Tell them to roll up silent. Everything in place inside?" His mind immediately went to Sophie, but he elbowed aside the concern. When trying to trap a predator, one had to use the right bait. They'd taken precautions for her safety. He concentrated on scrabbling up the hill without landing on his ass.

"Exactly as you wanted it."

"He'll be armed. The kids tonight said he had a gun." Once up the hill, he turned on his Maglite before plunging into the woods.

"We'll be ready."

Agent Corbin Boggs would be somewhere in the vicinity. Cam knew Boggs and Franks were more than capable, but he still cursed the time it would take him to arrive on scene. "No heroes. But I prefer the UNSUB alive, if possible."

Disconnecting the call, Cam made his way through the woods as quickly as he dared. If all went according to plan, by morning they'd have Vance trussed up so tightly that he'd never wiggle free. If the accomplice could be persuaded to flip on the other man, the whole case might never even have to go to trial. Sophie wouldn't have to testify. And Vance would never again see the outside of a prison cell.

And that was the thought that would sustain him on the race across town to Sophie's condo.

o o o

The first key was stiff in the lock. The initial time Vance had been there he'd had two made from wax impressions he'd taken of a set found inside. Eventually the key turned, and Sonny used the other on the dead bolt. The door swung open soundlessly.

He slipped the keys back in his pocket and took out a penlight. The next few seconds would tell the story. If Vance's tampering with the alarm had been discovered, the opening the man had fixed in the system would fail, and there would be only a thirty-second window to kill Channing and get out again.

Switching on the penlight as he opened the door quietly, he walked exactly to the spot where Vance had said he'd find the keypad for the alarm. If his entry was discovered, the light would switch from green to red, and an alarm would alert the security company and the woman inside of an unapproved entry. He scanned the area as he waited. Channing's bedroom would be through the kitchen, first door to the left of the living room. Even if the alarm were triggered, he'd be gone long before help could arrive if all went according to plan.

The light on the alarm winked green. Even better, no racket split the darkness.

He reached up to secure the night vision goggles and unzipped his hoodie partway, taking the pistol with its attached suppressor from the makeshift holster strapped around his chest. Then he tiptoed in the direction of Channing's room.

The place was still. Not even the ticking of a clock marred the silence. He sidled up to the door in question. Pushed it open and raised his weapon.

o o o

21

Seven-year-old Carter Hammel came awake slowly, wondering what he was doing in the sunroom. It took a minute to remember. The stuff his mom had given him for pain had made him fall asleep at, like, seven o'clock. But it was really dark out now.

Fretfully, he pushed aside the quilt his mom had spread over him. He was covered in sweat. Even his leg inside the cast felt sweaty and gross.

"Mom!" He wanted a drink of water. And he wanted to change his clothes and go to sleep in his own bed. "Mom!"

But she didn't answer. Her bedroom was too far away. He'd have to do it on his own. And he hated the crutches. They made his armpits hurt. Sulkily, he pushed himself up to a sitting position and looked out the window. That was about all he could do these days, and it really, really *sucked*. Mom said she'd call to see if Ryder or Zach could come over for a while tomorrow. But that was still a long time from now. And he was going to have this stupid cast on for five more weeks. That was more than a month before he could ride a bike or play ball. Why couldn't he have broken his leg when he was still in school?

Something moved in the darkness outside. Carter forgot his complaints and strained to see. Angel, Ryder's black lab, might have gotten loose again. If so, maybe he should call his friend's house. The last time Angel had gotten out, the animal control people had picked him up and it had cost money to get him back.

But it wasn't Angel. It was tall, like a man. It jumped over the fence and ran across Carter's yard.

"Mom!" He yelled louder this time, not taking his eyes off the window. Maybe it was a robber. Maybe he was coming *here*.

But the man ran clear across their yard into Dr. C's.

Forgetting his hatred of the crutches for the moment, Carter grabbed them and struggled to his feet. He went to the door of the sunroom and unlocked it. After pushing it open, he hopped awkwardly to the end of the patio and peeked around the corner of the condo. Just in time to see someone dressed all in black go into Dr. C's house.

His stomach felt as though he was going to throw up. Carter was the one who had seen the blue van in front of Dr. Channing's a while ago with the funny sign on its side. He'd had to talk to that agent guy about it. And yesterday he'd heard his mom talking on the phone, and she said Dr. C had been kidnapped and then gotten away.

He knew what kidnapped was. They'd heard all about stranger danger at school. And he wondered if Dr. C would've gotten kidnapped if Carter had seen the guy in the blue van. If he'd gotten a look at him so the police could've caught him before he hurt Dr. C.

Chewing his bottom lip, he considered going in to get his mom. But he already knew what she would say. That he was imagining things again and that he should go to bed.

He hadn't imagined the guy jumping over the fence. He knew he hadn't.

Positioning his crutches, he turned and hopped back into the house. Quiet this time. He didn't call for his mom. Instead he went to the kitchen and stood in front of the refrigerator. She'd put the BB pistol his dad had bought for him way up on top, saying she'd talk to his dad about it. Carter knew that meant that he wasn't going to get to keep it.

But right now he took one of his crutches and pushed the BB gun over the side of the fridge and then reached up to catch it when it fell.

Holding it in his hand, he immediately felt better. If there was a bad guy at Dr. C's house again, this time Carter was going to stop him.

o o o

The master bedroom was empty. The bed was stripped. No one had slept there recently.

To be sure, though, Sonny stepped inside the room and checked the adjoining bath. It was empty, too.

Nerves jittering through him, he slipped back into the living room and drew the penlight out of his pocket again. There was a second bedroom in the condo. Maybe Channing was sleeping in it because hers brought bad memories. Vance had taken her from her master bath. Just walked right up to the shower she was in and snatched her out of it. Vance might be an animal, but he didn't lack balls.

Aware of the passing seconds, Sonny moved swiftly through the living room, skirting the couch and end table to approach the bedroom door that led away from the room. It was partly open. And when he peeked inside, the tightness in his chest eased a little.

This bed was occupied. Although the room was dark, it would be hard to miss the figure under the covers. He shoved his goggles to his forehead, wanting to make sure. Channing was facing away from him, but he recognized the bright-blonde hair from Vance's description. Sonny took four long strides toward the bed, raising his weapon as he moved.

o o o

"Are you inside yet?"

There was a faint crackle in the radio transmitting Franks's voice to the whisper mic Boggs wore.

"No. I've got movement next door. You think this guy brought a friend?"

Franks was silent for a moment. "Did you see two approaching the condo?"

"Negative." But Boggs strained his eyes, scanning the area he'd seen the activity coming from.

"It could be the neighbor." Which, both of them knew, could spell a very different sort of trouble for them than an accomplice would.

Boggs caught another glimpse of movement. Someone was crouched on the next-door patio, pressed against the house in the shadows. He conveyed the information to the other agent, adding, "Let me know when you're in place. I'll go in, and you can take the second guy. How far away is backup?"

"Another five."

Boggs's gaze traveled from the next-door patio to Channing's condo, and he knew they didn't have that long.

o o o

A passing headlight speared through the blinds and washed the corner of the room in light for a moment. Sonny held his breath, wondering if Channing would wake. Turn over and open her eyes when he killed her.

He didn't like it when they looked at him. He always turned them away first. Otherwise their eyes turned into Mommy's eyes as they bulged and bugged from a face that turned into her face. Sonny didn't like that at all.

But Channing didn't turn over. The alarm on her bedside table clicked to the next minute, reminding him of the need for haste. *Three shots. Do it now.*

He drew closer until he was standing over the bed. Drawing a breath to steady his aim, he squeezed the trigger.

The shots came in quick succession, and even with the suppressor there was a sharp pop, pop, pop. Sonny was prepared for it. He'd been shooting since he was a teenager. But he'd never shot at anything live before. He wasn't prepared for the blood. It spattered his clothes, his face, the gun in his hand. Panicked, he jumped back.

Wiped the wetness from his chin with his sleeve and realized it was wet, too. His stomach lurched in disgust. Lowering the gun, he yanked the goggles back in place as he turned to run from the room, from the house, forgetting the need for caution.

"DCI! Put your weapon down!"

A figure was standing behind the couch in the next room, gun drawn. Flinging himself sideways, Sonny fired twice, hitting the floor as the man returned fire. He scrabbled along the carpet on his knees and elbows. The stranger had taken shelter behind the couch. Sonny didn't wait for him to raise his head to fire again. Instead he sent three shots through the back of the couch in the area where he'd last seen the man and raced toward the door he'd entered through. Caution was no longer an issue. Speed was. He burst through the back door, ran across the patio, and was stung by a volley of what appeared to be a swarm of bees, stinging his ankles and legs.

"DCI! Lay down your weapon!"

The goggles painted the man standing before him in a ghostly green glow. The weapon he had pointed directly at Sonny's chest looked all too real. "Don't shoot." Slowly he bent to let his gun clatter to the patio. "I'm unarmed."

"Hands behind your head. Kick the weapon to the side. Now!"

"I heard you shooting at Dr. Channing, mister," a small voice said almost simultaneously. "So I'm gonna shoot you!" Another volley of bees. Which weren't bees at all, Sonny realized then, but BBs.

"Go back in the house, son. Now! Now!"

Sonny dove toward the small shadow crouched on the next patio even as a bullet sang by. He tackled a miniature body— a kid—rolling, then came to his feet with the writhing boy held tightly before him.

"You don't want to do that," the DCI agent warned, but Sonny couldn't hear him. It was Mommy's voice that screamed through his mind, echoes of fear and anger clawing through him.

"Drop your gun or I break his neck." Sonny knocked the puny BB gun out of the kid's hand as he tried to aim it over his shoulder. He hefted him up, caught the boy's neck in the crook of his elbow. For a kid he was heavy; one leg hung uselessly down in front of him. "Don't think I won't."

The agent made no attempt to comply. "You're just digging a deeper hole for yourself," he warned. "Maybe you were justified for what you did inside. We can talk about that. But there's no going back from this."

Sonny bent awkwardly to pick up the gun he'd dropped, making sure the kid's head was shielding his own. The boy was *heavy*. In a flash of comprehension he realized the weight came from a cast on his leg. "Put your gun down. Do it!" he demanded fiercely when the agent didn't comply. "Do you want me to kill this kid?"

"There's no need to bring the boy into it. Let's settle this ourselves, man to man." The agent began to inch to the side. Sonny knew he was looking for an opening. In a flash of brilliance, he hoisted the kid up and over one shoulder in a fireman's carry, one arm clamped across his cast and free hand. The kid made a perfect human shield. And then Sonny turned and ran like a deer.

Not in the direction he'd come, but in the most direct route that would take him to his vehicle. He ran as fast as he could, but the boy was making it difficult. No longer rigid with fear, the kid was pounding his free fist into Sonny's back. Kneeing him in the side.

He yanked sharply on the kid's injured leg, smiled when he heard his high-pitched screech. The little bastard would behave or he wouldn't live through this. It made no difference to Sonny either way.

He swung around to fire several shots before running again. The cop didn't return fire. He wouldn't dare risk hitting the kid in the dark. But he was still chasing them. Sonny shot again, causing the man to duck for cover.

Lights were flicking on in house after house. One large dog, barking ferociously, sped along the fence line Sonny was running by. Sonny paused for an instant and undid the latch on the gate before resituating the kid on his shoulders and stumbling awkwardly toward his car. With a backward glance, he smiled in satisfaction as the dog tore toward the agent who had risen to give chase again. The man halted for a few precious moments, earning Sonny the most valuable of commodities: time.

The vehicle was just yards away now. Sonny ducked down and dumped the kid on the ground, then sprinted for his car. A volley of shots sounded, and something sharp and hot sliced into his thigh. He howled and returned fire before jumping painfully into the car, turning the key in the ignition, and squealing away.

○ ○ ○

Agent Micki Loring met Cam at his front door, a questioning look in her ebony gaze. "We had a quiet night here."

"Glad someone did."

"I heard things didn't go as planned." He toed off his shoes, and she followed him through the family room. "But if you hadn't had the foresight to move Sophia out of her condo and into protective custody, it could have been far worse."

Cam's skin prickled at the reminder. He took a quick glance at his watch. Barely 7:30 a.m. Sophie was probably still asleep. At least he hoped like hell that she was. "Listen, if you want to run home, grab a shower, and some sleep, I can get someone else in here—" he started.

"I slept on the couch, and I've already used your shower." She aimed a meaningful look at him. "From the sounds of things, you need to take your own advice."

"Probably." He rubbed the back of his neck wearily. A drill of frustration was jackhammering through him. Vance's accomplice had taken the bait they'd laid so carefully. But he'd slipped through their fingers, less than two minutes before backup had arrived. The near miss was bitter.

"You talk to Franks?" From her words he assumed she'd gotten the rundown on the last few hours from someone. The scene in Sophie's guest bedroom earlier had been chilling. If that had, in fact, been Sophie laying in the bed, and not a wig-clad dummy sporting fake blood packets . . . an icy finger traced down his spine at the thought. Rationally he knew Sophie was fine. Safely ensconced in his condo with an agent at her side at all times.

But right now emotion trumped logic. He needed to see for himself. Just a glimpse of her sleeping peacefully might be enough to dispel the sight of that dummy blown to bits, fake blood sprayed all over the room.

Swallowing hard, he headed in the direction of his spare bedroom. And tried not to recall the times, not all that long ago, that Sophie had spent her nights in *his* bedroom. With him at her side.

That was history. Recent enough, unfortunately, for the details to remain stubbornly, erotically vivid.

"No, I haven't talked to Franks. Special Agent Gonzalez filled me in."

Cam froze in his tracks. He turned to look at Loring. "She called you?" He couldn't figure why she would. He'd talked to Maria twice to apprise her of the events of the night as they'd unfolded.

Loring snorted indelicately. "As if. She's here. In your office with Dr. Channing. Didn't you see her car in the drive?"

Lack of sleep must have made him slow. "I thought it was yours," he said numbly. Gonzalez was here. Talking to Sophie. And he had a sinking feeling that he knew exactly what that conversation entailed. Striding rapidly toward the hallway that would lead to the office at the back of the condo, he barely heard the agent behind him say, "My car is in your garage. Remember? You told me—"

"I don't want to press you." Special Agent Maria Gonzalez's voice drifted through the half-open doorway to the office. "Of course, time is of the essence, but you've been through a terrible ordeal. Take some time to consider it." Cam was certain he was the only one to find her words fraught with irony.

"Glad you at least recognize that Dr. Channing has been through a trauma." Cam propped a palm on either side of the open doorway, glancing pointedly at Maria.

As usual her black hair, liberally laced with silver, was pulled back; its severe style was reflected in the plain dark pants and jacket she wore. She returned his gaze imperturbably. "I'm not without sympathy for what Sophia's been through. That's why I told her to take some time before deciding whether to resume her assistance on the task force."

"Dr. Channing"—Sophie's spirited response held just a hint of irritation—"is standing right here. And while I appreciate every-one's concern, it's unnecessary. I'm going crazy sitting around while everyone else tiptoes around me as if I'm a bomb ready to detonate. If I can continue to be of help in light of last night's developments, of course I want to do so. Vance terrorized me while I was his cap-tive, but I didn't suffer what his other victims did. I'm fine."

Cam studied her, mingled resignation and concern threading through him. Her slender frame was wrapped in a thin thigh-length robe, her long, blonde hair tumbling down her back. But it was her injuries that brought a clutching feeling to his chest. "You look fine," he drawled, a dangerous heat to the words.

As if on cue, she flushed. The bruise on her jaw had graduated from navy to purple, ringed with yellow. Her lip was still puffy and her left arm in a splint. From the careful way she moved, he realized her injuries weren't limited to those visible.

But it was the emotional injuries that concerned him most. He knew they were there, even while she continued to deny it. Cam still suffered the occasional post-traumatic stress flashback himself from the nearly two years he'd spent undercover on a multiagency drug task force. He knew from personal experience that there was no way someone could have survived what Sophie had without some collateral emotional damage.

Which is why he no longer wanted her anywhere near this case.

Clearly believing that she'd gotten what she'd come for, Maria said, "Take all the time you need, Sophia. You can call me when you make your decision."

Cam stared at Sophie, as if by sheer force of will alone he could alter what she would say next. Their gazes did battle as she responded, "I don't need time. I'm ready to resume my consulting duties whenever you need me."

Maria switched her attention to Cam. "Nine o'clock briefing?" He gave a curt nod before she exited the room. He walked over to the overstuffed chair in front of the desk and sank down heavily. Leaning forward, he rested his elbows on his knees and scrubbed his hands over his face. He'd been up more than twenty-four hours. It was going to be a lot longer before he'd get any rest.

But it wasn't sleep that concerned him most right now. Dropping his hands, he studied the woman who was watching him soberly. Aside from her physical injuries, she looked none the worse for wear. The bruises provided stark contrast to her gilded angel appearance, highlighted the refined features and intelligent brow. Most wouldn't notice the mauve shadows under her eyes. They were silent testament that she was anything but *fine*. She wasn't sleeping. After what she'd been through, who the hell could?

Her smile was tentative. "I know what you're thinking—"

"I made you a promise." He heard the bleakness in his tone, but was unable to temper it. Not now. Not when there was just the two of them. "Three days ago. Do you remember it?"

Something in her expression softened, and she came over to lean a hip against the overstuffed arm of his chair. "You said you wouldn't let anyone hurt me again. I believe you. That's what this around-the-clock protection detail has been all about, hasn't it? And it's been successful. You and the rest of the team are working yourselves into the ground toward that end. The least I can do is make myself useful."

Useful. The word was a masterful understatement. No one looking at the petite blonde in the filmy pink robe would ever imagine the mind housed behind those cultured looks. Dr. Sophia Channing was a leading international expert in forensic psychology. She had trained under the legendary Louis Frein of the FBI's Behavioral Science Unit. In the course of her career she'd interviewed the most notorious serial killers in captivity, and her services were highly sought after by law enforcement around the country. It was in her professional capacity that she'd signed on to develop the criminal profile when they were hunting Vance.

But it wasn't Dr. Sophia Channing the professional that concerned Cam now. It was Sophie the woman.

"I really am okay . . ." she began. But the look he gave her then had her voice tapering off.

"Don't bullshit a bullshitter. You're anything but fine." He bit the words out, incapable of finesse or diplomacy. He'd have to find those traits again in an hour or so when he briefed the rest of the team, but they were beyond him now. "You told me once that you could tell when I'm lying. The same goes. Last I noticed you weren't wearing a cape and tights, so drop the superwoman act. Vance beat the hell out of you. The only reason you weren't raped is because you convinced him to give you time to write a new profile on him. But thoughts of what he did to his other victims were in your mind the entire time. They had to be. It isn't your outward injuries that concern me—it's what's going on in here." He tapped her temple lightly, and she flinched a little.

"As it happens, I do have a cape." He snorted and looked away. "It's pink. Studded with rhinestones along the edge, elegant but not too flashy."

Dammit, he wasn't going to smile, although she was clearly trying to lighten the tension. "As I recall, you have a purse to match."

"Well, it's all about accessorizing."

Against his will, a corner of his mouth quirked. She reached over then, laid her hand gently on his arm, and Cam froze. His gaze fell to where she was touching him. Her flesh was pale. Smooth. The fingernails painted a pastel color he'd never be able to name. A few short days ago, after they'd found her escaping with Vance's other victim along a lonely gravel road in rural Polk County, her nails had been bloody and broken from the efforts of breaking out of the cell the man had kept her in. Sometime since they'd been repaired, as if the damage had never occurred. She'd have him believe that she was recovering from all her injuries that easily. He wasn't buying it.

Rivers of heat traced on his skin beneath her fingers, and he mentally cursed his response. Their affair had been short and spectacularly hot, but those twelve days had been just long enough for Sophie Channing to lodge herself under his skin, to take up residence in the corners of his mind. And he needed to distance himself from the personal to retain his objectivity.

As if reading his mind, she said, "Since this case is ongoing, I can be a valuable resource." When he raised his brows, she gave his arm a quick pinch. "False modesty aside, you need another offender profile, and then there's Rhonda Klaussen to be interviewed. She might be able to shed insight on Vance and the accomplice."

"She claims she doesn't know anything about an accomplice."

When Sophie just looked at him, his jaw snapped shut. That was what Klaussen had told *him*, but Sophie was adept at drawing out information from criminals and witnesses alike that law enforcement couldn't. It was one of the skills that had her services in such high demand.

"You know I can be of assistance, so to use one of your expressions, you're just going to have to suck it up. If I were anyone else, would you still be resisting?"

If she were anyone else they'd put in protective custody, how much time would he spend worrying about her emotional health? The reminder was useless. It wasn't a stranger; it was Sophie. He stretched out his legs, crossed one ankle deliberately over the other. This wasn't an argument he needed to have with the woman pinning him right now with shrewd blue eyes that saw too much. He'd have it instead with his superior.

"What'd Maria tell you?"

"She said another victim has been found. That the UNSUB was revisiting her burial site when he was interrupted by some kids."

"Revisiting." He settled himself more comfortably in the chair. "That's one word for it. He was sexually assaulting the corpse. I have a feeling that will be the last time those kids stage a kegger in the woods at night." He glanced up at Sophie. "So your first impression about there being two offenders was spot-on. One assaulting the victims when they were alive and the other postmortem. Which means as bad as Vance is, this other guy is a very sick fuck."

If her hand hadn't remained on his arm, he might have missed her subtle shudder at the mention of Vance. "Under the circumstances I wish my theory had been wrong. The victimology concerns me, though. I didn't think there were any other missing persons cases fitting the profile of the six already recovered." All the victims had been single, attractive, and wealthy. All had withdrawn a healthy amount of cash from their accounts on the days they vanished.

"There aren't any cases identical, no. Other women have gone missing, of course. But the case detectives couldn't be sure they didn't disappear on their own."

"Of course, as Vance and his accomplice evolved, their selection of victims might have, as well. I look forward to talking to the ME . . . Will Lucy be on the case?"

"She was there last night." The irony of her mention of Benally didn't escape him. He'd been vehement when he'd spoken to the ME that Sophie wouldn't be linked to this case any longer. Gonzalez had effectively changed all that this morning. And he was increasingly anxious to have a word with the SAC about that.

He looked at his watch. "I need to shower and shave."

Sophie let him get halfway out of the chair before she said, "Did you really think I'd let you leave before telling me the rest of it?"

"The rest . . ." *Damn.* He sank back into the chair. "You and Maria had quite the little chat before I arrived." Another mark against his superior. Gonzalez was racking them up lately where Sophie was concerned.

"Good thing, too." She smoothed her hand down the front of her robe. "You're maddeningly reticent. She said the UNSUB took the bait and entered my apartment. Since she didn't mention an arrest, I assume something went wrong."

"Try everything." Briefly he gave her a summary of the events, downplaying the details. His careful parsing, however, didn't stem the outpouring of concern.

"Oh, my God." With a flash of thigh she surged from her perch on the arm of the chair and proceeded to pace. "Is Corbin all right?"

35

"Boggs wore a vest. He'll be sore for a while, but he's fine." Cam wasn't without sympathy for the agent's injury. Even with the body-protecting armor, taking a bullet packed a helluva punch. Boggs had been out of commission until well after the UNSUB had fled the scene. "Your couch and the spare bedroom weren't as fortunate."

"And Carter." She rounded the desk, came to a stop for a moment as horror flickered over her expression. "He could have been killed. He has to be traumatized. Livvie must be frantic. I'll never forgive myself for involving him in this."

"You didn't involve him," Cam reminded her. "The UNSUB did. You're no more to blame than his dad is for buying him a BB gun that made him think he was invincible."

"I never should have agreed to the idea." Sophie wasn't finished berating herself. "I never considered—"

"It was a good plan." Cam leaned his head back, pushing aside the urge to close his eyes. Just for a minute. "Almost worked, too. None of us could have envisioned a seven-year-old being awake and seeing the guy enter your house. We're not going to spend time crying over how things went down." Although admittedly, he and Franks had spent more than a few minutes bemoaning their bad luck. "That's the way it goes, more frequently than you might think."

She was looking at him with an arrested expression on her face. "You said my spare bedroom sustained damage?"

Cam chose his words carefully. "The offender used a gun. We . . . ah . . . planned for every contingency. I'll have someone in there to take care of the cleanup." The room would have to be stripped, painted, and recarpeted. Somehow he'd have to arrange to get that done before she saw her place again. There were already enough memories there to haunt her. She didn't need more.

"Well." Sophie took a deep breath, as if fortifying herself. "I take back every complaint I've made about the tedium of protective—" Her voice broke off abruptly. "The UNSUB believes he succeeded.

He thinks I'm dead." She didn't wait for his slow nod before going on. "This is perfect. It changes everything. All we have to do now is continue to let him think that."

Chapter 3

Y ou want to fake your own death."

There was no inflection in Cam's voice. Shooting him a glance, Sophia couldn't tell what he was thinking. "Vance's accomplice set it up. I'm just suggesting letting it spin out. If he and Vance think I'm dead, I'm free. No more protective custody. I'd need to change my appearance, of course, but then I could move around openly, which means I can continue working this case at your side, instead of through reports."

It didn't bear mentioning how many of the cases she consulted on with law enforcement across the country consisted solely of long-distance involvement. She needed to get out, to immerse herself personally in the case. She had to have something, anything, to focus on besides the memories of the hours Vance held her captive.

She needed to escape the screams of his other victim that reverberated in her mind like a horror-filled echo chamber.

"This is a valuable weapon. If Vance believes I'm out of the picture, he might relax his guard. Courtney Van Wheton is still in a coma." A tight band of grief tightened in her chest at the memory of the woman Vance had kidnapped days before he'd lain in wait for Sophia. "He'll have every reason to think he's going to beat the charges. We already know he's impulsive and ego driven. A talented interviewer might get him to open up a little."

"Since he's lawyered up, the chances of an interviewer getting at him are slim. The first thing his attorney is going to do is press to drop the charges." Cam's eyes were hooded. "With your 'death,' the two main witnesses are out of the way and the case gets weaker."

"But you have trace evidence proving Vance was in my house." Sophia leaned against the corner of his desk, facing him, falling into the rhythm of debate seamlessly. "The most recent evidence collected by the crime team still hasn't been processed by the lab, right? If they find proof tying Vance to the barn Courtney and I escaped from, the case still goes to trial. And if Rhonda Klaussen can be persuaded to testify against Vance, she'll be another effective weapon against him, as well."

"I'd be lying if I said the thought hadn't occurred." Cam's admission stopped Sophia short. "For some of the same reasons you mentioned, yeah, but mainly because letting Vance think you're dead takes his focus off you. You can be damn sure his partner was following orders last night. If he and Vance think the assassination was successful, you're far safer than before. But I think there are a few details you haven't considered yet."

"Such as?"

"Faking your death means *everyone* thinks you're dead. Not just Vance and his sidekick. Your parents. Your friends. Neighbors. Colleagues." Sophia deflated a bit at the listing, hating his sardonic expression as he noted her response. "Reports of your demise would have to be public, because that's the only thing that would convince Vance. So that complicates things a bit."

She chewed her lip. "My parents are still in Europe." A fact that she gave thanks for daily. It meant she had been able to sugarcoat most of the details about her kidnapping. Both academics, Helen and Martin Channing had never approved of Sophia's gravitation toward forensic psychology. Had they heard the truth, they would have cut their sabbatical short to fly to her side and would currently be trying to whisk her off to their home in Michigan. "I could get in touch with them before any public announcement was released."

Another thought occurred. "Oh. And I'd have to let Livvie and Carrie know the truth." The women were not only neighbors but also dear friends. And after everything Carter had been through last night on Sophia's behalf, there was no way she'd add to Livvie's stress by letting her believe the farce. "And Dr. Redlow. Since he's handling my private practice he has to be clued in so he can decide how to best handle any client concerns that arise."

"That was quick."

Sophia didn't trust Cam's tone. He took an exaggerated look at his watch. "After planning to announce your death to the world, it took you all of three seconds to start reeling off exceptions. News flash, something like this works only if everyone really thinks you're dead."

"You get snotty when you're tired." The observation was mild, but her movements as she tightened the knot on her robe were jerky with irritation. "Five exceptions aren't going to sink the pretense."

"Five plus most of the DCI," he countered. He'd given in to exhaustion and shut his eyes for a moment, but she knew better than to believe he'd take any well-deserved rest before heading back into headquarters. "The more people who know the truth about you, the greater the risk that Vance learns you're alive."

"Stop being a naysayer. This could work. And you know it. You just said that you'd considered it." His eyes snapped open then, and something in them stopped her.

"Because letting the world believe you're dead is the best way to keep you safe." The starkness of his words, the intensity in his gaze had everything inside her going still. There was a time when just a look from him had her heart stuttering in her chest. She hadn't recognized the woman she'd become in the brief time they'd been together. The feelings he'd elicited in just twelve short days had been thrilling. Frightening. With the benefit of hindsight, she could see now how those unfamiliar feelings had impacted her decision to break it off.

It hadn't been the fact that he was totally different from any man she'd ever been involved with. It had been that free fall of emotion he'd elicited, which she'd been quite certain had been one-sided. For a woman who had spent most of her life making safe choices, her loss of control had been terrifying.

And then Mason Vance had walked off the pages of the offender profile she'd developed and into her life. And she'd learned the definition of real terror.

Unable to meet his gaze any longer, she looked away. "The entire time Vance had me, I felt helpless. Impotent. Completely at his mercy. The only thing that kept me sane was looking for an escape. Trying to outwit him. And now, hiding in your apartment with Micki or some other agent at my side . . . I feel defenseless again. Like he still has power over me. And I hate that. I *hate* it." Her fist clenched at her side, tightly enough that her nails bit into her palm. "Maybe you'll catch this second UNSUB as quickly as you did Vance. Or maybe he'll leave the state now that he thinks he succeeded last night. But I can't just float from one day to the next, not knowing, not doing anything proactive on my own behalf."

"You need time to heal," he started, but his words ended when she fixed him with a look.

"I'll *heal* by having a hand in putting that bastard away." The heat in her words surprised even her. "Sitting on the sidelines of the investigation is like being locked in that cell again. Different surroundings but still imprisoned. You should know how I feel. You hated being kept off the job while you were dealing with PTSD a while back." He flinched imperceptibly, and she felt a stab of shame for what in retrospect seemed like a cheap shot.

"I'm sorry." Leaning forward, she reached for his hand. "I shouldn't have brought that up."

His fingers curled around hers. Tightened. "I just want to spare you." The raw emotion in his words shook her to the core. "You may not have suffered the same fate as Vance's other victims, but you still suffered. Hate me if you want, but I'm going to do everything in my power to talk Maria out of this idea."

"I could never hate you." The flare of intensity in his gaze made the words falter on her tongue. "We both want the same thing. Vance and his accomplice behind bars for a very long time. So we'll make a pact, you and me. I'm going to present my case to Maria. But if you talk her out of it, I'll accept my role of sidelined consultant gracefully." And somehow she'd manage to keep her word about that. "Otherwise, you'll welcome me back on the team with . . ." She searched for the right phrase.

"With my usual abrasive charm?"

Hearing her onetime description of him had a small smile pulling at her lips. "I was going to say with a similar grace, but abrasive charm works for me. Is it a deal?"

With her hand in his, he returned her handshake. "I'm going to do everything in my power to make sure you lose," he informed her solemnly.

For some reason his words made her feel lighter than she had in days. "I know. I'd expect nothing less."

o o o

Sonny waited impatiently in the back of the rutted parking lot, with only a handful of aspirin to fight the waves of agony eddying from the wound in his leg. Every once in a while a whimper of pain escaped his clenched jaw. *It fucking hurts!* He hoped he'd killed that cop in the woman's condo. And he wished he'd snapped that kid's neck. Then the cop who'd shot him would have been blamed for letting the situation go so wrong. Sonny hadn't wanted to deal with a hostage, and, like a dumbass, he'd dropped the kid too soon.

He'd pulled off the headgear, hoodie, and gloves, then turned the sweatshirt inside out and tried to scrub Channing's blood from his face. Pain radiated from the wound in his leg. He might have injured himself even further when he'd pulled into an alley after getting away to steal different plates for the vehicle. But if the cop had gotten close enough to shoot him, he might have been near enough to see his license plates, too. Sonny could switch the plates yet again when he got home, but first he had to get treatment. He knew better than to go to a hospital with an unexplained gunshot wound. Which was why he was sitting behind the peeling single-story concrete block building waiting for a man he'd despised for most of the last twenty years.

The sun had been up for the better part of two hours before a midsize sedan pulled into the lot and parked near the back door of the building. The car gleamed with polish, but that didn't hide the scratches and dings on the doors or the rust forming over the back wheel well. The driver who slid out from behind the wheel was also showing his age. His thin shoulders were beginning to droop, and the bald spot on the back of his head was noticeable even from a distance. Sonny waited for him to let himself into the building before putting his vehicle in gear and backing up to pull in right next to the other car.

He slipped silently through the back door, every movement an agony. The man was crouched in front of an aging computer, his gaze intent on the screen.

"Let me guess. Kiddie porn?"

Jerking around, the man fumbled for the keyboard, finally finding the key to turn the screen black. But not before Sonny had gotten the glimpse he needed to affirm his suspicions. Disgusted, he snapped, "Still a pervert, Davis? Still bringing little boys to your clinic to show them the animals and then proving that you're the only real animal in the place?"

Davis rose and cast a quick look around as if in search of help. "I told you before, I don't want you to come here anymore."

Painfully, Sonny moved farther into the room before stopping and locking the door behind him. "Way I recall it, you were the only one to *come* in this room."

The other man flushed. "My employees will be arriving shortly. What do you want?"

In answer, Sonny unwrapped the crumpled blood-soaked Kleenex tissues he had stuffed against the wound and turned to show the man. "You have to get this bullet out of me."

Davis gaped. "Are you crazy?" he hissed. "I'm not risking my license for you. Go to a damn hospital."

"They'd have to report gunshot wounds." Sonny limped carefully to the door that led to the front of the clinic. Locked it, too. "And you will operate because if you don't I'll go straight to your wife and tell her that her husband likes to fuck little boys. I'm guessing she already suspects. And then I'm going to tell the cops the same thing. Losing your license is the least of your worries."

The older man blanched. "I stopped." The whine in his voice scraped down Sonny's nerves. "After just a few times, I stopped—you know I did. And I made it up to you. I gave you that drug you asked for a few months ago. It's not fair the way you keep coming back."

The gun was in his hand so fast, the man blinked before staggering backward in an attempt to put distance between them. "You don't want to talk to me about fair. Not after what you did to me. Now get the tools you'll need. If you're quick, maybe I can be gone before your workers get here."

Davis's whole body jolted at the reminder. "It wasn't just me. Your mother . . ."

A red wash of rage flooded Sonny's vision. Fogged his brain. He was six again. Cowering in the closet, trying to shit himself in the vain hopes of so disgusting the man who would come through his bedroom door that he'd be left alone. "Mommy is *dead*. She was a monster, and so are you." One-handed, Sonny fumbled to unfasten his pants, peel them down his legs. "And you're going to want to make sure I don't feel a thing when you take that bullet out, or you'll end up the same way she did."

o o o

Winding down his summary of the events of last night for the team members present for the hastily arranged briefing, Cam ended with, "Agent Franks is certain he wounded the UNSUB as he fled, so Des Moines Police Department officers are checking the local hospitals and clinics for patients who came in with gunshot wounds in the last few hours. The crime scene team found some small samples that might prove to be the UNSUB's blood at the site where his vehicle was parked." Cam couldn't help glancing toward the chair Franks usually commandeered. It was an empty reminder of what the scene last night had cost them. Boggs in the hospital. Both he and Franks on paid administrative leave until the internal review board cleared them of wrongdoing in the shootout with the UNSUB. Cam was going to do his damnedest to ensure that review was expedited.

"Franks got the license plate number, so we've got a BOLO out on the offender's car."

"There's a short window of opportunity on the be-on-the-look-out alert," Agent Alex Beachum observed. "After kidnapping Van Wheton, he switched the plates sometime while transporting her to Iowa."

Cam nodded. "And the van used in that crime was likely tinted navy before it was spotted in Channing's neighborhood, then switched back to white later. So this guy might have the skill to change more than just the plates on his vehicle. DMPD officers are canvassing the neighborhood to see if anyone can offer more details. Patrick, you'll go over the footage from the security cameras we installed in Dr. Channing's apartment, but for now we're operating under the assumption that the guy who went there to kill her is the same man who was seen assaulting a corpse a few hours earlier." The man had been wearing a hood and goggles when Boggs and Franks saw him, but maybe at some point during his time inside the condo he'd removed one or both.

He stopped for a moment to scan the group assembled before him, noting in a dim part of his brain that contrary to her stated intentions, Special Agent Gonzalez was not in the room. "One of the witnesses at the river has positively identified the man he saw. He ID'd him from the sketch Agent Turner drew of the man who kidnapped Van Wheton and was caught on camera transporting her from Edina to Iowa. From there the accomplice apparently handed her over to Vance. It goes to follow that the same man was doing Vance's bidding when he attempted to kill Dr. Channing early this morning."

And he'd pay dearly, Cam vowed silently, for that attempt on Sophie's life. He'd make sure of that.

Looking down to consult his notes, he said, "We've got one crime scene team finishing up at the Raccoon River site and another still dispatched at Channing's condo. It'll be hours yet before they're done there, but there will be plenty of ballistics evidence at the second scene."

"What's the latest on Corbin?" Brody Robbins, the youngest agent on the team asked. He'd transferred to the Major Crime Unit only months ago, and with this investigation he was gaining experience fast.

"The couch slowed the velocity of the bullets, and Boggs was wearing a vest, so both of those facts worked in his favor." Cam could be thankful the man wasn't hurt worse while remaining cognizant that Boggs's medical leave was likely going to extend well beyond his administrative leave. "One slug was buried in the couch, the vest stopped another, but he was hit in the arm by the third. He won't be released from the hospital until tomorrow, depending on the damage. Our best bet is the slugs the criminalists will retrieve from Channing's spare bedroom, and the spent cartridges expelled from the offender's weapon. I've submitted a request to have the ballistics evidence fast-tracked, so we can expect a quick turnaround with the results." Cam saw a few of the agents straighten in their chairs, looking slightly less grim. Although it was too soon for optimism, he was similarly anxious to see if the brass left behind from the offender's gun would provide them with a lead.

"We're due for some luck," Cam continued. God knows last night hadn't brought any. "The kids who found the body last night voluntarily surrendered their cell phones. They claimed they hadn't taken any pictures . . ." There was an audible snort of disbelief from one of the agents. "But I left the phones with the Cybercrime Unit to make sure. Channing's neighbor's boy, Carter Hammel, is at the hospital. While he's unharmed, we're having swabs done to see if he has any of the offender's DNA on his body." The chances of that were slim, but no avenue would be left unexplored. "Turner is conducting formal interviews with the three witnesses from last night and finishing up sketches of the UNSUB with two of them."

"Any chance this offender will head to Vance's house to lay low for a while?" This from Agent Samuels.

Cam resisted the urge to look at his watch. Gonzalez's absence from this briefing after her stated intention to attend was beginning to worry him. He hoped like hell that whatever had kept her away wasn't associated with this case. But he suspected otherwise. "Polk County Sheriff Jackson has had the house under surveillance since we arrested Vance and got proof he hadn't been working alone. If the UNSUB heads there, he'll be picked up."

He wasn't pinning his hopes on that. It would be too easy. And nothing about this case so far had been simple. "But you can head over to Alleman and talk to the townspeople. Show Rhonda Klaussen's picture around. See if you can get a feel for whether she was seen in public, how freely she moved around." A thought struck him then. "Take a copy of the first sketch Turner did of the UNSUB. May as well see if any of Vance's neighbors recognize him."

In addition to the events of last night, they were still faced with the task of building an airtight case against Vance. Discovering the true nature of Klaussen's involvement with the man was a priority. And Vance had to have met with the accomplice somewhere. "Beachum, you'll work the BOLO tip line. Robbins, head back to Channing's place. Once the crime team is done, I want her condo kept under surveillance." Hopefully he'd be able to get the DMPD to take over that duty. He needed every agent actively working this case.

A startled expression on his face, the younger agent questioned, "You think the offender will go back there?"

"Well, the guy does seem to get lonely for his victims," drawled Beachum, drawing a few laughs.

The remark brought an answering tightness to Cam's chest, but he tamped down the emotion. "That he does. We got a positive ID on the container by the river that the corpse was kept in. It's called a Ziegler Transfer Case, commonly used by funeral homes to transport dead bodies without a casket." He turned to the computer on the table next to him and brought up the photos of it. "It'd also work to keep animals away."

"Was this body doused with insecticide, too?" Beachum wanted to know.

"We'll find out when the ME has time to examine the body." But if it had been, that would be another clear link to the other six victims they'd found. Cam brought up another set of pictures. "The case was mounted on this flat gurney so the UNSUB could move it in and out of the cave more easily." The next pictures were of the cave they'd found yards away from the clearing used for the assault. It was directly below the rocky area the teenagers had watched the man from. "This chamber is barely wide enough to house the cart, and about eight foot deep." He switched to close-ups taken of the interior. "One small bone was discovered near the back of the cave, near the river. We'll know soon if it's animal or human."

The next picture showed a stack of stones next to the cave's entrance. "We think the UNSUB collected good-size stones from the area to block the opening from view and keep out wildlife. Then he moved them whenever he wanted access."

"You think he's used this spot before? For other victims?"

Agent Samuels had just nailed Cam's worst fear. He kept his reply neutral. "Too soon to tell. We don't know enough about this offender to predict what he's done or might do, outside of immediately seeking medical assistance for his injury. Given the fact that this body was embalmed, it might not have even been a victim. Maybe the guy was practicing. Maybe he was in between vics and snatched a body for his own twisted perversion. We have to consider every possibility. Keep me posted regarding your progress. Unless something major comes up between now and then, we'll meet here tomorrow, same time."

Gathering up his things, he headed toward the door, his earlier agreement with Sophie ringing in his ears. He needed to see SAC Gonzalez and do what he could to dissuade the woman from Sophie's plan. It behooved him to act first before she called the SAC. He'd already lost the battle of keeping Sophie out of the investigation. Cam was going to do his best to ensure her involvement was limited to consulting from afar.

His progress down the hallway was halted when he heard his name called from behind him. Turning, he saw Mark Kohler shuffling toward him. Cam had never seen the tall lanky cybercrime agent move at any pace above a slow amble. His mind, in contrast, moved at Mach-1 speed. "Hope your news is better than the luck you had at the races Saturday."

The other man reached up to touch the back of his neck, which sported a wince-worthy sunburn acquired, he'd told Cam earlier, at the Newton racetrack the past weekend. Although Cam wasn't a race fan, he could easily imagine why it appealed to Kohler. The cars' speeds had to rival that of the man's mind.

"Depends on what you were hoping for, I suppose." The other agent halted beside him. "A more detailed analysis of those three phones you dropped off will have to wait at least a day or two. But I can tell you for sure that one of their owners lied to you about not taking any pictures."

Cam uttered a distinctly unprofessional oath. Kohler's head bobbed in agreement. Each of the kids who'd witnessed the scene at the Raccoon River had fervently denied snapping a picture while there, and when they had all three freely given up their phones as proof, he'd hoped that meant they'd been truthful. The image, if it had been shared widely, could mean they were headed for a PR nightmare. "Which one?"

"The Samsung Galaxy S4. Belonging to the Pals boy. How is it these kids all have newer phones than mine?" The man's voice was aggrieved.

Cam was unsympathetic. "Because your wife clamped down on your budget for useless technological gadgetry?"

That earned him a quick grin. "Nothing about technology is useless, my friend, but point taken. Anyway, your little buddy activated his Snapchat app during the time frame you described. Took a ten-second video, which wasn't stored on his phone, but I was able to retrieve it. Pretty good clarity, given that it was taken at night, but sick subject matter. I can't tell you right now who the recipient might be or whether there were multiples. And I won't be able to get at that task until late tomorrow afternoon, probably."

A hot burn of anger spread through Cam's chest. Being lied to came with the job, but in this instance it might just turn into a media nightmare for them. Which didn't have him feeling charitable at all toward that little weasel Pals. "Tell me about this app. You said it wasn't in his gallery. Does that mean he deleted it from his phone after sending it?"

"He could have, or he could have failed to save it. Snapchat allows a user to set a time limit in which the recipients can view it. Anywhere from one to ten seconds. Then it supposedly disappears."

A dull spike of tension started to hammer in Cam's left temple. "Supposedly?"

"Well . . ." Kohler again rubbed his neck, albeit gingerly. "There are glitches. It takes minimal skill to retrieve a photo or video after it's supposed to disappear. And if a viewer doesn't open the snap, it can exist on the Snapchat server for thirty days. There are also utilities that a viewer can use to save a sent snap without notifying the sender."

The ramifications were clear. "So any one of Pals's viewers could have saved it and sent it out to their own viewers without Pals being aware of it."

"Pretty much."

"Appreciate it. Hang on to the phones. I'll let you know if we need more."

"No problem."

Cam watched the other man stroll away for a moment, his mind working furiously as he mentally switched gears. That meeting with

Gonzalez seemed even more important than ever, and she wasn't going to be pleased with this news. It occurred to him that he'd lost the last argument he'd had with her regarding media releases when she'd released Sophie's offender profile to the public. It had been that act, Cam was convinced, that had drawn Vance's attention to Sophie and led to her abduction.

Pivoting, he pulled out his own cell and called Jenna as he made his way to the area housing the interview rooms. When she answered, he wasted no time. "Where are you on the forensic sketches with Pals and Adams?"

"I'm finishing with Spencer right now. He's done a terrific job. You'll be interested in the composite sketch that's emerging."

Her comment was laden with meaning, but right now there was only one aspect about Pals that concerned him. "I'm on my way. Keep him there."

"You got it. We're in interview room four."

Slipping the phone back in his pocket, he lengthened his stride. The minute Pals sent those photos, he'd compromised the agency's options when it came to public dissemination of information about last night. Before seeing Gonzalez, Cam knew he'd better be armed with the full extent of the potential damage those pictures might cause.

His mood darkened. Kohler might be in love with all new facets of technology, but there were times when it was just a major pain in the ass.

Slowing in front of interview door four, Cam gave a perfunctory rap before entering. The first person in the room that he noted was Jason Drew, legal counsel for IPI Home Products. The attorney was wearing a suit that Cam suspected cost more than everything in Cam's closet combined. The man had been at the scene last night, too. The elder Pals was apparently too busy to tend to the minor matter of his son being chased by a gun-wielding necrophiliac.

Normally the realization would have elicited a stab of empathy. Right now, however, compassion was the last thing he was feeling toward the kid currently twisting in his seat to check out the new arrival.

He sent a questioning glance at Jenna, who had risen from her seat next to Spencer and approached him with a sheet in her hand. "All done. Spencer's been a trouper." She handed the composite sketch to Cam, and he glanced at it, familiarity striking him with the force of a blow.

The subject in the sketch had some significant differences from the one Jenna had done with a witness in Edina, the one Cam had shown to Jonah last night. This man wasn't wearing a hat, and his dark hair was shorter. The features weren't arranged in a pleasant mask this time, but twisted in rage. However, the nose was the same, as was the slightly narrowed jaw and the mouth that Sophie had dubbed "sensitive."

After studying the drawing for a moment, he handed it back to Jenna, careful to keep his face expressionless. He rounded the table then, nodding to the attorney. "Mr. Drew. Spencer. I want to thank you both for being here."

Drew made a point of looking at his watch. "Spencer has been quite cooperative, but he needs to get to school. I assume I'm free to leave with him?"

"In a minute. I just have a couple follow-up questions. That okay with you, Spencer?"

The kid started a little as Cam turned his attention to him, but he never glanced at the attorney before shrugging. "Sure. I guess."

Drawing out the chair beside Drew, Cam sank into it to face the boy. "We've still got your cell, but I'm working on getting that back to you as soon as possible." He offered a smile he was far from feeling. "Guessing a teenager feels lost without his phone these days, even if it's just for a few days."

Another shrug. "I can just activate my old one."

"Good. Glad we won't be putting you out. I can probably get that phone back to you sooner if you come clean about what you did with it last night before you ran back to your car."

That had the kid's head jerking up, a flare of guilt in his eyes. Drew's voice was controlled. "Are you accusing my client of a crime, Agent Prescott?"

"Just an omission." Cam never looked in the attorney's direction. He was focused on Spencer. "I asked if you had used the phone while you were watching that man. You said you hadn't. Cyberforensics says otherwise. You took a short video. You used the Snapchat app and transmitted it. Good clarity, I'm told."

A look of incredulity on his face, Pals blurted out, "You can't trace anything on Snapchat! The pictures disappear."

"Spencer!" The attorney's expression was thunderous. "Not another word."

Cam looked at the lawyer. "He's not being charged with anything, but he gave misleading information that might have bearing on this case. I don't think you want him to further obstruct our investigation."

"That's bull, Mr. Drew. They can't access anything that goes out—"

"Quiet," the man snapped. His gaze never left Cam's. "I want your word that his involvement is ended after this. That includes no misdemeanor or false reporting charges."

"You have it. All I want is an answer to the question so I can act accordingly."

After a long moment, the attorney nodded and switched his attention to Spencer. "Whom did you send the pictures to?"

The kid slouched in his chair, clearly disgusted with the proceedings. "I don't know."

"We can find out." Cam made sure none of his frustration was apparent in his tone. "It'll take another day or two, but forensics can trace the recipients of your messages. You tell me now, it'll build up some goodwill. Make up for lying about it in the first place."

"I mean, I'm not sure. All my contacts are grouped, and I sent it out to some friends."

"How many in the group?" Drew asked.

"I don't . . ." With a quick glance toward Cam, the kid backtracked. "I'm just saying I can't be sure without looking at my phone and counting. Not many, I know that. I'm guessing . . . thirty or so?"

o o o

Cam knocked at the SAC's closed door, a sense of urgency riding him. He was taken aback, however, when Major Crime Unit Assistant Director Paul Miller opened the door.

"Sir." It didn't take much guessing to figure what had brought the man from his office at DCI headquarters to the agents' field office. Gazing past the man, he could see Gonzalez behind her desk, her expression inscrutable as always. "I can come back."

"No, come in. We were just discussing your case." Miller stood aside and waved him to a chair, demand implicit in the gesture. Feeling like a fly settling on a spider's web, Cam walked past the man and sat in one of the two chairs facing the SAC's desk.

He wasn't given to paranoia, but he had a healthy sense of self-preservation. Miller's involvement in this investigation had all his instincts screaming. Cam had been serving in California on a multiagency drug task force when the former assistant director of MCU had suffered career suicide. Miller had been named in his stead, and the man had always been a little too concerned about public relations to suit Cam. Given the recent twist in this case, however, there was real cause for worry.

"How long will it take for the internal review on Boggs and Franks to be conducted?" he started when Miller had reseated himself.

Miller frowned at him. "Just concern yourself with the investigation, Agent. I'll manage the personnel matters."

"With all due respect, sir, I need to know how long I'm going to be down two agents on the task force." The assistant director exchanged a glance with Gonzalez. "I can't afford to wait days—or weeks—to be fully staffed again."

"The agents have already submitted reports of the events. We can probably have Franks's hearing conducted late afternoon. Tomorrow morning at the latest." He gave a shrug. "Boggs isn't going anywhere for a while, so his can wait."

The timeline was quicker than Cam had expected. And, unfortunately, no one could be certain at this point how soon Boggs would be granted a medical discharge allowing him to resume his duties. "I've just come from reinterviewing one of the witnesses to the sexual assault last night. Cybercrimes did a preliminary check and discovered one of the kids took a video on his camera phone. He sent it to a group of friends that he believes numbers around thirty recipients."

Miller's face visibly grayed at the news. "God, this gets worse by the minute." He took out a handkerchief to mop his balding dome. "Multiply thirty kids who all might've sent it out to thirty more . . . Has anyone seen TV? It could already be on the morning news."

"We need to prepare a statement about the events of last night and get it out to the media sooner rather than later." He was aware of Gonzalez's sharp look. The words were a first, coming from him. But he was not unmindful of the nightmare ahead of them if the investigation became dogged with sensationalism. "In the meantime, I've directed Spencer Pals to make a list of people that may be on that list, and I'll request that Cybercrimes cross-check the group. Agent Turner can contact each of the individuals on the list the boy is making. If the video hasn't been made public yet, maybe we can prevent it from happening." Jenna would be free for the task after the sketch session with Trina Adams was completed. The last thing he wanted was for the family of the victim discovered last night to stumble across that video online.

Miller nodded. "That's the best we can hope for, I suppose. I'll take care of the press release myself. Maria, I'd appreciate you making yourself available for the news conference."

"Within the hour we'll have our third composite drawing of the man seen on the riverbank, if you decide you want to release them."

The assistant director switched his attention to Cam. "Have copies of the sketches sent to me. How soon before you can determine whether the same man attempted to kill Dr. Channing last night?"

"I've got someone on the way to go over the security footage as we speak. We'll know shortly."

Miller nodded decisively. "I'll arrange for the news conference as soon as possible, but the focus will be on the man seen by the teenagers without mentioning the attempt on Channing's life. I believe Maria has already discussed with you her intention of continuing Dr. Channing's consultation on this case. She believes, and I concur, that Channing's input can help us narrow our focus on Vance's accomplice."

It was easy to see that he was outnumbered in his feelings about that action, so Cam reserved his argument for the scope of Sophie's involvement. He shifted in his chair, looking for a more comfortable spot. There wasn't one. "I can have complete case files at Dr. Channing's disposal," he began. "Her involvement can be done safely in a controlled setting, with an agent at her side at all times—"

He stopped when he noted the meaningful look exchanged between Gonzalez and Miller. "I've spoken to Dr. Channing again since I left her this morning," Maria began. "And although I have a few reservations about her idea, I think it has some merit."

"She wants to fake her death," Cam stressed. He looked at Miller. "It would involve deceiving the public."

"A deception that is forgivable if it leads to her safety." Cam's stomach tightened at the other man's reply. "Dr. Channing is probably more secure right now than she has been since her abduction. If Vance and his accomplice believe she's dead, she doesn't have to work in a controlled environment, although certainly I believe we should continue to offer protection. With the right precautions in place, she could move around freely, conduct interviews, and attend scenes."

With a hitch of his trousers, the man stood. "I believe hers is a reasonable request, one that will offer more safety for her. She's emailing an obit notice to be released to the press, and we've agreed to a handful of her family and friends who can be let in on the truth. I've directed Special Agent Gonzalez to agree to her plan. You will, of course, personally see that she's accompanied by an agent at all times."

"Of course." It was difficult to force even those words out of his mouth, so Cam said nothing else while Miller issued a few more directives for Maria before leaving the office. Only then did he lean back in his chair, pressing the heels of his palms to his eyes.

"Relax. The news of her death will be greatly exaggerated."

"Spare me the literary references."

"We're not going to announce it," Maria went on. "The obit will be buried in the newspaper with minimal information, pending the notification of next of kin. Hopefully that will be enough to satisfy anyone following up to make sure Channing is really dead."

"This is totally unnecessary." Frustration had Cam biting out the words. "She could consult from her current location where she's already safe with an agent at her side. No one knows where she's at."

"I believe she can be more useful when she's not kept at a distance. And I agree with Dr. Channing that we lose a valuable element of surprise if Vance and his partner discover she's alive. We can make sure she's no longer a target, and, properly disguised, she can be mobile. Once this thing is solved, we'll have public sentiment on our side, and there shouldn't be any blowback for the false obit, since we're doing it as a matter of protection." Cam lowered his hands to see Maria lifting her shoulders in a gesture that was oddly reminiscent of Spencer Pals. "I don't see a downside."

He lowered his hands to stare at her. "You don't see a downside," he repeated incredulously. "Jesus, Maria, you're the same one who told me only days ago that you had second thoughts before naming me lead in this investigation." And the memory of that conversation still held a bite. "And I've been back on the job for *a year* since my stint undercover on that multiagency task force." An assignment that had resulted in recurring PTSD, which had kept him from returning to work for far longer than he'd liked.

An assignment that continued to haunt him to this day.

"But you don't think that Soph—Dr. Channing might be too traumatized to consult after being abducted, beaten, terrorized, and nearly raped just three days ago?" He surged to his feet, unable to contain his frustration any longer. "Try explaining that reasoning to me."

From the looks of her expression, he imagined she was gritting her teeth. "I'm not placing the outcome of this case and the well-being of a material witness in Dr. Channing's hands," she snapped. "She's not in charge of the investigation. Are you really saying that her experience a few days ago damaged her credibility? Her expertise? You don't believe her work on this case can result in any valuable leads?"

It was his turn to clench his jaw. It was the resulting emotional cost to Sophie that he was really worried about, but there was no way to share that without revealing that his concern stemmed from the personal and not the emotional. But he wasn't done trying.

He took a turn around the office as he spoke, making an effort to level his tone. "I'm just asking you to weigh the potential personal cost to Channing. Is it worth it in exchange for the possible leads she can give us?"

"She's an adult. She's responsible for her own choices, and I respect her too much to try to second-guess them." Although some of the temper had dissipated from Maria's words, there was still an edge to them. "And I'll tell you one thing, I have a feeling she wouldn't welcome your paternalistic questioning of her capabilities."

He stopped to arrow a look at her then, one she returned unblinkingly. Rationally he recognized this was his out. Better that the SAC thought he was a chauvinist than to suspect that his concern for Sophie stemmed from something else.

Something far more intimate.

He was zero for two since walking into her office. Cam recognized there were no battles left to fight here. Silently he went to the door.

"Assistant Director Miller has been in contact with lab manager Fenton, and your request last night for priority status on the ballistics testing has been granted. As soon as the evidence has been logged in, they'll start the tests."

It was a sop, but better than nothing. Cam figured the brass and spent bullets collected at the two scenes were their best lead so far, and the sooner they yielded results, the better. He'd left orders that the collected brass at the scenes be taken to the lab immediately. Maybe the tests would be started soon.

"Oh, and Prescott?"

He aimed a look over his shoulder.

Maria's gaze was shrewd. "I'm hoping that the concern for Channing that you've stated so eloquently comes from a sincere lack of faith in her abilities. Because if I start to believe you're more worried about Dr. Channing the woman . . . The case already has two agents on administrative leave. We can't afford to lose a third."

The warning implicit in her words was impossible to miss, and one he knew better than to respond to. Cam shut the door behind him almost silently, a stark contrast to the resentment seething inside him.

Chapter 4

It had been ridiculously easy to find the woman he'd seen last night. Sonny stared at the computer screen, his throbbing leg propped on a pillow and stretched out on the recliner. IOSME, he'd discovered, stood for Iowa Office of State Medical Examiner. Which made sense, given that she'd been at the scene last night for Janice. Barely a pang accompanied the thought of the dead woman. All his focus was reserved for the new one.

Dr. Lucy Benally, forensic pathologist. Lucy. He said the name aloud, savoring it. It fit exactly the woman he felt as though he already knew. The IOSME website showed the office personnel, and there was a picture of the female he'd seen last night. Although the others wore a bright smile for the camera, Lucy's lips were only slightly curved. Fitting, Sonny thought approvingly, for the seriousness of the job she was entrusted with. A second page on the site informed him that she'd been employed by the agency for the last five years, and it listed her schooling and previous jobs.

A sharp pain arrowed into his wounded leg, and he muttered a curse. Picking up the bottle of pain pills on the table beside the couch, he shook another out into his palm and popped it in his mouth. Davis had done a ham-handed job. He should have shot the bastard while he'd had the chance. Sonny had ordered Davis to supply him with enough pain medication to get him through his recovery, and the man had been so eager to see the last of him that he'd done so uncomplainingly.

Sonny turned his attention to courthouse searches. Homeowners gave up a great deal of information about themselves in the simple act of buying property. Of course, he couldn't be sure that Lucy Benally owned a house, but he hoped she did. Not just because it made her easier to find. But because the woman he suspected she was would be anxious to have a home to call her own. To tend to it as lovingly as she had tended to Janice last night.

A few minutes later, he reached for his cell to log in the address his search had yielded. A bit more digging, and he found her home just outside Bondurant, less than twenty miles east of Ankeny, where she worked. Returning to the computer, he typed the address into Google Maps Street View. Instants later his screen filled with the image of a neat older two-story sitting on shaded acreage, a detached two-stall garage behind it.

Sometimes you really had to love the Internet.

Sonny played with the image, zooming in and out, looking at the property from different angles. Although the house wasn't fancy, it was plenty big for someone living alone.

After opening another window on the browser, he set to work combing public databases for a marriage license listing for Lucy Yanaha Benally. Not finding one, he leaned back against the pillow and smiled. It was easy to believe that a clear path toward Lucy meant only one thing.

They were fated to be together.

o o o

"You're right." Cam peered closely at the enhanced image on the computer screen over Agent Samuels's shoulder before looking down at the composite sketch in his hands again. "It's the same guy. Not that there was much doubt."

"Good thing you added cameras in all the rooms. This is the only place he removed the goggles," the other agent said, squinting from the screen to the drawing and back again. "What's he look like . . . five ten, one sixty?"

Cam was silent for a moment as he judged the height and weight of the image on the screen. "I'd say so. And that's a close match to the description given by Franks and Boggs, not to mention that of the kids."

John Samuels looked up at Cam. "Gonna give a description of the guy with the press release?"

"The news conference was a couple hours ago. This sketch was released at that time." But Cam would apprise the SAC that they had positive ID. The same man that had kidnapped Vance's last victim in Edina had been found assaulting a corpse last night. And had then tried to kill Sophie Channing.

He pulled out his cell to text the SAC. "Make a copy of the security feed and bring it back to headquarters with you."

"But secure the place first?"

"Robbins is taking care of it." They had deliberately left the security breach Vance had exploited here the first time he'd gained access, as well as the hole he'd left in her system that allowed reentry. "You can team up with Beachum on the tip line. Nothing panned out on the BOLO this morning, but calls are starting to come in on the sketches." A valuable lead could be gleaned from a tip line, but they were also laborious to operate. Every call that came in had to be evaluated for possible helpfulness, then prioritized. The ones that had the most potential were then checked out. The manpower required was not insignificant. And it was never far from Cam's mind that he was down two agents.

"Cam, that neighbor you said to watch for just pulled in her drive." Criminalist Aubrey Hartley turned sideways in the doorway to ease the girth from her pregnancy through it. She and some of her colleagues were packing up their equipment to return to the lab. Another who was focused on retrieving the bullets from where they were embedded around the condo would remain to finish that task.

He gave Aubrey a wide berth as he passed, an action that drew a glare from the woman. "I'm not *that* big, wise guy. You want to see how fast this pregnant lady can move, just keep being a smart-ass."

He shot her a grin. "How much longer?"

"Seven weeks." He didn't miss the subtle movement as she pressed a hand to her lower back.

"Fenton would let you stick to lab work for the duration." He knew for a fact that the lab manager wouldn't protest at the idea.

"And let these clowns have all the fun?" Aubrey jerked a thumb in the direction of her coworkers. "I told my husband I'd give it a couple more weeks. After that I doubt I'll be able to get up off the floor even if I can squat down. I'm hoping that by then . . ." Her voice tapered off, but he knew exactly what she was thinking. That by then this investigation would be ended, finally. Vance and his accomplice would both be behind bars, with an ironclad case built against them to ensure they stayed that way.

"I hope so, too." He went out the door and jogged next door to where Livvie Hammel, Sophie's friend and neighbor, lived. When the frazzled redhead opened the door and saw him, her expression wasn't exactly friendly.

Silently, she opened the door for him. When he walked inside, she swung it shut behind him. Locked it. "I talked to Sophia. And you're not leaving again until you promise to talk her out of this crazy idea. Pretending she's dead? Diving into this investigation again? I can't believe you're allowing that. She could have been killed last night. So could Carter." Tears welled up in her eyes. "That man touched him. He hurt him and could have done worse. And you damn well better be doing something to catch him. Why aren't you out there looking for him?"

Her voice broke on that, and she ducked her head, but not before he saw the tears spilling down her cheeks. Cam shifted uneasily. He had a male's natural unease when faced with a crying woman. "The entire area is searching for him. We released a description on a news conference a few hours ago. And Sophie's safer while the assassin thinks he succeeded than she would be otherwise." As much as it pained him to echo Sophie and Maria's argument, there was an element of truth in it. "She called you?"

Livvie wiped her face on the sleeve of her T-shirt, nodding silently.

"Delete her number from your cell or change the contact name," he ordered. "Get rid of any records of past calls to or from her, any texts or messages. Tell that other friend of yours, Carrie from down the street, to do the same. It's safer for everyone that way."

"Safer?" The word hitched up at the end, and for a moment he thought she'd break down in sobs. "There hasn't been a lot of that in the last twenty-four hours. What if that man comes back for Carter? He didn't get a good look at him, but the guy doesn't know that. What if—"

Consciously gentling his voice, Cam said, "There's no reason for him to come back. But for your peace of mind, you and Carter should stay somewhere else for a while. Just until we have a handle on this guy."

Livvie looked torn. "I couldn't possibly leave while Sophia is still in danger."

"She isn't." At least not the type of danger Livvie was talking about. "She's under protection, but you'll feel better if you get a break from this. The phony obit has already hit the news, and, given your proximity to Sophie's home, there might be nosy reporters wanting a word with you."

She stepped back, a look of horror on her face. "Oh, God, Carter will hear the news. He'll think . . ."

Cam nodded grimly. There were ramifications for this plan of Sophie's that eddied further than she'd considered. "Better that he doesn't hear about it at all. Where can you take him?"

Livvie chewed her bottom lip. "My mom lives in Branson. It's a drive but we could stay there a few days. And if necessary, she'll keep him longer, after I have to get back to work. She was going to come here to do it, but . . ."

"Sounds like a plan. Do you mind if I talk to him?" At the uncertainty on her expression, he assured her, "I just want to ask a few more questions."

"He's answered plenty already. The kid should be exhausted, but I swear he's more wired than usual from the excitement." She made a face. "Whatever you do, don't encourage him. Right now he thinks he's a superhero. I'm waiting for the nightmares to start."

Cam followed her through the condo to the small sunroom in the back. Carter was ensconced on the couch there, gaze intent on a handheld video device. "Hey, buddy." Sitting down next to him, Cam waited until the boy's attention shifted from his game to him.

"Mom says Dr. C didn't get hurt last night." The boy dropped the game system in his lap and pinned Cam with a bright-blue gaze. "She says Dr. C wasn't even home."

With a glance at the silent Livvie, who had propped herself against the doorjamb, he responded, "Well, your mom is right. But you didn't know that, did you?"

The boy shook his head. "I thought when the guy told me to go inside that he was with the bad guy who was going to hurt Dr. C. But he wasn't, was he?"

"No, that was another agent who works with me. What you did was a real brave thing. But it was foolish, too. Do you understand the difference?"

With a hunch of his shoulder, Carter said, "It means I lose my BB gun."

"Well, that." Cam stifled a smile. "You did something most kids your age would be too afraid to do. That's brave. But seven-year-olds are too young to chase bad guys. You'll have to wait until you're older to do that." He paused a beat before saying, "Did you see the bad guy's face at all?"

Carter gave a vehement shake of his head. "He had a hood and something over his eyes. I couldn't even see the agent guy real good because it was dark when he was chasing us."

It was exactly what had been in Franks's report, so Cam had expected no different. "You tried to help, and that's important. I have another thing you can do. You want to help Dr. C, don't you?" He saw Livvie straighten warily.

"Why does she need help? Mom said she wasn't hurt." Worry clouded the boy's eyes.

"She wasn't. But we have to keep quiet about what happened here last night. And we need you to keep what you saw a secret. Do you know what a secret is?"

The boy looked decidedly unenthusiastic at the topic. "I would only tell Zach. Not even Ryder, because he blabs everything. No one else, though, I swear."

Cam shook his head solemnly. "That's not the way secrets work. There are lots of things I'm not allowed to tell when I'm working a case. Because if the wrong person hears it, a bad guy might get away.

I know it's hard, but you can't tell Zach or Ryder or anyone else, even if they ask you questions about it."

The faster Livvie got the kid out of the state, the better. There was no way to predict how many news organizations would pick up on the fake obit and, when they did, how long it would take them to piece together facts about last night. Hopefully reporters couldn't track the kid down in Missouri, but that didn't mean Carter couldn't still communicate with his friends.

"Not even my dad?"

"Just Mom and Dad," Cam answered. He watched the boy's expression. "Do we have a deal? Until I catch the bad guy?"

"Okay." Resignation heavy in his tone, Carter picked up his game again. "But I hope you catch him quick. I'm not real good at keeping secrets."

"True enough," Livvie murmured as she stepped away to let Cam go by. "But we can be on the road in an hour. I'll make sure he doesn't have any opportunities before then. And I'll be sure his dad understands the need for secrecy, too."

"It'd be best." He slowed so she could fall into step with him, their voices low. "The neighborhood is going to be abuzz in a couple hours, and people will be calling to get your take on the news of Sophie's death. Might be best to avoid the calls even while you're on the road. Get settled in with your mom, get your story straight so you can feign sorrow like the rest of your friends."

"I'll do my job." She leveled a look at him from eyes that were eerily similar to her son's. "You just be sure that you do yours. Keep my friend safe."

"Believe me—Sophie's my top priority."

o o o

Cam opened his office door and stepped inside, stopping short in the entrance. "What are you doing here? Where's Dr. Channing?"

Agent Micki Loring turned. "Maybe you don't read the obits. Dr. Sophia Channing passed away last night. More information will be released upon notification of family. I would like you to meet her replacement, Dr. Mona Kilby." She stepped aside, and only then did Cam see the shorter woman who'd been blocked from his view. He blinked.

The foundation she wore covered the bruises on her face, but they also made her skin look several shades darker. She wore a simple navy blazer and pants with matching blue flats. The image was functional utilitarianism and completely unlike the pastel suits, skirts, and death-defying heels Sophie usually favored. It was the hair that gave him pause, however. An unassuming shade of brown, it was worn straight to barely the top of her shoulders, with a fringe of bangs. He felt a sudden and inexplicable pang of panic. "You cut your hair." It wasn't meant to sound like an accusation, but the two women exchanged a knowing look.

"Relax, it's a wig. Mine, actually, so no judging please." Micki gave Sophie a quick once-over. "Not bad for a few hours' time, I say. Once I completed the makeover, we stopped at an optometric center and ordered brown contacts. In another day or two we can change her eye color, too. I think it's good enough to fool anyone looking for a blue-eyed blonde."

"And it has the added benefit of allowing me to rejoin the investigation." It was actually a jolt to hear Sophie's voice coming from the other woman. They'd done something with lipstick to make her normally full mouth appear thinner, although the split and swollen bottom lip was still obvious. With a quick glance, he noted they hadn't forgotten to use the darker shade of foundation on her hands.

"Not bad," he said grudgingly. Cam would still prefer that she assist from the comfort of his apartment if at all, but even he had to admit that the disguise the women had come up with passed the casual observer test.

"Not bad is synonymous with genius in Prescott-speak," Loring said in an aside to Sophie.

"I'm familiar with his dialect," came Sophie's dry answer. "He's the master of the left-handed compliment."

"If no one's looking for the deception, you'll pass cursory observation." He strode past them to gather up the contents of the case file that was strewn across his desk. "But if there is someone who suspects, someone who monitors our movements, they won't be fooled for long."

He took photos from the file of the Ziegler box and the gurney and passed them to Loring. "As long as you're free, I want you to contact funeral homes in Polk and surrounding counties and ask if any of them had a theft of these items in the last year or so. I just got a call from the lab, and this gurney has been identified as a one-man cart used by funeral homes and coroners to load and unload bodies into vehicles. If you strike out with the funeral homes, try county MEs and coroners." He flipped the file shut and rounded his desk. "If that doesn't pan out, we'll need to take a look at the local companies that supply the two industries."

Loring looked distinctly unenthusiastic about the task. "If he was smart, he would have just ordered them off the Internet."

"Let's hope he didn't." Their chances of getting any web-based company to cooperate by turning over customer lists without a subpoena were far more remote than the task he'd just given the agent. "I checked the crime feed and didn't find any crimes in the state involving a body snatching, from either a funeral home or a cemetery. So we need to consider the fact that the offender has some experience in the area. I've got Robbins calling funeral homes to check on employee lists for the last fifteen years."

"Okay, I'm on it. Let me know when you want me back on protection duty." With a wave to Sophie, the agent opened the door to exit and very nearly ran into Jenna, who held two steaming cups of coffee.

"Whoa." Jenna stepped back hastily. "That could easily have been a work-related accident. Not the way I like to get my caffeine."

"Sorry." The taller agent held the door for her. "Need me to take one off your hands?"

"I got it, thanks. Although I didn't realize Cam had company." Jenna stopped just inside the door. "Should I come back?"

"Not without leaving these. You don't mind if I give one to my guest, do you?"

Jenna grinned. "I'll give her yours. Hey, Sophia. Like the new look."

Cam shot a glance at Sophie, noted her downcast expression. "She's a composite sketch artist. Tough to fool." Although he hoped like hell Sophie's disguise worked better on others they encountered, Agent Jenna Turner was the one person who should see through it.

"I'll take your word for it," Sophie replied. "And thanks, but I'll pass on the coffee. My caffeine intake the last few days has reached staggering levels."

Taking a cup from the other agent, Cam said, "You finish up with Pals and Adams without strangling one of them?"

"The girl was still pretty worked up. And she freely offered the information that Pals had taken a video. After your little talk with him, the boy listed closer to forty names that might have been contained in the group he sent that video to." Deftly Jenna shifted the file folder she'd carried under one arm to her hand and gave it a slight wave. "Have the names right here. Along with the sketches of your UNSUB. Want a peek?"

He sipped from the cup, giving a slight wince at the first taste. If there was anyone at headquarters who could make a decent pot of coffee, he or she had long managed to hide the talent. "Let's see what we've got."

Jenna handed him the file. Sophie moved closer as he flipped it open to reveal three sketches. One was the original composite drawing she'd completed from a witness account in Edina, Minnesota, when Courtney Van Wheton had been kidnapped. He recognized the second sketch as the one she'd finished with Pals. Cam studied the third that had been drawn with Trina Adams. Given the fact that eyewitness accounts were notoriously unreliable, its likeness to the other two drawings was startling.

"No question that we're looking at the same man," Sophie murmured, and he nodded. Vance's accomplice had snatched Van Wheton. Had been seen last night assaulting the corpse of an unknown victim. And was almost certainly the same man who had tried to kill Sophie just hours ago. "We already released the first sketch to the public. The new ones can be disseminated at the next press conference."

When Jenna's eyes widened a bit, he smiled grimly. Usually taking details public was anathema for him. "I want to turn the screws on this guy. He has every reason to flee the area. He thinks his job is completed, and he realizes there's a chance he can be identified by those kids last night. We may not have much time. The public now knows what he drives and what he looks like. With any luck, somebody has seen him and will let us know."

"I'll get copies to SAC Gonzalez."

"After that you can start contacting those kids on Pals's list. Leave messages. Better yet, contact their schools about the need to have the students call in regarding a sensitive matter they may be involved in. Maybe we'll hear from them sooner that way."

"You got it." Jenna flashed a grin to the woman by her side. "Good to have you back on the case, Sophia."

"I appreciate everyone's enthusiastic welcome. Present company excluded." She nodded in Cam's direction.

"Are you kidding? That's Prescott brimming with enthusiasm."

"No, this is Prescott telling you to get on your next assignment," Cam said pointedly.

The two women laughed, and his cell pinged, signaling an incoming text. Withdrawing the phone, he read the terse message. His gut did a quick vicious twist.

"And what's Dr. Mona Kilby going to be doing?" Sophie asked.

With a feeling of resignation, he slipped the phone back in his pocket, gathered up the case file, and headed for the door. "Dr. Kilby is coming with me."

"Where are we going?"

He held the door long enough for the women to walk through it, then closed it behind them. "We're returning to the scene of the crime."

o o o

Sophia hung back as they emerged from the woods that would take them down to the banks of the Raccoon River. When Cam looked over his shoulder questioningly, she waved him on without speaking, and he made his way down a rocky slope to where the criminalists still worked below. Although she had consulted on some of the most hideous crimes in the country, it was rare to actually be on scene. Especially only hours after a body was discovered.

A slight breeze whispered through the leaves, hushed gossip among the arboreal sentries about the events that had transpired here hours earlier. She stood quietly, immersing herself in the setting. Seeing it as the offender had seen it. Trying to get a feel for the man who had selected the place to enact his stomach-churning fetish.

Mason Vance had set up house in his grandfather's vacant home nearly forty minutes away in the tiny town of Alleman, east of Ankeny. According to her GPS, they were close to Van Meter right now, whose population was slightly larger than Alleman's at a thousand plus. Each of the six victims found so far had been buried atop burial vaults in rural cemeteries ringing the Des Moines metropolis area.

She was trained to look for patterns in offender behavior, and this pattern couldn't be any clearer than if the UNSUB marked his territory with a dot-to-dot drawing.

The wooded area they'd walked through would seem dark and sinister at night, but right now sun slanted through the dense canopy above, painting the ground with fingers of light. Six feet below was a grassy area that faced the river. Only the lazy drone of insects and the sound of the water lapping gently at the foot of the bank broke the silence. Under other circumstances it would seem idyllic.

Sophia was willing to bet that it was the seclusion that had called to the UNSUB. Her gaze tracked Cam's path as he and one of the Tyvek-garbed criminalists walked a short distance to an opening in the embankment. Squatted down to peer inside the dark entrance.

Remembering the isolated barn where Vance had kept his victims to practice his atrocities had a chill tracing down her spine. Where he'd kept *her*. The offender they were seeking might have a different MO, but he'd have reasons for choosing this site. Reasons that had everything to do with his ability to enact his crimes in secret.

She made her way carefully down the slope, aware of the occasional curious glance thrown her way. When she reached Cam's side, she bent down next to him.

"What are we looking at?" She recognized the criminalist at Cam's side, although she couldn't recall a name. With a flash of amusement, she realized from his expression that he either didn't remember her or didn't recognize her. Under the circumstances, she hoped it was the latter.

"I was just showing Agent Prescott," the man replied. He held an LED light aimed inside the entrance. "I'd be willing to bet this enclosure has been here for centuries. You can tell by the rough stony pattern on the walls here." He painted the area in question with his light. "They're natural. Rocks in the area are mostly clay based. Likely glaciers carved these bluffs when they moved through. Along with a slight opening here."

Following his meaning she said, "This is more than a slight indentation now."

"Seth thinks the natural part of this cave was only a couple feet deep," Cam put in. He had his own Maglite out and was pointing it deeper into the cave.

Memory flickered. *Seth.* Sophia remembered the criminalist now. Seth Dietz. She'd met him when she'd worked the rest stop rapist case for the agency last winter. An absurd sense of satisfaction flickered. Her disguise was apparently good enough to fool people she'd met only once, months ago. It was something, anyway.

"I've been inside. Shot pictures. The marker is still in place where we found the bone toward the back. Once you go deeper, the walls smooth out. There are rocks here and there, but the earth around them is much more uniform."

"You think the offender found this place and enlarged it to suit his needs."

The criminalist nodded as he moved aside to allow Cam room to belly crawl into the enclosure. "The cave ends on a slope about forty inches from the water. That entrance was covered with stones, too, but its mouth looks completely man-made. Nature didn't get that far."

"Maybe he wanted access to the river, too," Sophia said slowly. The first element of forensic profiling was to remember every choice the offender made was relevant to his wants and needs. He'd seen the secluded spot and thought of the privacy it would afford for his nighttime assaults. The cave had been tailored to that end. But the man-made back entrance might be the most telling of all.

"He'd have needed a place to put the dirt," the criminalist agreed. "But it's still supposition at this point, Miss. . . ."

"Kilby." She shot him a quick smile. "Dr. Mona Kilby. I'm the forensic psychologist consulting on the case."

The man looked at her in surprise. "Oh. I figured . . ." Obviously thinking better of whatever he was about to say, he swallowed the rest of the statement. "Nice to meet you, Doctor."

Sophia stepped aside to allow Cam to wiggle out of the enclosure. As he stood and brushed off his clothes, she decided that in this instance she was perfectly willing to look at the photos Dietz had shot of the interior of the cave rather than getting an up-close-and-personal look at it herself.

"I'm surprised it took Lucy so long to determine the bone was human." Cam had told her on the way over here that his earlier text had been from the ME, verifying the source of the remains found.

"They weren't found until after she'd left the scene." Dietz squatted and pointed inside the cave. "We discovered it just inside the back entrance. We got a better look at things when the sun came up." Looking at Cam, he asked, "From what I saw last night, it didn't look likely that the bone could have come from last night's victim."

"It didn't," Cam agreed grimly. "The body found last night is intact. Lucy would only say from the size of the one found that it likely belonged to a small-boned adult."

"With its proximity to the river, the cave would be prone to flooding," Sophia noted.

"It would if we had a year like five years ago," Cam agreed. "Rivers were up record levels. And with the spring rains, the Raccoon was definitely out of its banks. But not high enough to make it up that slope and into the cave."

"The Ziegler box wouldn't be waterproof," Seth informed her. "But if river water has gotten inside it, we'll be able to tell at the lab."

Sophia took a step back and looked at the site with new eyes. Dense woods above the bluff flanked the grassy clearing on two sides. On another it was bordered by a rocky hill that hid the tunnel. Scattered trees and underbrush on the shoreline blocked the clearing from view of the river. The seclusion it offered would have been perfect for the UNSUB's activities.

"How much time would it take him to dig out that tunnel?" she wondered aloud. It wouldn't be unusual for an offender to invest copious amounts of time looking for exactly the right spot to enact his atrocities. Some killers spent years fitting a cellar with cells and torture equipment, acting out their fantasies in the meantime with a mate or prostitutes. Others found spots that required little repurposing for their needs, like the abandoned livestock barn Vance had used. "I imagine this river is heavily fished. Although he'd be shielded from view, he still ran the risk of being seen, unless he came here only at night."

"People fish at night, too," Cam informed her. He'd put on his suit jacket before exiting the car, and his hands were in the pockets, his expression enigmatic. "And he wouldn't have had to dig it by hand. If he used a power shovel, he could have done it in one or two nights. Probably two, because he would have needed to haul the dirt out and dump it. It would still have been risky. But he's already proved he's not risk averse."

Sophia silently agreed. The second offender had been seen stalking Vance's last victim. He'd waited outside a bank while his victim went outside and made a large withdrawal, under his orders. But it hadn't been until he'd been captured on a security camera outside a gas station en route to Iowa that they'd matched him to the eyewitness sketch from Edina. "That would be a lot of work to go through for one victim."

"It sure as hell would be." Cam was already taking his cell from his pocket. Dialing in a number. "I'll call Story County emergency services and the HRD liaison. Get a STAR 1 team out here."

The words left her shaken, although they echoed her own thoughts. The Story County emergency services would dispatch a civilian human remains detection canine team trained to alert to clandestine graves or to determine the location of bodies in the water. The discovery of that finger bone meant the UNSUB had likely brought other victims to this site.

The trill of a songbird sounded. An inquisitive squirrel paused at the bottom of a tree on the ridgeline, as if puzzled by the human interruption of its normal tranquil routine.

Staring out over the peaceful scene, she wondered bleakly what sort of macabre secrets its serene facade might mask.

Chapter 5

The excitement of being this close to Lucy Benally's home almost made him giddy.

Carefully he opened the door and eased out of the borrowed car, pausing for his bag of tools before turning to squint at the nearby house. The picture on the web was obviously outdated. It hadn't done justice to the place. The home glistened with a new coat of green paint. The windows were neatly trimmed in a purplish color that provided nice contrast. The lawn looked freshly mowed, and there were pots of flowers on the front and back decks.

A call to the IOSME had told him what he needed to know— Lucy was on duty. But that didn't necessarily mean her house was empty. He walked the few remaining yards to the detached garage and peered in the side window. No cars.

He crossed the yard and climbed the two steps to the back deck. Pulling out a chair, he cautiously sat down at the outdoor patio set there and looked around. He was seated where she sat. Looking out over the scene she saw every day.

The area was peaceful. Secluded. A windbreak of fat pines surrounded the property on three sides. The nearest neighbor was a quarter mile away. Lucy Benally obviously valued her privacy. Just like him.

The knowledge made him feel closer to her. As close as he'd felt last night when he watched her tend Janice. In a way she'd come to his *yard* then. To his private area away from prying eyes and a demanding world with its never-ending static.

The pills had reduced the pain in Sonny's leg to a dull throb. It was bearable, even when walking short distances. And the slight mind haze that came with the medication was not altogether unpleasant.

Davis had said it was a flesh wound. The man was only a vet, and not a very successful one from the looks of his business. But Sonny was hoping he was right.

He'd gone to the drugstore for first aid supplies and picked up hair dye and clear-lens glasses. The box had promised ash blond but had delivered an unappealing red. Probably better, since his facial hair would be dark as it grew out. Sonny was resigning himself to the fact that he might have to shave his head eventually. But that would be a last resort.

The car had presented a problem. He knew how to disguise a vehicle. He'd tinted the van to navy before returning it to its natural white a while back. But he didn't have supplies on hand to do the car. And physically he probably wasn't up to the task right now. It hadn't taken him long to devise an alternate plan. On the way home from the drugstore he'd stopped at a bakery.

Old lady Moxley next door was eighty if she was a day. And the old sow would do anything for a willing ear and a handful of cookies. He'd taken a dozen to her house, sat through an excruciating fifteen-minute rundown on the story lines from all her soaps, and then, when she'd finally run out of breath, presented his sob story about a broken-down car. As expected, the old bat had offered the use of hers. Sonny just hoped she didn't forget she'd loaned it out and report it stolen later.

He got up, pulled gloves from his pocket, and drew them on. Then he examined the back door. The outer screen was open, but the newer-looking interior was secured. A shiny dead bolt was mounted above the knob. He took out his bump key and slipped it first into the door lock. Applied just the right pressure and felt it turn in his hand. Then he withdrew the key to perform the same action in the dead bolt. He felt a jolt of satisfaction when the lock gave. Lock picking was an art, one that had taken time and patience to perfect.

Easing the door open, he walked inside and started searching the area nearest the door for a security panel that would signal the presence of an alarm. Finding nothing in the kitchen, he strode quickly to the front door and performed a similar search. It took less than a minute to determine that the extent of Lucy's security started and ended with new doors and dead bolts.

Sonny gave a mental tsk at her carelessness. He'd have to teach her to be more safety conscious. There were few alarm systems that would have kept him out. Years of experience had taught him how to disable most of the ones on the market. But a common burglar wouldn't have that knowledge. He didn't like the thought of Lucy leaving herself vulnerable.

He moved into her living room, sat down on the comfy-looking overstuffed couch. There were things on the wall, pictures on the shelves, and a bookcase overflowing with books. Her TV was on the small side, but the overall effect was cozy comfort. It was a nice area. Homey.

With some effort he got up and resumed his exploration. The downstairs yielded a bath and another room that was used as an office. Upstairs he found three bedrooms, but only two were furnished. There was no men's clothing in any of the closets. No male items in the bathrooms. He smiled to himself when he found a loaded pistol hidden among her panties and bras.

Maybe Lucy Benally wasn't so vulnerable after all.

He emptied the weapon, slipping the cartridge into his pocket. Then he devoted a few more minutes to searching for the rest of the ammunition he was certain she'd have. Found it on the top shelf of the hallway closet. Sonny took that, too.

Opening the door next to the closet, he found a narrow stairwell. Out of curiosity he ascended it, found himself in a surprisingly well-lit attic. Three sets of dormer windows let the early afternoon sun in. It reminded him of his bedroom at the second foster home he'd been placed in. Or maybe it had been the third. The home had been a story and a half, and the entire upstairs had been remodeled into a large bedroom and bath he'd shared with three other boys. It had almost—almost seemed like a family.

Until the foster parents discovered how he'd ended up a ward of the state. Then he'd continued the foster home shuffle. Like most of the other places he'd stayed, he'd never been given a chance to show that he wasn't bad or scary. He was just an ordinary nine-year-old boy.

Mommy's good boy. The voice blew through his mind on a chill wind. *Come help Mommy.*

He shuddered, although it was hot in the attic. Stuffy in a way his other room all those years ago hadn't been.

Get your ass over here, you fucking little prick. Untie me. Now!

His heart was jackhammering in his chest. His breathing came fast and hard. Whirling, his gaze searched the barren space frantically, half expecting to see Mommy standing there. Yelling from across the space, the mean in her eyes dark and violent.

But it was empty save for some neatly stacked boxes and dust motes dancing in the sunlight.

Mommy wasn't here.

He was safe.

Safe in Lucy Benally's house.

o o o

Sophia followed Cam back to his car. "Aren't you planning to wait for the search team?"

"Oh, I'm waiting." He consciously slowed his long strides so that she could catch up, then helped her over a downed tree. "The idea is to multitask."

Of course. He was directing the investigation, responding to the regular updates coming in from all his agents. In the short time they'd been here, he'd spent more than half of it reading emails or texts on his phone or sending his own.

They walked out of the stand of trees and toward his car. "I fed the facial photo of the corpse we found yesterday evening into various missing persons databases last night. Went through the photos on the Iowa and FBI sites but found nothing. I've got the State Radio Center submitting the picture to NCIC. But I still need to look through other online missing persons sites." He slanted a glance at her. "Figured you could use the time to work on the new profile."

"I have some thoughts," she admitted. Sophia had been completely unaware of the temperatures when she'd been at the water's edge. She'd been too immersed in learning everything she could about the man who had chosen that spot. But the sun was warm after the relative coolness of the woods. The warmth made her scalp under the wig itch.

Reaching the car, he walked around to open her door. The old-fashioned gallantry in the gesture was oddly charming. Continuing on to the driver's side, he slid into the vehicle but left his door open.

She did the same to allow the slight breeze to channel through the vehicle.

Noting the fact gave her an idea. "Maybe the back entrance of the cave was to access the water. Or he might have built it to allow the cave to air out. The smell of decomposition has to get pretty overpowering in an enclosed space like that."

Cam held out his sleeved arm. "If you want proof, smell my clothes."

The invitation had her ducking away. A faint stench of decay would hang over the area at any time. But it had been far worse with the mouth of the cave open.

"You might be right. Even if he didn't remove the stones at the back entrance, the cracks between them would allow in some fresh air to provide ventilation. In any case, this place is in keeping with the pattern so far." Cam shrugged out of his suit jacket. "It's rural. Near the Des Moines metropolis, but he hasn't chosen an urban setting yet for a body dump."

"That pattern only fits the MO," she pointed out. "It doesn't tell us anything about this offender's signature. But one point I made in Vance's profile remains true. There will be an anchor that ties his accomplice to central Iowa. Vance's anchor turned out to be his grandfather's home, and the fact that he spent summers with the man. We need to figure out what this second UNSUB's bond is. And why he broke pattern on this site."

At Cam's quizzical look, she explained. "The bone here means the offender may have used this site more than once. He never did that before." Only one body had been found atop each burial vault, reburied at each rural cemetery that dotted several counties outside Des Moines.

"We'll see. At this point we don't know if those bones have anything to do with the body we found last night."

Sophia knew he was hoping to discover just that. But she recognized what his instincts were telling him. The discovery of that
first body in the cemetery at Slater had led to five more excavations.
"I tend to believe Vance used this UNSUB for the grunt work. We
know he snatched Van Wheton."

She withdrew her iPad from her bag. "Given what you found
here last night, this man may have also been tasked with disposal of
all Vance's victims." The first six victims had suffered pre- and postmortem sexual assaults, but the attacks differed dramatically. Vance
was brutal, given to sudden bursts of rage. Part of his satisfaction
in the rapes had come from his ability to control and torture the
victims, in keeping with the behavior of a sexual sadist.

But whoever had been charged with getting rid of the bodies
had first bathed them. Perhaps primarily to erase evidence, but the
care hadn't stopped there. The bodies had been rubbed down with
Mother's Touch, a lotion identified by the lab. Then they had been
doused with insecticide, either to slow down the decomposition and
stymie an investigation or to aid the postmortem sexual assaults.

"What makes you so sure this UNSUB was charged with the
body dumps?"

"The kids' interviews." Sophia powered up the laptop and found
the file she'd begun on this UNSUB. "They all said they thought the
man was talking to a girlfriend. His tone—his words—were loving.
That seems to fit with the care taken with the bodies. And while
each victim bore evidence of postmortem sexual assault, there were
no signs, at least with the first six, that they were physically abused
after death, as well." A clearer picture was forming in her mind of
the offender they were seeking. And while he might not be as violent as Vance, he just might prove to be a great deal sicker.

Twisting in his seat, Cam turned toward her, reaching in the
back for his laptop. His long-sleeved shirt was a dark dusty blue. It
looked good on him, providing contrast to his short-cropped brown

hair that still bore no hints of gray despite the fact that forty, while not exactly around the corner, was certainly within sight. The shirt's color softened the lines and angles of a face that was too hard to be called handsome but bull's-eyed on sexy.

He caught her gaze on him as he turned forward, computer in hand. "What?"

"Nothing. I was thinking of the profile." At least she would be. As soon as she could tuck away a vivid mental picture of what he looked like without a shirt. Or anything at all. The last thought had heat flooding up her throat to her cheeks.

Cam seemed unconvinced. "That dark makeup you're wearing might hide the fact, but I'd be willing to bet you were embarrassed about something."

With effort, she tore her gaze away. If the foundation hid her annoying penchant for blushing, she might be tempted to continue with it long after the need for a disguise was gone. "Over what, work?"

"You know, if this is too much for you, I'm sure Gonzalez would understand."

Sophia froze. Stricken, her gaze met his. He continued, deadpan. "I mean this." He stabbed an index finger in his own direction, made a small circle. "All this potent male virility in one smokin'-hot package. You wouldn't be the first female to be too overcome to work."

Her mouth twitched. Before she'd allowed herself to be weak with Cam Prescott for twelve gloriously hot days, he never would have veered from the professional. And a few months ago, she would have been much too reserved to summon a response.

"You're right, of course," she responded dryly. "It's only through great personal resolve and heroic effort that I can keep from throwing myself at your feet at this minute." She paused a beat before adding, "Coupled with the fact that you smell vaguely of decomposing roadkill."

His teeth flashed, and her heart did a slow lazy spin in her chest. She could have worked alongside Cam Prescott, the agent, for several more years and never felt this foreign level of attraction. It hadn't been until she'd seen him like this a few short weeks ago that her defenses had started abruptly eroding.

"Since you seem to be weathering my overpowering allure, we may as well go to work."

A companionable silence grew, broken only by the periodic alerts of texts Cam was receiving from the other agents. Sophia quickly typed up her observations of this area and then focused on the man who had chosen this spot to enact his perverted fantasies.

She had firsthand knowledge of Mason Vance's personality. Her kidnap and captivity by him had been a harrowing nightmare. But it'd also given her a unique perspective of the criminal, the likes of which was unmatched by any of the interviews she'd conducted over the years of similar criminals behind bars. Sophia had seen Vance in his element, in control and brutally violent. He was capable of any brutality one could enact on another human being.

Even before they had known he was working with an accomplice, she'd had a hard time reconciling the man she'd come to know too well with the postmortem sexual assaults. Vance fed off the victim's pain and suffering. But there had been no evidence of postmortem mutilation. And while he'd uttered many threats about her death while she'd been held, his verbal details had been reserved for the sexual assaults he had planned. The torture. Not once had he mentioned how he would kill her.

Many of the violent sexual offenders she'd interviewed spoke at length detailing how they had murdered their victims. The deaths had been an extension of the fantasies they'd created, the ultimate finale to the sexual torture leading up to it.

The fact that Vance had never mentioned more than the certainty of her eventual demise seemed telling.

Thoughts of the man who'd kidnapped her had Sophia's fingers going stiff and awkward on the keyboard. The rhythm of her heart kicked a faster beat. Despite the warmth in the vehicle she felt chilled to the bone. Surreptitiously she wiped her damp palms on her no-nonsense navy slacks and took a long deep breath. Released it slowly.

She knew all the techniques to calm her physical response to the memories. But even given her expertise, she couldn't prevent the recollections from exacting an emotional toll. So she took a few moments to practice deep breathing, hoping Cam would think her pause was only to collect her thoughts.

At her side he made an inaudible sound. Sophia glanced over to find him with a photo of the victim from last night in one hand, his gaze intent on the computer screen. He was scrolling through pictures at a dizzying pace. They represented dozens of stories. Some could have disappeared voluntarily. With others, mental illness may have entered the equation.

And a few might have fallen prey to a predator like Vance or his accomplice.

The thought of all those lost and missing women fortified something inside her. Lent her the strength to wall off the memories and return to her task. Perhaps the body found last night would be one of the faces in the databases Cam was mining. Or it may be someone who was never reported missing at all. In any case, the victim deserved justice. Her family deserved answers.

Sophia resumed typing. Vance's interest in his victims had primarily been limited to the money he acquired through their abduction and the sexual torture. She didn't doubt that he was capable of killing. With an icy finger tracing down her spine, she recalled his sudden bouts of rage and erratic violence. But after coming in far too close contact with the man, she could be fairly certain that once the women were dead, they lost all appeal for him.

Enter UNSUB number two.

Her typing began to pick up speed as the profile for the second offender began to take shape. He had a proven sexual affinity for long-dead victims. Given the link between him and Vance, it seemed probable that the UNSUB had been responsible for the postmortem sexual assaults of the bodies disposed at the cemeteries that had been discovered weeks earlier.

The lotion used on the corpses suggested something of a personal nature for the offender. Something his parent had used on him, perhaps? Or a sharp contrast to a childhood devoid of the care the brand name denoted? She made a note to check out how long the product had been on the market. In any event, its selection was telling. Vance had been an egomaniacal offender motivated by power and control who had exulted in degrading and torturing his victims. Perhaps the accomplice had been given access to the victims only after their deaths. Or, more probably, his perversion was titillated by the dead or near-dead women.

Perhaps the most puzzling thing about the second offender was the lack of evidence of accompanying paraphilias. The absence of postmortem sexual sadism and mutilation made him unlike many lust murderers.

Cam's cell rang then, and Sophia listened unabashedly to his side of the conversation. When he finished he turned to look at her. "Beachum and Samuels might have a real lead. They were following up on the most promising of the tips coming in since the sketch of the offender was released. Most of them turn out to be people claiming the drawing is an exact match to an ex, or an ex's new boyfriend, but they just finished interviewing Becky Gainer, a cashier at the Pinter's on East Euclid."

Sophia nodded. Pinter's was a chain of grocery stores that didn't exist outside the Midwest, but one couldn't drive more than five miles in any direction in the urban Des Moines metropolis without seeing one. "She thinks she saw the offender?"

"Identified him from the sketch we released. The first one Jenna did, of the offender in Edina. According to Gainer, he shops there occasionally. She sees him at least once or twice a month."

"Did she actually date him or just want to?"

He stopped then, drilled a gaze at her. "Did I have it on speakerphone?"

Sophia smiled faintly. "The first sketch depicted a man who was fairly attractive." His features hadn't been nearly as pleasant in the drawings done earlier that morning when Jenna had interviewed the kids. But it was the face in the first sketch that the UNSUB would be showing the world. It was the one that would be recognized. And regardless of his true personality, at least initially some women would respond to him.

"Beachum said he got the impression Gainer was interested in the guy, but that he didn't always come to her lane and they never exchanged more than a few words. She described him as a cash customer. Always alone. No wedding band, so you're probably right about her interest. Polite and a little shy . . . 'A perfect gentleman' were the words she used."

"What about the store security footage?"

"Gainer thought she'd last seen him in the store about ten or twelve days ago. The agents are in the process of getting the store surveillance footage, both for the interior and exterior. Then we'll see how well he matches our sketches. But the agents said the woman seemed pretty certain. It'll also give us a time stamp so we can get an idea of his schedule."

Excitement thrummed in her veins. If the match was verified, this was valuable information, indeed. "If it does prove to be him, you'll need to prioritize tips of individuals living or working in the area. Triangulate a grid between all the nearby Pinter's, focusing on the neighborhoods and businesses closest to this one. Likely he either lives or works within a few miles of this grocery store. Oh." A thought occurred to her. "Most of the Pinter's stores have a pharmacy. See if he had prescriptions filled there."

"All the store employees will be shown the sketch," he agreed. "If it comes down to getting a look at his prescription history, it'll take a warrant, but I can get it. Do you have something specific in mind?"

"It's just a thought. He could be under treatment for some diagnosed mental illness, I suppose. But I'm wondering if he might have some condition that caused him to lose his sense of smell." Close proximity to the odor of decomposition would be overpowering. Even protective covering over the nose didn't mask the smell. "The kids at the scene hadn't described the man with a mask. So with this offender's perverted predilection for corpses, maybe he dealt readily with the odor because he couldn't smell them."

"Your mind . . ." The admiration in his expression warmed something inside her. "What medical condition would cause a permanent loss of smell?"

She thought for a moment. "There are several. Advanced diabetes and MS are two, but I can't imagine this offender having the strength needed for these crimes if he were in the advanced stages of either. That also rules out Alzheimer's and old age. But there are medications that can lead to a loss of smell, too. Also trauma to the nose, nasal polyps, radiation, chronic cocaine use . . ." She gave a little shrug. "The possibilities are there."

"Yeah, they are. It's a good thought." For the first time she noticed the small smile playing about his mouth.

"What?"

"I know we've had this conversation before, but you would have made a helluva cop."

It was hard to think with the intensity of his gaze trained on her. His eyes seemed more gold than brown when they were focused on something, and right now she was the object of his attention. Muscles in her stomach quivered.

"My reasons for using my training strictly for research and as a civilian forensic consultant haven't changed."

"You said it was because you were too big a coward to do otherwise." His voice had lowered. The slightly raspy tone scraped over nerve endings that seemed overly sensitive. "But it wasn't a coward who outwitted Vance. Who saved Courtney Van Wheton and escaped from the barn you were kept in. Somehow I'm going to find a way to convince you of that much."

Sophia forced herself to look away, oddly shaken at how easily the conversation had veered to the personal. She wished fervently that he could convince her of just that. Wished he could make her believe that her success in diverting Vance from assaulting her in exchange for time to create a more "accurate" profile to release to the public had been solely due to bravery.

Because when she'd discovered that he'd used the intervening time to sexually brutalize another victim . . . her cleverness had seemed like something much less admirable. And until she could extricate Courtney Van Wheton's screams from her mind, she knew she wouldn't be able to forgive herself.

It was with a degree of relief that she noted the plume of dust rising from the road before them. Within moments she could make out the approach of a dark Tahoe. The cadaver dog and handler had arrived.

She wasn't altogether certain what it said about her that the arrival and what it entailed was a welcome distraction from her memories.

Chapter 6

George." The two men shook hands. "Never sure who's going to respond to the callout. Glad to have you." Cam had worked with George Roberts several times before. The man belonged to the STAR 1 civilian team that had an agreement with DCI and were dispatched through the Story County emergency services. Most recently Roberts had helped on a case Cam had worked involving a missing five-year-old girl. The handler knew what he was doing.

"Dr. Mona Kilby is working with us on this investigation." The name sounded foreign on his tongue, but he delivered the falsehood without batting an eye. Before transferring to DCI, Cam had worked for DNE, the narcotics enforcement branch. He'd spent more time than he wanted to consider working undercover, where his survival depended on his ability to lie convincingly. It was that earlier undercover experience that had landed him on the multiagency task force a couple of years ago. To Sophie he said, "George runs his own marketing firm."

The man pulled a dark cap over his longish brown hair. "And my boss is a real pain. Took some arguing to get the time off." Tall and lanky, he had a lean face and an irreverent sense of humor. His navy T-shirt read, "Z-Pack. We Find Zombies."

Cam's mouth quirked as he read it. The cadaver dog handlers, like major crime agents, were present at some pretty grisly discoveries. It wasn't unusual to use humor to establish some sort of emotional distance. And even then there would be sights that were impossible to scrub from the mind.

"I want you to meet someone new." He went to the backseat and opened the door to let out a black-and-white border collie.

Cam eyed the dog. "Where's Deke?" Every time he'd worked with the man before he'd worked with an intelligent-looking German shepherd.

Roberts grimaced. "Participated in that search over by Elkader last month. You hear about it?"

He had. An elderly man with Alzheimer's had wandered away from his caregiver. His body had been found miles out in the country, on an abandoned farmstead.

"On the way back to the vehicle, Deke got his foot caught in the rotted cover of a cistern. I even had him on a leash, but the place was so overgrown, I just didn't see it." Remorse was evident in his voice. "Had some pretty nasty splinters taken out of his paw. He's still favoring it, so he's not up for work quite yet. This is Veyda. She was a rescue pup a couple years ago. She's met all the training standards and has proved herself several times over. She'll do fine."

Cam watched the dog beeline for Sophie and was unsurprised to see the delight in the woman's expression. They'd spent several hours one afternoon in a shelter looking for a pet for Livvie to present Carter for his birthday. Their progress had been slowed by Sophie's inability to pass a cage without stopping to coo over the animal inside, no matter how homely or battle scarred.

Sophie lowered herself carefully to one knee to pet the animal. Stopped herself, hand midway in the air, to look at George. "Will I distract her?"

The man grinned. "You'd distract any of us, Doctor. But she hasn't gotten the work command yet. You can pet her."

Cam watched Sophie fuss over the dog and the canine's blissful response. It occurred to him that in that regard, dogs and men weren't all that different. With or without a disguise, Sophie would rate a second glance from any male with a pulse.

In concise words he brought the other man up to speed. Roberts nodded. "Dispatch said you had a small search area, so it shouldn't take long. Where do you want us to start?"

Cam pointed toward the path into the woods. "Through the trees and down a bluff there's a clearing. That's where the corpse was found. Another, unrelated bone was discovered in a cave down there."

Roberts called to the dog, and she reluctantly left Sophie to return to her owner. He snapped a leash on Veyda's harness.

"They brought the body out on the path that way," Sophie ventured. "Won't she alert to the scent?"

"She'll definitely pick it up. But I won't give her the command until we're at the search area. Once she's working, nothing can disturb her focus." The handler started off and Sophie followed, Cam falling into step behind her.

George and Veyda led the way toward the path that would take them to the ridge above the clearing. Roberts was the chatty type, and he kept up a constant monologue as they walked. He had a fascinated audience in Sophie. "Dogs can identify smells at least a thousand times better than humans. They've even been known to alert to thirty-year-old body dumps."

"Does she work from air scent or ground?" Cam asked as he reached out to steady Sophie as she stumbled on the uneven terrain. If she fell with her injured wrist, she'd have difficulty breaking her fall.

"Both." They walked through the dense trees. "You'll see her working nose up, and then once she gets a scent she'll have it down, trying to find the source. These dogs search specifically for human remains, and they alert to the gases that decomposing bodies release into the air. Where we've got about five million olfactory receptors in our noses, dogs have nearly fifty times as many." As if in demonstration of her handler's words, Veyda turned her head first in one direction, then another as her entire body quivered with the act of sorting out the scents. Occasionally she looked back at her owner, as if questioning why she hadn't been given the start command when there were clearly so many target scents in the area.

When they came to the clearing, Cam hung back to help Sophie maneuver the descent. "By the time I'm done with this, I should be able to find the place in my sleep." He reached out to catch her around the waist when one of her feet skidded out from under her on the treacherous incline.

"Let's hope that's never required. Although I'm beginning to think we may be spending far more time in this place than either of us had intended."

He shot her a look and noted her grim expression. He had a similar feeling of foreboding. It was hard to hope for a positive outcome in this search, given what they knew about this UNSUB's connection to Vance.

Cam showed George the spot where the body had been found and the cave where it had been kept.

Roberts looked pensive as he scanned the area. "If someone disposed of a body, he'd want to do so with the least amount of physical labor. Here that means dumping it in the river or digging a shallow grave somewhere in this clearing, so the body doesn't have to be hauled off-site through those woods. Can't see him dumping in the river around here, though."

Sophie looked at Cam for confirmation. "Why not?"

"The Raccoon is heavily fished. According to the Department of Natural Resources, this area is a fairly popular spot. And that means increased chances of discovery. Fishing lines getting snagged on the body." Cam was deeply regretting his decision to re-don the jacket. Although the morning temperature had been mild, it had to be at least in the mideighties right now. He plucked a pair of mirrored sunglasses from his inside coat pocket and settled them on his nose.

George refolded the map, tucked it away. "They've pulled more than one car chassis and washing machine out of this river in places, though. If it was me, I'd haul the body by boat farther down the river. Closer to West Des Moines, the Raccoon gets a lot deeper."

"That's what you'd do, huh?" Cam's voice was dry. Roberts grinned.

"You don't know how lucky you are that I didn't turn to a life of crime." The handler returned his attention to the dog, who was straining at the leash, clearly anxious to begin. "How recent do you think the dump occurred?"

"We don't know. We can't even be sure there is a dump here," Cam said, as much to remind Sophie as himself. "The gurney would have enabled the UNSUB to transport the box and body from the vehicle on the road to the cave. It could have just as easily been used to cart it back." The words were true but lacked conviction. Maybe the offender had planned that this corpse would find a home in a rural cemetery like Vance's first six victims had. If that were the case, this site had been selected solely based on the seclusion it afforded the UNSUB to act out his perversions in secret.

It'd be easier to believe that scenario if not for that human bone they'd found.

As if plucking the thought from his head, Sophie murmured, "It would help if we could age the bone. I know Lucy has some expertise in the area, but she's swamped right now. It's too bad Gavin Connerly's not still consulting."

"He's on a plane back." Her head swiveled toward his, surprise in her expression. "Got a text from Gonzalez earlier. He had called her concerning your . . . article in the paper." Meaning her obit, but there was no reason to let the handler in on the secret. Too many people knew the truth already. "The SAC filled him in, and he volunteered to come back immediately and consult, free of charge."

There was a slight smile on her lips he didn't quite trust. "How very altruistic of Gavin."

He grunted at that. The forensic anthropologist from Berkeley had been a huge help aging the human remains they'd excavated from the rural cemeteries. Cam didn't know what was bringing the man back, and he didn't care. He'd welcome any insight the anthropologist could offer.

A side benefit was that he'd be stationed once again at the medical examiner's suites and that he seemed to drive Benally crazy. That was a talent Cam could appreciate.

"Start with the clearing then?"

Cam nodded at the handler. "Fine by me."

Roberts shrugged out of his backpack to take out a well-worn tug toy. He told Sophie, "The dogs are trained using positive reinforcement. The breeds we use will do anything to play. So we start them with play, and reward them the same way."

He turned to the dog. "C'mere, girl. Come tug." Veyda launched herself at the other end of the toy and grabbed on with a show of teeth. Bracing her feet, she pulled mightily, letting out a mock ferocious growl. The two played for a minute or two before Grady replaced the toy in the pack and reshouldered it. He led the dog to the farthermost corner of the clearing, where they could work downwind, reached down to unleash the dog, and said, "Game on."

The dog shifted from play to work mode with an alacrity Cam didn't always see in humans. Veyda tested the air carefully and then put her head down to scent the ground. Over and over she performed the same act, moving in a pattern discernible only to the handler. Roberts stood a slight distance away, subtly keeping the dog to a grid that Cam knew the man had mapped in his mind upon his first sighting of the scene.

"Why did he take the leash off her?" Sophie's gaze was riveted on the pair.

"Some of the handlers I've worked with leave the animals off leash. George tends to keep the dogs leashed unless he's working an area where he can see it at all times. It's too easy for the animal to get hurt by something unseen in tall grasses, or to fall down unused cisterns or wells. With this small an area, the dog can be unleashed without risk. When we're working a big scene, there will be dozens of personnel on site and an entire team of handlers and dogs. Leashes are used then, and everyone wears high-visibility clothing for identification purposes. It can get confusing."

Criminalist Seth Dietz headed over. "Did you want us to check the woods before we leave? We examined the path and either side but didn't spread out any farther than a few yards on both sides of it." The rest of his team was hauling equipment up the ridge and through the woods to the waiting vehicle on the road.

Cam considered. "Take soil samples from a few areas to go with the others." Seth had painstakingly collected samples from above and below the bluff. They'd managed to narrow down Vance's location from sediment he'd left behind in Sophie's apartment. Maybe they'd get lucky again and connect these surroundings with Vance's accomplice, once they caught him. An enterprising defense attorney would argue that the kids were too far away to make a positive ID. That they'd collaborated on the description.

It was harder to argue away trace evidence.

The criminalist didn't seem in any hurry to leave, although none of his colleagues were in sight. Together they watched the dog for another quarter hour. Every passing minute that the dog didn't alert should have had the knot in Cam's gut loosening a bit more.

But he couldn't forget that solitary bone in the cave. Under the circumstances it was hard to think of a credible explanation for its presence there. So he watched with the others, not with the fascination shown by Seth and Sophie, but with a sense of dread that increased with each passing moment.

The dog had her nose to the ground, occasionally lifting her snout to test the air before it was lowered again. She had paused in a six-foot-wide area, testing and retesting the scent. When she dropped to the ground, Cam's gut dropped with her.

Veyda barked to alert her owner, never moving from place, her sides trembling from the excitement of her discovery. George looked up to the group and called, "I think you're going to want to get an excavation team in here to check this area out."

○ ○ ○

Lucy Benally pulled into her drive, temper still simmering. She'd intended to finish up a few outstanding details and then focus on the crime victim discovered last night. After only a few more hours, she'd be ready to start the autopsy first thing in the morning. No matter that she wasn't slated to work the next day. No one else would be allowed to autopsy that victim. Once she started a case, she saw it through to the end.

Unfortunately a family of four was at the head of the line. All had died in a house fire that had been deemed suspicious. Her day had been consumed with those victims. Two still required autopsies.

And Steven Benson, the chief medical examiner, had sent her home early, citing her late night as his reason. No amount of arguing had swayed him.

Her ire was such that she was unusually unobservant when she pulled into the long drive to park the car in the detached garage. But she had taken only a few steps toward the house before she saw the figure seated on the back deck. Watching her.

Her steps faltered. Even at this distance, the man was instantly recognizable. There was a curl of something weak and cowardly deep in the pit of her stomach. Infuriated by it, she shoved it aside and strolled up the deck to confront the devil head-on.

"They have this thing these days," she said conversationally. "GPS. Marvelous invention. Helps people with directions. For instance, west is that way." She jabbed a finger in the appropriate direction.

Gavin Connerly hooked the chair next to him with one foot and dragged it closer so he could stretch his legs out on it. "I've heard of it," he agreed mildly. "Plane I was on probably even has a similar instrument. But Iowa is east of California, so that's why I'm here. The plane I boarded was headed east."

Grinding her teeth, Lucy ducked her head to dig in her bag for her house key. The man got under her skin like a needle-sharp splinter and took up residence there with the determination of a tick. "Sort of a long way to travel for a booty call."

He threw his head back and laughed, genuine amusement in the sound. Lucy had decided long ago that his affability was one of his most annoying attributes. That and the fact that he seemed to find humor in *her*. In her world, life—and death—was serious business. No one had ever been amused by her before.

Quite the opposite.

Finding the key, her fingers closed around it, tightly enough for it to dig into her palm. "So. I don't see a car." She made a point to look in both directions. "Either you parachuted out over my property or you had a taxi drop you off. In either case you're out of luck. You aren't staying here."

"No, I'm not," he surprised her by saying. "I've got a place at the Marriott in Ankeny. There was a problem with my car rental. They're going to deliver it." His voice lowered. Became intimate. "You didn't answer my calls. How are you, Luce?"

His expression was guileless. But she didn't spend more than a second looking at his face. Staring at Gavin Connerly could be entirely too pleasurable, and pleasure made a woman weak. Lucy knew that from experience. She'd spent her teenage years parenting her siblings while her mother chased booze and men with the kind of single-minded devotion she'd never shown her kids. Stacy Benally had been prone to forget minutiae like food, bills, and schoolwork. She couldn't even be trusted to take the medication needed to control her mood swings and depression. Lucy had shouldered all those responsibilities.

But like the pest he was, Connerly's image imprinted on her mind as she fitted the key into the lock of the back door. His blond hair was pulled back as usual in the ponytail he favored, but she'd once seen it loose around his shoulders. Ran her fingers through it and felt the fall of it over her skin when his mouth had been wickedly busy. His face was sharp and intelligent, with a narrowed jaw and cheekbones that could have been etched in ice. An earring dangled from one lobe. Topped with shrewd green eyes that saw entirely too much, the entire package was encased in one long lounging specimen of manhood. He was entirely too comfortable in his own skin.

Like her Navajo forefathers, Lucy had a firm grasp on who and what she was. She'd risen above circumstance, charted her own course, and navigated around the obstacles that life had strewn in her path. But nothing in her experience had prepared her for a man like Gavin Connerly.

"Knowing your work habits, I figured I'd have to wait here longer."

"The chief examiner has views that parallel yours when it comes to hours spent on work," she said shortly. The door open, she chanced another look at him. "Better get that taxi out here to take you back to the hotel."

His eyes, damn them, were alight with amusement. "Been a long trip. I'm sort of parched. Got a bottle of water in there?"

She surveyed him for a moment. Lucy knew the man well enough to know that there'd be no moving him until he'd said whatever it was he'd come here to say. She moved resignedly into the kitchen, snatched a bottle of water from the fridge, and went back to the porch. Set it on the table before him with slightly more force than was necessary.

Moving to the next chair she dumped his feet from it so she could sit down. "Why are you here, Connerly?"

After screwing off the cap of the bottle, he tipped it to his lips and took a long drink. "To talk to you, obviously." When her eyes narrowed, he smiled. "Actually I called Gonzalez when I saw the *Des Moines Register*'s obituary for Sophia online. Got sort of panicked."

Ice filtered through her system, freezing her organs from the inside. "Obituary? What are you talking about? I spoke to Sophia a couple days ago." He simply had to be wrong. There was no way something had happened to her friend without her having heard about it. Was there?

He reached a hand over to cover one of hers. "Relax. She's fine. Gonzalez wouldn't tell me what the deal was, but she did tell me there was nothing to worry about. She also filled me in on the case I was consulting on until a few days ago. Looks like it isn't over."

Relief had her insides thawing. Lucy didn't have any close friends, and that was by design. But Sophia Channing was closer than most, simply because she was adept at slipping through defenses. Whether through training or personality, Lucy didn't know, but the woman was hard to keep at a distance.

A trait she shared with the man sitting next to her.

"So again, I'll ask. Why are you here?" She didn't flatter herself by believing it had anything to do with her. Lucy had used every tool in her not inconsiderable arsenal to make it clear that his help with the last six victims in Prescott's case was unnecessary and unwelcome. His presence had been solely at the behest of the DCI.

Of course, she mentally squirmed, that message might have been muddied a bit when she slept with him the night before he flew back to California. She'd thought they'd never see each other again.

Which just went to prove that fates always, always extracted a payment for indulging in any weakness.

The man drank again. Took his time screwing the cap back on the bottle. "The bone, of course."

"The bone."

"The one Gonzalez said was found with the corpse in Prescott's case. Apparently there isn't a body to go along with it." With his thumb he traced a line in the condensation collected on the bottle. "I have vacation time accrued. I offered to come back and do what I could to age it for them."

She didn't believe him. The office of the medical examiner was perfectly capable of extracting whatever information could be gotten from a lone finger bone. But the only other answer that made sense was that he'd returned to see *her*, and that was just as unthinkable. They'd hooked up for one night.

Lucy might keep her intimate experience with men limited, but she knew it was illogical for a man who looked like this one to fly across the country to see a woman he'd slept with one time. A woman who didn't even *like* him. Much.

Whatever game he was playing, she was abruptly tired of participating in it. "Great. Maybe I'll see you at work then." Or maybe, out of a strong sense of self-preservation she could arrange to work nights for the duration of his visit and avoid him completely. "I'm going in. You're going to want to call a—"

His cell rang then, and he answered it with an ease that shattered her airy dismissal. She should go inside and leave the man to his own devices. Curiosity kept her rooted to her chair. Especially when Connerly kept glancing at her as he listened.

After saying very little else, he finally said, "Not a problem. I'll catch a ride and be there shortly." Slipping the cell back in his pocket he said, "You might be stuck with me longer than you thought."

Wariness surged, mingled with a single and quickly extinguished traitorous flare of joy. "And why is that?"

Gavin rose. "That was Prescott. They're starting a dig at the site where the body was found last night. I need to get a ride over there."

Surging to her feet, Lucy went to lock the door again. "I'll take you."

That damned amusement reappeared in his voice. "Hard to figure out if you're more anxious to get rid of me or to take part in that dig."

"It's a tie." She jogged down the steps. "In this case, my having to deliver you gives me a reason to void Stevens's order and to be at the site. As Prescott likes to say, it's a win-win."

o o o

"So while I was sweating through the usual pleasantries of a shooting review, you were enjoying a day at the river. Typical." Tommy Franks leaned down to brush off the dirt on his pants acquired by his ignominious descent down the bluff.

Cam eyed him with a glint of humor. It had been a relief to hear the agent had been cleared. Not only because it would lend another experienced agent to the case, but also because Franks was a damn fine investigator and a personal friend. Cam valued the older man's insights. "You know there's a path down the hill, right?"

Franks straightened. "I do now. What'd I miss?"

Since they'd last talked less than an hour ago, the question should have been rhetorical. But the buzz of activity in the area meant it was anything but.

"The HDR handler took the dog to the back entrance of the cave. All along the shoreline." Cam turned to gesture toward the area. He pitched his voice over the intermittent whine of the power shovel the team was using and tried not to consider that the UNSUB might have used one very like it to enlarge the cave. "The dog alerted, so they're bringing in another handler who will work from a boat while George uses the dog onshore." A dull throb had taken up residence in his temples. He had a feeling before the day was over it'd elevate to jackhammer status. "In the meantime, the dig is progressing slowly."

Excavating clandestine graves was a laborious affair. After breaking ground, trowels were used more than shovels, and the process was slow. Right now the site was nearly hidden from view, with medical examiner personnel and evidence techs surrounding it. One criminalist was using ground-penetrating radar to direct the parameters of the dig. Although another ME had taken the call, twenty minutes ago Gavin Connerly had shown up with Lucy Benally in tow. Or vice versa. Cam neither knew nor cared how their arrival had coincided. But from what he could see, the two were in the center of things, supervising the activity.

Franks pulled a fat sheaf of folded pages from his suit coat pocket and handed it to him. Already the man's face bore a faint sheen of perspiration. Cam had shed his jacket and rolled up his shirtsleeves hours ago, and he still craved a long cold shower followed by an icy beer. The likelihood of either in the coming hours was slim.

"The ballistics report? That's record time for the lab." Unfolding the pages, Cam skimmed them rapidly. He'd been briefed on the results by a call from the lab manager earlier that day. The news contained in it represented the first real break they'd gotten in the case. Ordinarily he'd be excited by the possibility. But the grim scene unfolding before him muted that emotion.

"Ballistics testing matched the offender's weapon that discharged in Dr. Channing's home with one used nearly fifteen years ago in a robbery of a convenience store." Franks pulled a half-full bottle of water from his other suit coat pocket and unscrewed it, taking a long drink. "Kid swiped it from his foster father's collection. The punk got caught, and the weapon was eventually returned to its rightful owner."

"Only to be stolen again six years ago along with the rest of the guns in the collection." Cam flipped to another page. "Either that guy has incredibly bad luck or he's a completely moronic gun owner."

"Think there's more since you last talked to the lab." Interest sharpening, Cam looked away from the report to focus on the man next to him. Franks screwed the top back on the bottle as he spoke. "Three years ago a matching bullet was dug out of the ceiling of a garage in Urbandale. The man who owns the house had reported his wife missing. Family and friends claimed they hadn't seen her either, so a Detective Timmons conducted a search of the property. Findings were inconclusive. Her car, purse, and some clothes were missing, and she maxed out her credit cards in the days following the report before her husband canceled them. Her cell phone was never used again. Absolutely nothing in the house to suggest foul play, but CSU did find the bullet. No way to tell how long it had been there."

His mind working rapidly, Cam asked, "What's the owner's name? How long had he been at the property?"

"Kevin Stallsmith. And four years."

"So the bullet could have been there since before he moved in." He felt a stab of disappointment. "You talked to Timmons?" At Franks's nod, he asked, "What was bought on the credit card?"

Franks took a small notebook from his pocket to consult. "Mostly electronics. A laptop. Large-screen TV. Stereo. That sort of thing. Some clothes in sizes that matched the ones in her closet. Gift cards for large amounts."

In other words, things that could be easily sold or pawned for quick cash. "What's her family say?"

"She was estranged from her mother. They hadn't talked in several years at the time of Emily Stallsmith's disappearance. Her two sisters claimed they haven't heard from her. Word was that all was not rosy in the marriage, so Timmons looked at the husband pretty hard. But he was alibied, and the detective never could put together enough answers to close the case. He tends to think Stallsmith fled an unhappy marriage and used the credit cards to finance her getaway."

Sophie had disengaged from the group around the dig when Franks had come on scene and joined them in time to hear the agent's words. "You've got a missing persons report that matches Vance's MO?" she asked.

At the sound of her voice, Franks did a comical double take, surprise on his normally taciturn features. "Dr. Channing? Almost didn't recognize you."

She smiled. "I'll take that as a compliment. Although the disguise is mostly Agent Loring's doing."

As Cam filled her in on the conversation, her smile faded and her expression went pensive.

"She disappeared three years ago? Vance was released . . . what, four years ago from that Nebraska prison?" She didn't wait for the men's nods before going on. "And his former cellmate told you Vance had planned his crimes in prison. Stalking wealthy women, kidnapping them, and forcing them to withdraw large sums from their banks before the sexual assaults . . . Even if this woman you're speaking of was the victim of foul play, it certainly doesn't sound like Vance's MO. Unless . . ."

When she trailed off, Cam prompted, "Unless?"

Whatever Sophie might have said was interrupted when there was a shout from the group gathered around the dig. The three of them rejoined the others. Lucy, Gavin, and Pete Lerdahl, the first ME on scene, were gloved and on their hands and knees around the deepening hole. Cam stepped around the wood-framed screen they'd been using to sift the dirt for small bone or tooth fragments. The area was littered with their tools. Shovels, trowels, a large white plastic bucket, and some brushes lay nearby. An ME tech and a crime lab photographer were documenting every step of the process.

"Gavin, help me dig from here." Lucy's voice was remarkably calm. "Pete, you want to take a turn with the screen?"

"It'll give my back a break." The stout, balding ME backed away, making room for Cam at the side of the hole. Once there he saw immediately what had caused their excitement.

The hole was only about two feet by three feet at this point. But the partially uncovered grimy wizened face with its nest of stringy dark hair was unmistakably human.

Chapter 7

Y ou," Cam pronounced as he drove through the light traffic with
relative ease, "are a bully."

Not raising her head from the iPad screen in her lap,
Sophie's voice was imperturbable. "I prefer the word *assertive*. And
in this case, I was absolutely correct, and you know it."

"I don't know it," he countered, slowing to a stop at a red light
on Hickman. Then proceeded to drum his fingers impatiently on
the steering wheel. "I could have had Agent Loring come pick you
up to take you home for the night. I mean"—the slip was awkward,
the correction more so—"to my place."

She gave a tiny sigh, the kind he usually got before she told
him, in an absolutely civil and concise way, that he was being an ass.
"The point isn't that I'm tired, although I am. It's that you haven't
slept in almost forty-eight hours. You're no good to the case if you
work yourself into exhaustion."

The light changed again, and he accelerated. And reflected that
she was always at her most irritating when she was right. "The dig
will go on all night." Cam had relieved Seth with a new crime scene
team. They'd unloaded the generators and large portable lights to
ensure that the work continued. The IOSME office had sent more

personnel. "Williams—the criminalist operating the GPR—thinks there could be two or three more bodies in that hole." It was difficult to determine without enlarging the hole significantly. If the UNSUB had used a mass grave to dump bodies in before reburying them, the victims might be positioned in a pile, and a body could be hidden beneath the others. The only way to know for certain was to continue the dig. And the thought of not being on scene for any future discoveries burned.

"You're kept updated constantly on every detail of this case." Without bothering to ask, she dug in her purse and withdrew a bottle of Tylenol. Shook two out into her palm and handed them to him. "You have that little crease above your brow that you get when your head hurts you," she explained when he glanced at the pills, then at her.

The fact that she knew him so well was a little disconcerting. And since the headache had gained villainous strength in the last few hours, he scooped up the pills and popped them in his mouth, ignoring the open bottle of water she offered as he swallowed.

"How bad is it?"

At any other time, the sympathy in her voice would have warmed him. But he wasn't any too happy about having to take time away from the case for minor things like eating and sleeping. "It's a couple notches down from the headache I get if I have to listen to Taylor Swift."

She laughed. He'd walked in on her one morning during their brief time together, making coffee and singing a duet with the country/pop artist and had never let her live it down. "And here I was going to suggest a little easy listening as just the thing to ease your stress." She reached for the radio teasingly.

"You're living dangerously, woman." But the banter had him relaxing a fraction for the first time since he'd taken Sheriff Feinstein's call last night. "I need to update the report for the briefing tomorrow." The headlights of oncoming traffic only worsened the pounding in his skull. The paperwork required to pull the details that had been coming in all day into one cohesive report would take a couple of hours, at least. Maybe it wouldn't hurt to shower, put the report together over a cold beer, and grab a few hours' sleep. Like Sophie had said, he'd know the instant the crew at the dig found anything more.

And it wasn't the bodies hidden in that grave that were the most pressing details at this point, anyway. It was the offender himself, who could possibly still be in the area.

"Warrant came in on the Pinter's pharmacy a few hours ago." The drive at least gave him time to catch Sophie up on some of the facts that had been steadily streaming in that afternoon from the rest of the team. "We struck out there. One of the employees recalled seeing the UNSUB in the store before, but none ID'd him as a pharmacy customer. We still might get something on the security footage, but right now all we've found is an image of him walking to his car."

"Does the vehicle match the one Tommy ID'd leaving my condo?"

Sophie's voice sounded remarkably controlled for someone talking about a failed attempt on her life. Too controlled, in fact. Cam glanced at her. She wasn't the only one who had picked up on a few personal nuances during their time together. "We don't have to talk about this now. A few hours' break from the case isn't going to kill either of us."

"Meaning that it did. It's all right, Cam. I've been in the thick of things all day." The pills rattled a little in the bottle as she dropped it back into her purse. "I'm not likely to break down over a vehicle description."

"No." It was difficult to keep his gaze on the road and off her. "You aren't. They didn't get a view of the license plate number off the car he got into, but Tommy says it's absolutely the one he saw at your place. I've got Des Moines Police Department officers going door-to-door in the area showing Jenna's initial sketch to employers and residents. But that's going to take a few days."

"Someone will have seen him." She leaned against the headrest for a moment and gave a nearly imperceptible sigh. And he was reminded that she had gotten almost as little sleep as he had last night. "I honestly think this line of investigating will be our best—"

His cell rang then, and Cam mentally cursed as she straightened expectantly beside him. Drawing it from the pocket of his suit coat folded over the console beside him, he brought it to his ear. Answered tersely. It was John Samuels. The agent sounded as tired as Cam felt.

"I'm at home but DMPD just reported a tip that came through. Got a guy who claims to have seen our UNSUB. Says he bartends over on Franklin in the River Bend neighborhood at a dive called Screwball's. He took a picture on his cell and sent it to the officer manning the line who forwarded it to me. I sent it along to you for a look. I don't know if it's our guy or not. It's hard to say. If he shaved his head maybe, yeah. Something about the shape of his face could be a match. Want me to give it a look tonight?"

"No, I'm in the car. If I think it's worth it, I'll go. What's the address?" The River Bend neighborhood was slowly being transformed. Renovated historical old Victorians and a few new businesses were sparkling gems set alongside crumbling buildings and low-rent tenements. But its crime rate was still among the worst in Des Moines. Although the city had poured funds into restoring the area, it would take another few years of determined TLC to offset the rampant prostitution, drug deals, and gang activity reported there.

Signing off, he waited for the telltale alert of an incoming text. When the photo arrived, he took a hard look at it before handing it to Sophie. "What do you think?"

She glanced at the photo of the man and then reached up to turn on the interior light. "Is that . . . Who is that?"

"Some bartender. At a bar that would be"—he did a quick mental calculation—"about eight blocks south of the Pinter's where our UNSUB was seen."

After several more moments she said, "I don't know. The features aren't quite as regular, and with that scruff of a beard and shaved head . . . But there's something about the shape of his face."

"Yeah." Cam turned at the next corner and headed east. "It's probably close enough to be worth checking out."

Screwball's was aptly named, and all eyes turned in Cam's direction the moment he walked in the door. The interior was dimly lit, neon beer signs providing most of the atmosphere. He was definitely overdressed. Most of the patrons were wearing wifebeaters or tees, with ripped jeans or shorts. The dress code, he noted as he made his way through the scattered customers, was unisex.

And everyone in the place immediately made him as a cop.

He saw a couple of men sidle not quite nonchalantly to the hallway leading toward the back of the bar, which probably housed either a restroom of questionable sanitation or an exit. After a hard look, he dismissed both of them. They didn't match the photo he'd been sent, and right now he didn't care about the sources of their guilty consciences.

His focus was on the bartender. Who was definitely not the man in the picture.

Choosing a spot at the bar for its proximity to the door, he leaned against it in a position guaranteeing him the best visual access of the place. With the exception of the two who had gone to the back, after that first inspection the customers had returned to their drinks and their pool games.

The lone bartender fluffed her jet-black hair and sauntered in his direction. She leaned toward him over the bar, giving him an up-close-and-personal view of her ample cleavage, which was spilling from the skimpy top she was wearing. "What can I get you, Tall, Dark, and Coplike?"

"You have me all wrong." There was an argument escalating between two pool players and what looked a lot like a drug deal going down in the corner booth under one cracked plate glass window. "Me, I'm an accountant."

She flashed a smile that was likely supposed to be sultry. "Me, I'm really a nun. My disguise is better than yours, though, ain't it?"

"It's masterful." He pulled out his cell and brought up the picture Samuels had sent. He turned it around so she could peer at the screen. "Know this guy?"

After a long moment she shook her head. "Uh-uh. Should I?"

Cam speared a look at her. "I'm told he bartends here."

"Lots of guys have tried that. None stick around, though. How long ago did you say he was here?"

"I didn't."

Lifting a shoulder, the woman half turned away to grab a bar rag to wipe down the nicked and graffiti-scrawled bar top. "I've been here eight months and never seen him. Think someone's giving you a line of shit."

Cam tended to agree, but that someone was standing before him. And lying through her hygienically challenged teeth. He slipped the phone back in his pocket. "Yeah, you're right. There are probably a lot of bars that have a Fat Tire sign situated behind the bar in that exact position. And I'd probably see a bar mirror with a chip in the same place at any number of rat holes like this one." He got up. "Thanks. Think I'll just ask your customers. I'll start with those two in the corner who just finished conducting their drug deal. After that I'll shut the place down for housing illicit activity and wait for vice to get here."

The bartender grabbed his arm. "Jeez, calm down. I said I hadn't seen the dude. Could have been any lowlife who came in here and got tanked enough to jump over the bar and try to pour himself a free one. The manager's in the back. Let me go get him to come out and take a look, okay?"

He gave her a hard look. "You do that."

She scurried away from the bar, ignoring the calls of the patrons waiting to be served, and headed for a side door several feet away. Cam gave her a moment and then trailed after her.

He followed her into a dimly lit cramped area stacked with cases of beer and liquor cartons. And was just in time to see a flash of sagging denim disappearing through the room's exit.

The woman placed herself in his path as he attempted to follow. Cam shoved her aside and reached the doorway. Saw a skinny, bald man tearing through the alley. As he started after him, the bartender launched at him, clinging to his back like a determined monkey, one arm around his neck and the other beating him in his already pounding head with a balled-up fist.

Prying her arm away, he unceremoniously dumped her on her ass and ran after the fleeing man.

The neighborhood was poorly lit, with many broken street-lights. But while the man stuck to the pavement, there were enough lighted business signs to keep him in sight. When they hit a more residential area, however, chasing him through backyards and down rutted alleys became trickier.

The man slowed, looked over his shoulder. Seeing Cam, he put on a burst of speed and turned down a narrow passage between two dilapidated houses. Sensing a trap, Cam paused at the entry of the side yards. Drew his weapon. Pressing his back along the side of one dwelling, he sidled through the darkness, gun raised.

One of the buildings was dark. The other home had faint lights showing through the barred and shade-drawn windows. The canned laughter of a sitcom blared from it. Coming to the open area afforded by the houses' backyards, he swung around the corner, sweeping his weapon in both directions. A body launched itself at him like a heat-seeking missile; the force of the contact took him down.

Cam hit the ground hard and rolled, pressing an arm against the man's windpipe. His assailant bucked beneath him, and Cam saw the flash of a blade a split instant before he leveled his weapon against the man's temple. "You're going to want to drop that."

There was a pause as if the stranger was considering his options. Then slowly his fingers uncurled from the knife. As Cam reached for it, the man screeched, "Do it! Right now, Jesus!"

There were a couple of thuds behind him, and Cam scrabbled away with his captive, yanking the man up and around as he rose. Then blinked when he saw the woman from the bar on her knees, arms covering her head, a baseball bat on the ground before her.

And Sophie towering over her like an avenging angel, her splint-enclosed wrist still raised threateningly as she reached for the bat.

He gave a shake of his head to clear it. Was dimly aware that his headache hadn't receded. "What the hell . . . ?"

"I think"—Sophie sounded breathless as she used the bat in the center of the woman's back to urge her to sprawl facedown on the ground—"that the phrase you're searching for is 'thank you.'"

o o o

It was another twenty-five minutes before DMPD showed up and Cam explained the situation to the officers. "Neither of them have names, apparently. At least none they're admitting to. I'm guessing once you get their prints, you're going to see a sheet on both of them, and an outstanding warrant starring this guy." He jerked his head toward the man he'd chased, who was currently handcuffed and sitting in the back of the squad car at the curb next to them. The woman had been secured and hauled away to the police vehicle parked ahead, from which creative profanities could still be heard.

The officer next to him bore a graying buzz cut and the creased face of a seasoned veteran of the force. "You want to be alerted when we get their identities?"

Cam dug in his pocket and handed them a card. "You can give me a call. But I think I'm done with them." Once he'd gotten the man in the light afforded by the car's LED bar, Cam had immediately known he wasn't the UNSUB. He was the right height and weight, and there was enough of a resemblance along the jaw to give him a second look, but the mouth was wrong. The nose. He was obviously a scumbag. Just not the one they were looking for.

He strode back to his car still parked a couple of blocks away in front of Screwball's. And the closer he drew to the vehicle—and the woman in it—the more quickly his mind shifted away from the capture and arrest and landed squarely on the danger Sophie had placed herself in.

After opening the door of the vehicle, he got inside. Fitted the key in the ignition but didn't turn it. Instead he considered Sophie for a moment. Noted the way she was cradling her splinted wrist.

"How bad does your arm hurt right now," he asked conversationally.

Her gaze dropped to her wrist, seeming surprised to find herself holding it. "I took some pain relievers." Her voice was wry. "So ask me in the morning."

"Not to be a stickler, but I did tell you to stay in the car."

"And I did!" Her defense was spirited. "Right up to the time that the busty brunette chased after you from the bar wielding a baseball bat. Then I thought, 'Oh, hell no.' I had to follow to even the odds."

He did a double take. "Did you just swear?" Though the word was mild, he'd never heard anything remotely close to a cuss word cross her lips before. She was perfectly capable of verbal annihilation without raising her voice or resorting to profanity. He'd be willing to bet under the dark makeup she was blushing.

"I think *hell* ceases to be a considered a swear word by about age ten. And you're digressing. I just thought you needed some backup—that's all."

Cam couldn't stop staring at her. The woman was infinitely fascinating. "A fiberglass splint against a Louisville Slugger." He was unable to keep the amusement from his tone. "The woman didn't have a chance."

"I also had a small canister of pepper spray on my key chain," Sophie said sedately. "I was waiting for her to turn around so I could use it on her."

Lord help him. Every day he spent with this woman he learned something new about her. Something that solidified the tangle of emotion she elicited. Something that added a little bit of light to a world that all too often seemed crowded with darkness.

"Is that what you were waiting for? I thought you said you were waiting for a thank-you."

Her fall of hair shielded her profile as she pulled the shoulder harness over to fasten her seat belt. "I'm not going to hold my breath."

"You don't have to." Leaning toward, he cupped the back of her neck. Exerted subtle pressure to urge her closer. And in the first sweet moment that his lips met hers, he had an unmistakable sensation of homecoming. So he lingered, savoring the sense of familiarity, which beckoned a desire too long ignored.

He'd meant only to brush his mouth over hers. Not to open the floodgates to past intimacies she'd halted before he'd had enough. Long before. But then her lips opened under his, and his intentions abruptly dissipated. The taste of her filtered through his system, had his loins tightening in remembered response. And when their tongues tangled, he felt the blood in his veins rev to life.

He'd almost convinced himself that he'd imagined the explosiveness between them. But he hadn't. And he didn't know whether to be glad for that or sorry. Cam pressed closer for a deeper taste, and for a few instants he let the rest of the world recede.

A car door slamming nearby shattered the moment. Abruptly yanked back to their surroundings, Cam eased away, hauling in a long breath as he did so. "Thank you."

It was a moment before she responded. When she did so, her voice was shaky. "You're welcome."

o o o

Getting the wig off had been Sophia's first order of business once they got back to Cam's place. Such a simple thing, she reflected as she pulled a comb through her hair still damp from the shower, to provide such utter relief. Each time she'd caught a glimpse of herself in the mirror she'd been startled by the stranger staring back at her. After only one afternoon, she was already hoping her days of disguise would be numbered.

Wrapped in a towel, she peeked out of the bathroom to look down the hallway. Cam's bedroom had an attached bath, but the second bath was located in the hallway off the family room.

Ducking back inside to scoop up her clothes and toiletries, Sophia hurried back to her bedroom. A hot shower had done wonders to refresh her, but it hadn't been especially conducive for wiping the memory of Cam's kiss from her mind. That remained stubbornly, vividly implanted despite her best efforts to elbow it aside.

As kisses went it hadn't been nearly as passionate as many they'd shared in their brief time together, she reflected as she swung the bedroom door closed with her foot. It had lacked the new and exploratory nature of their first kiss. The exciting sense of discovery of subsequent ones.

But it had still managed to summon a memory reel of every sensual moment they had shared. To revive the temptation he'd presented from the instant he'd happened upon her that night last month at Mickey's. The single brief intimacy had opened the floodgates of memories and immersed her in a sensual onslaught she was helpless to escape. She'd struggled to barricade them away when she'd joined the investigation of Mason Vance's victims.

But her time in captivity had given her too much time to think. Too much time in which to finally admit to herself that her breakup with Cam had been due more to fear of the emotional risk he posed and far from the stilted reasons she'd given at the time.

The memory of Vance chilled her. The man was safely behind bars. He couldn't hurt her anymore.

And he'd never had a chance to hurt her the way he had his other victims. Terrorize her the way he had Courtney Van Wheton, who continued to lie in the hospital, still and lifeless.

Her feet halted, and she clutched her clothes and bag tightly to her chest. There had been plenty of time for regrets while she'd plotted her escape, terrified Vance would come back before she could get away. And seeing that body that had been uncovered today had been a devastating reminder that her fate could have been far worse.

Her brain ordered her feet forward. Walk to the closet. Take out her robe. Put her things away.

But the open closet morphed into the cell she'd been held in. *The cool cracked limestone wall at its back. The wooden slat sides and sturdy livestock gate secured at the top with heavy galvanized wire.*

And the blow-up mattress in the corner that Vance had once pinned her on, his intent obvious until she'd managed a distraction.

Her palms dampened. And the thudding of her heart grew faster, louder. Until the sound of it filled her ears. Kept beat with the rapid pulse in her veins. Tension crept through her muscles, and her stomach churned with nausea.

She struggled to haul in a breath. To shove the unwanted pictures of Vance and the stall that had become her prison out of her mind.

Sophia was a professional psychologist. But recognizing her physical response to the sudden flashback didn't make it easier to overcome it. She battled to find something else, anything else to focus on. To fill her lungs, then release the air slowly in an attempt to calm her breathing.

Before she could be successful, there was a knock at her door. "If you haven't turned in for the night already, I have something I want to run by you." Cam's voice sounded from the hallway. "Are you decent? Sophie?"

What she was was frozen. Rooted in place by an involuntarily reaction to events that should no longer wield this kind of power.

When she didn't answer—couldn't—the door eased open. And in one quick glance, Cam seemed to understand exactly what was happening.

"I . . . need to get dressed." There was a quaver in her voice that she hated. Was helpless to control. And still her feet didn't move.

"Yeah, you do." He crossed to her and matter-of-factly pried the items out of her grasp and tossed them nonchalantly on the dresser. Then he went to the closet—*the closet, not your former cell*— and pulled her robe off a hanger. Came back to drape it around her shoulders. Helped fit her stiff arms into it and tugged away the towel so he could tie the robe around her waist.

"I just . . ." Her tongue seemed thick, so she tried again. "I was thinking of Vance, and then the closet . . . For a moment it reminded me . . ."

"I know." Gently he turned her and guided her to the bed. Took a moment to yank back the bedcovers before scooping her up and laying her on the mattress. "Exhaustion makes the flashbacks worse. So does fighting them alone."

He stripped off his shirt and turned on the lamp at the bedside. Then crossed to flip off the overhead light. When the mattress gave beneath his weight, she felt a flare of panic that had nothing to do with the flashback. And everything to do with another sort of weakness, this one caused by his presence.

Cam crowded her on the bed. Fitted himself to her backside so they were spooned together in a way that was all too familiar. "Thing I wanted to ask you," he said, the low rumble of his voice soothing in the shadows, "I've been thinking about getting a dog."

"A . . ." The non sequitur was almost successful as a diversion. "That is so not what you came here to talk about."

"Sure it is." He stretched his legs along hers. "I need help selecting a breed, though. Remember when you dragged me to the shelter that day? We saw a lot of dogs there. Which one did you like best?"

"Umm . . ." A fraction of the tension seeped from her limbs as she thought about it. "It'd be hard to say. One that doesn't shed much."

She felt his smile against her hair. "Of course."

"And one that's friendly. Likes exercise, because you'd want one that could run with you."

"Again, you know me too well. So we can cross off the wimpy little yappy dogs. I think we're on a roll."

Her heart began to slow to a steadier beat. And Sophia knew the current molten pulsing in her veins had more to do with the man holding her close than the earlier panic-fueled fear that had ambushed her. Both were a type of weakness. But the long hours she'd spent as Vance's captive had resulted in a jarring shift to her earlier priorities. And she was no longer going to beat herself up for being weak with Cam Prescott.

She let her body soften against his. "Livvie mentioned Portuguese water spaniels as active dogs that don't shed. But I don't think you're going to find one in a shelter."

"Maybe a rescue dog then. I had looked into labradoodles because they like a lot of exercise. But active dogs might not like being cooped up in a condo all day. So maybe I need to start looking for a house. One with a yard."

"A house?" He'd managed to surprise her. "Have you looked at any properties?"

"Not yet. It's just something I've been kicking around. I'm not home that much, but I wouldn't mind more space. An extra bedroom that doesn't double as an office. A spot for a wet bar. Maybe an exercise room so I don't have to keep the treadmill in my bedroom."

There was something oddly intimate about conversing in bed, the shadows cocooning them from the stress of the case. From the rest of the world. Something comforting about the rumble of his voice in her ear. The weight of his arm around her waist.

There had been a time not too long ago when alarms would have gone off in her head as the steadiness of his presence lulled her. A time when she would have resisted feeling too much for a man so far outside her comfort zone.

Sleep beckoned, even as his words continued to come, low and soothing. Sophia focused on the sound of it, indulging for once in the freedom from her own personal restrictions. The sound of Cam's voice in her ears, the warmth of his body next to hers successfully banished Mason Vance from her mind. And when unconsciousness sucked her under, she thought only of the man beside her.

o o o

Sonny clapped his hands over his ears and paced. The static in his head had returned, picking up volume ever since he'd left Lucy Benally's house to go back to his own. Mommy's voice had lodged in his brain, a constant angry buzzing that no amount of effort could banish. He was done listening to it, though. He had something far more important to think about.

Vance had outlined a plan in case either of them got caught. He'd be counting on Sonny to stay around and follow it through. But Sonny wasn't stupid. He knew that if he was the one sitting in jail, Mason Vance would already be out of the state on his way to a new place where he could indulge his pastime in peace. Vance didn't give a shit about his partner, and Sonny returned the loathing. The man was a sadistic prick. And as long as Sonny remained in the vicinity, he was in danger of landing in a cell right next to him.

He wasn't sticking around for his former partner in any case. It wasn't Vance who had claimed his every waking thought; it was Lucy. Sweet, soft Lucy Benally who shared his affinity for the dead. Sonny didn't fool himself that she'd understand what he did at first. The things he'd had to do. But given time, he could teach her. Mold her. Eventually she'd come to realize that they were kindred spirits. Soul mates. Meant to be together.

And if she couldn't be taught . . . the thought had his throat closing. He shied away from it at first. Then forced himself to circle back to it.

If he was wrong about Lucy, there were always other women.

But he wasn't wrong about her. He knew he wasn't. Lucy Benally was perfect for him. They were meant to be together. He just had to shut off the noise in his head long enough to figure out a way to make that happen.

Dropping down on the couch, he picked up his laptop and began looking for his and Lucy's new home. Somewhere remote. Isolated. Sonny was a patient man, a gentle one, but the lessons would be easier once Lucy realized she had nowhere to run. No one to turn to.

No one but him.

Chapter 8

Sleep is known for its restorative powers, Lucy. That's why they invented beds." Gavin Connerly stifled a yawn as he helped the diminutive ME push the gurney holding the body discovered the evening before from the morgue's refrigerated room. The wheels of the cart clattered in the early morning silence as they pushed it down the sterile dimly lit hall toward the autopsy suite Lucy had claimed.

"If you're that tired, you can climb up on this cart once we transfer the body to the autopsy table." But Lucy's words lacked rancor. Unlike Gavin, the work they'd been involved in for the last several hours had exhilarated, rather than exhausted, her. Her mind couldn't rest until she had answers, and if her mind wasn't at rest, well . . . then her body was out of luck.

"I was shocked when you offered to accompany the ME assistants back here with the first two bodies." There was suspicion and a discomforting hint of insight in his words. "What gives, Luce?"

"Don't call me that." She opened the door into the suite, and they maneuvered the gurney inside. "The first station. Help me transfer her over to its table. Please."

His teeth flashed then, making his narrow face ridiculously attractive. Her stomach did a neat flip. From hunger, she assured herself as they brought the gurney beside the stainless steel table and carefully lifted the body onto it. She'd skipped dinner. And chances for breakfast were looking about as feasible as Gavin's pleas for sleep.

"I think that's only the second time I've ever heard you say *please*."

Because he so clearly wanted her to inquire, she ignored the remark. "I can handle it from here if you want to go back to the hotel."

"The first time was the night we spent together before I flew back to California." He wheeled the gurney to the opposite wall of the suite and returned with a saunter in his step. His green eyes were alight with amusement, and something else. Something she didn't want to identify. "As I recall it was after I touched you right—"

"I seem to recall that you were the one to do most of the begging." She turned to the cupboard several feet away and took out the tools she'd need and arranged them on the autopsy tray. She mentally damned herself for being drawn into the conversation after all. Lucy didn't need any verbal reminders about the hours she'd spent wrapped around Gavin Connerly. Her memory of that time was spectacularly vivid.

"You know, you're right." He followed her to the counter and propped his lean form against it. The man seemed to have a phobia about standing upright. "I wouldn't mind doing some more begging when we're through here. I'm not proud."

"I've noticed." After arranging the hammer, bone saw, scalpels, and knives on the sterile paper towel covering the tray, she placed the tray on top of a four-shelf rolling cart and returned to the table, careful to keep her back to him so he wouldn't see her smile. Hers was a somber job, and Lucy was a serious woman with little time for frivolity. Longer exposure to Gavin's seemingly constant affability would surely elevate him from irritant to unbearable annoyance.

Maybe that would be the trick to extricate him from her thoughts. The idea tantalized her. She could increase the time she spent with him rather than avoiding him altogether. It was almost certain that he wouldn't wear well.

That thought summoned another, one much more intimate. She cast a speculative glance in his direction. Perhaps the chemistry between them would burn itself out if she spent more hours stretched out with him in that hotel bed he mentioned. Enough to completely satiate her of this inexplicable attraction.

His brows rose. "Whatever you're thinking, I think I like it."

She turned away, and the sight of the three bodies waiting, still and silent on the gleaming stainless steel tables, jolted her focus back to the job. "I'm serious. I can take it from here. Go get some sleep. The victims aren't going anywhere."

There was a long, tension-filled silence behind her. Then Gavin appeared at her side. "I think we both know that you can't get rid of me. And sometime soon you and I are going to have that discussion you've successfully avoided since I got here."

"I think the matter at hand is a little more important than a conversation," she retorted. She brushed by him to retrieve the handheld oscillating saw and the pruning shears that she favored as rib cutters. Both instruments were placed on another tray and set on the second shelf of the cart.

"Agreed." He went to dig in the cupboard and collected measuring cups, a skull chisel, and toothed forceps to join the ones she'd set out. "The job first. But then . . ."

A shiver chased down Lucy's back at the promise imbued in his words. She'd been granted a reprieve, and it was one she gratefully accepted. Sometime in the intervening hours she'd manage to rebuild her usually stalwart defenses. Because it was going to take far more than sharp words and a prickly exterior to drive this man away.

She was going to need a fortress.

o o o

"You summoned?"

Masked and gowned, Cam and Sophia entered the autopsy suite. When the smell assailed her, Sophia reared back. The odor was as powerful as a weapon, strong enough to bring tears to her eyes. Blinking them away, she was again reminded that given the offender's predilection for the dead, he might be unable to smell or had deliberately rendered himself that way. The odor was different from the stench of putrefaction she'd expected. Formaldehyde was the uppermost in the scents stinging her nose despite the mask she wore.

Gavin Connerly gave them a lazy wave, but Lucy spared them only the briefest of glances. "I figured you'd be in a hurry for information. As it happens, I'm in a hurry to deliver it. I'd like to start the autopsy. Sophia. I assume that butt-ugly suit is part of the disguise?"

Until that moment it hadn't occurred to Sophia that Lucy, who was not considered part of the investigative team, wouldn't have been given the truth about the false obituary. And she felt a stab of remorse for that. "Not a very effective one, obviously." She strode to the woman's side. Touched her arm. "I'm sorry, Lucy. I was allowed to tell a few people the truth, but I didn't have your number."

"Well." The other woman gave her a small smile. "That'll teach me to be so miserly about giving it out. I wouldn't have known the truth if it weren't for blabbermouth over there." She jerked her head in Gavin's direction.

"And you're welcome," he inserted.

"Can you put off the autopsy for an hour?" Cam's request elicited a daggerlike stare from Lucy. "I've got a briefing in thirty minutes."

"And I've got three of your victims ready to give up information about their killer." She walked to the side of the first autopsy station and tapped the table impatiently. "I understand another body is being excavated as we speak."

Cam nodded. "There's even a possibility of a fourth in that grave. They'll be digging for a while. I've also got a dive team forming, so I'm probably going to be at the site most of the day. Which doesn't mean I don't want to be at the autopsy," Cam hastened to add as Lucy narrowed a look at him. "I just can't be in two places at once without cloning myself."

"Out of an abundance of concern for a world with two of you in it, I'd advise against the process."

Concentrating on breathing through her mouth, Sophia looked at the bodies. Back to Lucy. "You're doing all three autopsies today?"

The ME's mouth quirked. "I'm good. But not superhuman, unfortunately. I've done an exam and photos of all three already. They've all been weighed, cleaned, and X-rayed. I'll probably get one autopsy done myself before heading home for some sleep."

"Don't let her fool you. She's hoping that when other staff comes in and sees the second two victims ready, they'll start the autopsies sooner rather than later," Gavin said.

Cam grinned at him. "A woman after my own heart." He glanced at the sharpened tools on the tray next to the autopsy station. "Figuratively speaking."

"I'm just being efficient." Lucy's tone was dismissive. "But I plan to get this first victim done before I leave today. I'll just let you know when the final report is ready."

"I can have another agent here. Just give me some time."

Cam and Lucy exchanged glares. Sophia knew that being present at the autopsy meant the agent was privy to the ME's observations as she worked on the victim. And since they were in a hurry to glean whatever they could about the crime, it was imperative to have an observer from the task force at the autopsies, rather than wait for a report that could take days or longer.

"I can understand your hurry," she told Lucy, turning to scan the other tables. "You've got quite a job on your hands. We're in a hurry, too, to learn anything you can tell us." She turned back to smile at the woman by her side. "I'm not going to volunteer to be the one to observe your work, but someone from the team should be here. How much time can you spare us?"

"Oh, come on, Luce, tell them the truth." Pushing away from his stance against the counter, Gavin approached them. "She really just wants to get done as much as she can before the other examiners arrive and she has to share the fun." To Cam he said, "We can stay busy for another hour before beginning. But no more than that. Neither of us got any sleep last night."

The look Lucy was aiming at the forensic anthropologist should have flayed several layers of skin off him. "You're not in charge here, Connerly. You weren't even invited. And I say—"

"As Lucy said, we examined all three victims," he continued calmly, seemingly unconcerned by the woman seething at his side. "All have been embalmed, although maybe not professionally. There's embalming fluid leaking from two of them. All were vaginally and anally penetrated, but the . . . ah . . . damage from the sexual assault, at least outwardly, appears to be less extensive than that sustained by the first six victims."

Elbowing the man aside, Lucy marched to the computer atop a cart in the middle of the room and typed in a few commands. Sophia was relieved—and more than a little amused—to see a PowerPoint display of photos detailing every step of the excavation.

The ME was notoriously OCD about keeping digital files of her work.

Lucy scrolled to pictures that had obviously been taken in the lab. Then slowed to display them. "It's not just the sexual assaults that appear to be less brutal. The torture—while definitely evident—wasn't as ferocious as the others, either. You'll note here"—she flipped to another set of photos showing the leathery dehydrated skin from the backs of the bodies—"that all three victims have been numbered. If I enhance the pictures, rotate them . . ."

Cam and Sophia moved forward to examine the photos more carefully. "That looks like a seven. Or a one."

"Rhonda Klaussen, Vance's first victim, bears a one," Cam said tersely. His gaze was intent on the screen.

"A seven then." She peered more closely, felt more certain of her observation when Lucy highlighted the wounds in the photos using a tool to draw circles around each of them. "It is a seven. And the next . . ." She swallowed hard. Laid a casual hand on the nearby counter. Gripped its edge tightly. "Four." Without appearing to, she drew in a deep breath. Released it slowly. And struggled to keep a tight seal on the door against the memories that threatened to intrude.

It served no purpose to wonder about the number she would have borne if she hadn't escaped from Vance. Or to question the location chosen for the shallow grave her body would have been excavated from, had it been discovered at all.

"What's the next number? Shit."

Cam's voice succeeding in pulling Sophia from the nightmare that threatened to pounce. She refocused on the screen. Hissed out a breath. "Is that . . . ?"

"Yep. This is the victim found a couple night's ago when the sick fuck decided he was in the mood for romance." Lucy's voice was hard. And her eyes, like all of theirs were glued to the newest photo displayed on the screen. "I had to enhance the pictures to be sure of the number, but anyone disagree that she's number sixteen?"

o o o

"I've always wondered what that meant, that saying on the sign Lucy has sitting out." Cam parked the car in the lot of the Iowa State Patrol Post 1 building, where DCI Zone 1 field agents had their offices in Des Moines. The IOSME shared a campus with the state crime lab in Ankeny. Given the hour, they'd bucked traffic all the way there. Cam and Sophia walked across the pavement to the structure. "I know it's hers because I never see it unless she's the attending ME. But I'm not sure what language it is."

Sophia recognized the verbal distraction for what it was. Her mind was furiously circling the ramifications of what the ME had revealed. But the upcoming briefing would be soon enough to focus on that. So she accepted the reprieve his conversational gambit provided even as she struggled to keep up with his longer strides. Although not wearing the towering heels she usually favored, Sophia's steps were shorter than his. He unconsciously adjusted his stride to accommodate her. The small gesture softened something inside her. "The language is Navajo, I assume. Lucy grew up on the reservation."

He stopped in his tracks. Stared. "She's Native American?" Almost immediately he corrected himself. "Sure she is. She has the coloring. I just never thought . . . actually I try *not* to think about Benally when it doesn't directly involve a case. That's how I can sleep at night."

Sophia gave a smug smile. "You two do seem to have a rather caustic relationship. Too much in common, I think." She shot him a sidelong glance. "You share the same abrasive charm."

"I'm officially offended," he declared. He squinted a little against the bright overhead sun. The expression had tiny creases fanning from the corners of his eyes. This wasn't a man who was going to get less devastating over time, she realized. In the ultimate unfairness of fate, every crease, every line to his face was only going to make him sexier. And more and more, she was coming to realize that she wanted to be there to experience those years with him.

The thought yielded a familiar flare of panic, one that took effort to extinguish. She'd exerted careful control over every aspect of her life, including the men she allowed in it. Her brief intimate relationship with Cam had been an aberration, one she'd been quick to correct when she'd felt too much for the man much too soon. But Mason Vance had shattered the illusion that any amount of personal control could truly keep a person safe. And she was coming to recognize that some risks were worth taking.

Cam Prescott just might be one of them.

"Every time I'm in an autopsy suite with her, I leave feeling like she's used the scalpels on me rather than the victim," he complained as they drew closer to the building.

"When I meet someone with a prickly exterior like hers, I immediately wonder what experiences have caused it. Which is something she and I actually have in common," she declared as she walked briskly beside him. Women who wore wigs for health or other reasons would have her undying admiration in the future. Already her head itched. And the entire day still lay before her. "I dissect personalities. She dissects corpses."

He grunted, checked his watch. Whatever he saw there had him quickening his step. "Not just corpses. If Connerly spends too much time around her, he better watch his back."

A smile played around the corners of her mouth at the thought of the two. "Oh, I don't think Gavin is threatened by Lucy. Just the opposite."

It obviously took a moment for him to grasp her meaning. When he did he froze, his hand on the door handle to the entrance. "Are you saying . . . uh-uh. No way."

"Who's the expert on people here, Agent, you or me?" She reached out to pull open the door, and he had to step aside or risk getting beaned by it.

"You mean he . . . they . . . both of them . . . Holy shit." He seemed ridiculously dazed at what she was suggesting. "That would explain why he offered his services this time around, and pro bono at that. But sleeping with Lucy Benally." Cam gave his head a little shake as if to clear it as they walked down the hallway to the conference room that would hold the briefing. "Connerly's got balls—I'll give him that. Probably not for long, since it's Benally, but still."

Her elbow caught him in the ribs. "Stop. I think they're cute together."

His golden-brown eyes widened comically. "Cute? Sure, praying mantises are cute. Right up until the female devours the male's head." He opened the door to the conference room and waited for her to precede him.

His words were an almost jarring reminder of her earlier thoughts. "And yet the male mantis takes that chance. Proving that even in nature, love is never without risk."

o o o

"So far the excavation has yielded two more bodies." Scanning the team members gathered in the conference room, Cam saw identical grim expressions stamped on every face. "We know there's at least one more. All the bodies were embalmed, so none are skeletonized. That's going to be a huge help for us when it comes to identifying them, which is good because the embalming will make it real difficult to get a time of death."

The evidence team would have taken core samples from the soil as the digging continued, to look for plant life and other evidence that might give them hints about how long they'd been buried. "The excavation is continuing," Cam added. "The HRD team got three separate hits on the river. I've alerted Department of Natural Resources. They're bringing a boat with a side scan sonar."

"You've summoned a scuba crew?"

This from SAC Gonzalez, seated in the front row next to Sophie. Cam scanned the crowd, failed to see any of the top brass in it. And felt a measure of relief. "I've got the Underwater Search and Rescue Team sending one out this morning."

His sleep had been interrupted periodically with updates from the excavation crew, and none of the updates had contained good news. After each call and text, however, he'd quickly fallen back asleep. That could have been due to exhaustion, but he was more likely to credit Sophie. What had started as a way to distract her from the PTSD-induced flashbacks had wound up as comforting to him as it had been to her. And that realization made him more than a little uncomfortable.

"Doesn't make much sense that he would dump them in the river, does it?" The tips of Agent Robbins's ears reddened after blurting out the question. He sank a bit lower in his seat as he fumbled to explain himself. "I mean, why would he bury the ones at the cemetery and at this site, and then break routine with water dumps?"

"Since we're heading into Dr. Channing's territory now, I'll let her answer."

At Cam's words Sophie stood and turned to address the group. "That's a good question, Agent. I can make only an educated guess at this point. But I think we can assume that this second offender was subservient to Vance in some way. He was an accomplice to at least one of the kidnappings, that of Courtney Van Wheton, and it's probable that the partnership of the two men required this UNSUB to be in charge of the body dumps."

Sophie shifted slightly, angling her body so she could include Cam in her comments. "Given what was seen at the burial site the other night, the man we're seeking is most likely to be the one guilty of the postmortem sexual assaults. I think the river represents the same convenience the freshly dug graves at the cemeteries did. Ease of disposal."

"With Iowa winters," Cam inserted, "this guy wasn't digging graves year-round for the victims. He might have looked for a way to get rid of them that was a whole lot easier."

Sophie nodded. "Once the ground froze I'm guessing there was still open water on the river, which explains using both areas. After what we just learned from the ME, I have more questions than answers about this offender. The most pressing of which is why the bodies found at the river are embalmed and the first six discovered weren't. And the timing of the disposals interest me. The ME and forensic anthropologist agreed that the bodies discovered in the cemeteries had been buried in the last year to eighteen months. Identification of those victims verifies that estimate. There's no way to be certain at this point how long the bodies at the new site have been dead. But we now know the recently discovered victim is likely the most recent."

Cam took over. "All three bodies found at the river site bear numbers on their backs, just as Vance's other victims did." He waited for the murmur from the group to die down before continuing, "The two found in the grave bore the numbers four and seven. The one kept in the cave is sixteen."

"That makes no sense."

Cam waited for Tommy Franks to go on. He and the more senior agent were often on the same wavelength.

"The ViCAP files don't show any other crimes with the same details as those first six women we pulled out of cemeteries." The man's scowl was fierce. When Cam had needed fresh eyes to go through the copious information gleaned from the FBI's database on similar violent crimes, Franks had done so. And neither had come up with more victims than the ones discovered a few weeks ago. "Are you saying he varies his victim selection?"

"I think that might be possible." Sophie folded her hands before her sedately, her voice pensive. "Vance and his accomplice may not have partnered on all the crimes. Or they could have alternated victim selection. They may even have engaged in a sort of—for lack of a better word—individual competition. That would explain the difference in the severity of the attacks on the victims. The medical examiner believes that while the new victims were also viciously sexually assaulted, the exterior damage to the bodies at least isn't as great as the other six."

The room went abruptly silent as Sophie's words sank in. Cam found himself leaning forward a bit, in anticipation of her next words. She was given to movement when she addressed a group, and she paced a little now as she continued. "Vance's prior employment tended to be manual labor, so these two didn't meet on the job at a funeral home. But something brought them together. Maybe their pastimes."

"So they met up at a support group for sadistic necrophiles?" Micki Loring's question had a chuckle rippling through the agents. Cam could hear the answering smile in Sophie's voice.

"Possibly. Although I don't believe we'll discover that Vance's paraphilias ran to necrophilia, there is evidence of torture on bodies recovered from the cemeteries and the one discovered two nights ago. We already know that we're looking for a man in his late twenties, early thirties. Given his predilection, I'm guessing we'll find his name on an employee list—past or present—for a funeral home. Other possible occupations are morgue attendant, orderly, cemetery attendant—"

She broke off and glanced at Cam. "Although that list was exhausted when we searched for Vance." Facing the group again, she continued. "Whatever his occupation, he'll likely be underemployed and lacking in social skills. Inept with women. Living alone or with a single family member, likely a female."

"You're saying he's the disorganized one in the partnership, and Vance called the shots," Beachum observed from the back.

Cam could almost feel Sophie's wince. He'd been on the receiving end more than once of a lecture from her regarding the danger of stereotypes using the organized–disorganized dichotomy.

"I do think it likely that he was dominated by Vance, but I suspect we're looking for an offender who's a mix of the typographies. He's capable of highly organized behavior, despite likely being almost completely nonsocial. The methods of disposal, the selection of the dump sites, the stalking of Courtney Van Wheton shows that this man doesn't act at random."

Her words flowed more quickly now. And Cam noted that every person in the room, including the SAC, was listening intently. Sophie had once confided that she'd grown bored with the routine of teaching at the university level. But she was a natural speaker. And given the case, her subject matter was fascinating.

"He's equally likely to be a prisoner to his organization, a creature of routine. Even realizing that his near capture the other night means his image will be all over the media, he will tend to think he can successfully elude capture by changing his appearance, finding a new address in the same neighborhood, or both."

"You think he's still around?" Franks sounded startled.

"I think it's highly likely," Sophie said simply. "He's comfortable only with the familiar. He chose that spot by the river because he's been there before. He knew it well and recognized that its seclusion would serve his purposes. But the site would be seasonal. Wherever he lives he'll have an alternate space for his assaults. Look for a chest type or large upright freezer in his home."

"He likes his chicks chilly," cracked Samuels.

Sophie smiled. "Absolutely. It assists in his paraphilia. Refrigeration would slow decomposition a bit. Freezing would nearly halt it. He'll also have access to a boat and trailer. And I think it's possible that he suffers from some sort of mental illness." The room went silent. "Approximately sixty percent of necrophiliacs have been diagnosed with a personality disorder, and up to ten percent with a psychosis."

The door opened then, and Agent Jenna Turner walked in at a fast clip. Cam told her, "I want a forensic sketch done on all three victims in the morgue."

She didn't bother to sit. "I did the first one—the one on the riverbank yesterday. And I'm afraid you're going to need it sooner than you think." She paused a beat. Sent a nervous look toward the SAC. "I touched base with every kid on Pals's contact list yesterday. Corroborated the names with Cybercrimes when they finished with his phone. I did my best to put a scare into all of the high schoolers, but apparently I'm not as intimidating as I thought." She nodded toward the computer he had at the front of the room. It was used much as Benally's had been in the morgue, for presenting information visually. "May I?"

Cam gave a terse nod. He had a feeling he was going to be ambushed with new information, and it was a sensation he didn't much care for.

"I set a Google alert just in case one of them decided to get clever." Jenna was typing busily on the keyboard as she spoke. "Keywords *Raccoon River, Van Meter, Zombie Woman.*" She sent an apologetic look at Cam. "Just trying to think like kids would.

Wouldn't have told me if they were sharing the video on a social network, but if they uploaded the video to YouTube . . ." She stepped aside, turning to look at the screen behind Cam. He looked, as well. Mentally cursed.

The video was dark. The images shaky. But there was no denying it was the one Pals had taken of the offender at the river. "When was this posted?"

Jenna pulled a small notebook from her pocket to consult it. "About one a.m. this morning. And it has two thousand views already."

A chair scraped. Gonzalez was walking rapidly to the door. And Cam knew she was already in full damage-control mode. "Send a copy of the victim sketch to SAC Gonzalez's office. Alert Cybercrimes. First priority is getting it off YouTube. Second is finding the punk who put it up and nailing him for obstructing an ongoing state investigation."

Cam paused a moment to tamp down the temper that had flared to life. If he found out Pals was responsible for this, Jason Drew, his high-powered attorney, was going to have the fight of his life keeping the little prick out of jail. But whoever was to blame, there would be no mercy. "Any way of knowing who posted it?"

"Not yet."

Cam nodded. "I'll update you later. Leave a hard copy of the sketch for me, too. When you get done at Cybercrimes, go ahead with the sketches at the morgue."

Nodding, Turner headed for the door. If anything, the mood in the room had grown more somber. "The clock just started ticking." A muscle tightened in Cam's jaw as he issued the words. "The last thing we want is for the victim's family to ID her from that video before we can alert them. Getting it off the web as soon as possible will help, but every single one of those kids on Pals's contact list is a potential leak." He waited a moment for his words to sink in. "We didn't get a hit off NCIC or any of the other databases I submitted the photo of the victim to. Patrick, you done in Alleman?"

The agent nodded. Of the group, he was the most flashily dressed as usual in a dark-blue suit, bright-purple shirt, and matching patterned tie. "No one recognized the UNSUB as someone seen around the Vance house. Got varying accounts regarding Klaussen. A few people saw her occasionally in the van with Vance. One old lady, who quite possibly wears the thickest glasses made in this country, swears she'd seen Klaussen coming and going alone." He shrugged. "I don't have corroboration of that, and I'm pretty sure I talked to every resident of the town above the age of ten."

"Good. I want you to take the copy of the sketch Jenna leaves for me and submit it to every law enforcement agency in Iowa and surrounding states." It was a task Cam would have done himself today, anyway, but the matter had just gained urgency. Interstate dissemination wasn't a problem. Iowa's Law Enforcement Intelligence Network shared crime information between the law enforcement agencies. But other states had a patchwork of systems that all had to be accessed separately. And Vance had cast a wide net, sometimes hunting out of state. He wanted to make sure not to exclude any of the surrounding locales. "Flag it as a priority."

He shifted his gaze to Loring. "Want to catch the group up on what you discovered?"

Micki rose lithely. She would tower over some of the men in the room if placed next to them, something she never tired of pointing out. "I had a couple funeral homes that reported break-ins and thefts. Ended up visiting them and showing them pictures of the Ziegler case and one-man gurney. Neither of the places could positively ID them as the items they were missing. I figure the UNSUB shopped online. But I did contact the vendors in the state that sell funeral home equipment. Needed a warrant to get their client list, but it came through this morning."

She strode to the front of the room to hand the list to Cam. He glanced at it. Then at her. "You keep a copy?" At her nod he continued. "Good. I want you to cross-reference the client list with the one Robbins compiled of the past and present employees of funeral homes in the area." He reached for the sheaf of papers on the table before him, riffling through them until he found a copy of the list in question to hand to her.

While she returned to her seat, he said, "I followed up a lead that came in last night on the tip line regarding our UNSUB." Briefly Cam updated the group about the events of last night, omitting the more colorful details. "Although the man arrested wasn't our guy, he bore enough resemblance to him to make the trip to the area worthwhile. Beachum and Samuels, I want you to continue with the BOLO tip line." Although the men didn't utter a word, he could see the weary acceptance on their expressions.

Cam smiled slightly. "Tomorrow we'll switch it up. No use letting you two have all the fun."

"It's a laugh a minute," Beachum assured the others. "Available to the highest bidder. Submit your bids early."

"Robbins." Cam looked at the youngest member of the group. "You have DMPD officers at Channing's place?"

The agent bobbed his head. "Got a pretty steady stream of media knocking at the door, and that of the neighbors'. One guy in particular was pretty persistent." Robbins addressed Sophie. "Told the DMPD officer stationed outside that he was your ex, Dr. Channing. Demanded to know the details related to your death. I understand he wasn't too happy when he was sent on his way."

"Under the circumstances," Sophie said dryly, "It's hard to muster any sympathy for him."

"Head back to her place, and from there you can follow up on the employee names you got from the funeral homes. Start checking out place of residence and contact records. Run the names through the system for criminal records. Let me know if any of them pop." Switching his attention to Franks, Cam said, "You want to provide the ballistics update?"

After the man did so in his usual terse and spare manner, Beachum drawled doubtfully, "I don't know. If Timmons was right, this could just be a case of a woman who wanted out and found a way to do so, while taking Stallsmith to the cleaners. Which isn't as unusual as you might think."

"Until we nail down the alternate victim selection, we can't afford to overlook the ballistics match." To Franks, Cam said, "Benally is waiting—not patiently—for one of us to attend the autopsy on the victim found a couple nights ago. Head over there and then to the river to oversee the operation until I can arrive."

Tommy raised a brow. "And where are you going to be?"

With a glance toward Sophie, he responded, "Following up on the ballistics match. I'll meet you later." With a nod, the older man joined the other agents heading toward the door.

"I'd like you to accompany me on the stops," he informed Sophie when she gathered up her purse. It was in a functional black like her suit, and he had to agree with Benally's earlier assessment. The outfit was butt-ugly, and completely unlike the bright butterfly colors Sophie usually wore. That made it as effective as the wig and newly arrived contact lenses at disguise. "I'll want your take on both these men." He found the information that Franks had brought yesterday and circled the names of the foster parent and Stallsmith. "While you're waiting, contact them and see if you can get a meeting set up for this morning. As soon as possible." He started from the room.

"Okay . . . but where are you going?"

"To Gonzalez's office." Something other than intuition told him the upcoming conversation was going to be far from pleasant.

Chapter 9

Sonny had put a rush on the online order of materials to tint his car a different color. Bouncing through the foster care system hadn't been pleasant, but he'd picked up a lot of skills along the way. He could have bought what he needed at a local auto supply store, but he preferred the anonymity of the web. Online orders were difficult to trace, and it was important to be careful.

Especially now that he had plans for Lucy Benally.

Once he'd seen the inside of her house, he'd been certain his original instinct about her had been right. They were perfect for each other. There hadn't been an item out of place in her home. Sonny had been taught to appreciate orderliness. His own place was equally tidy. Everything precisely placed in a given spot for a reason. He smiled indulgently. Tidiness, at least, was one lesson he wouldn't have to teach her.

His leg throbbed. Sonny was beginning to think that Davis, the bastard, had deliberately put something in the wound to make it more painful. He reached behind him for the bottle of pain relievers he kept on the table next to the couch. Empty. He'd have to drive the mile and a half to Pinter's and get some more.

His leg sent up a howl of protest at the thought of the effort the trip would take.

Awkwardly, he swung his feet off the couch, rising with some difficulty. The old woman next door probably had something. The old cow took enough pills to drop a horse. Surely she had some pain pills in the mix.

He banged out of the side door off the kitchen and crossed the pitted drive to the identical stoop at Moxley's house. Because he knew the old bat was half-deaf, he let himself in and announced his arrival from her kitchen.

The tiger-striped cat the old lady kept arched its back and hissed at him. Sonny gave it a well-aimed kick, satisfied when it yowled and ran under the table.

"Carleton?" came the familiar quavery voice. "Here kitty, kitty. Come here, Carleton."

"It's just me, Mrs. Moxley." Sonny pitched his voice above the sound of the TV blaring in front of her. He stepped through the dark cramped dining room to the living area, where Moxley spent most of her time.

"Oh, Sonny." The old lady chuckled. "I must have dozed off. I dreamed that I heard Carleton. You didn't see him, did you?"

"No, sorry. Do you want me to find him for you?"

"Such a good boy," she said good-humoredly. "But it's probably just as well. He's never liked you. He'll come out when he's hungry, I'm guessing." Fumbling on the TV stand she had set up next to her easy chair, she picked up a thick pair of glasses and peered at him. "Oh." Her voice was disappointed. "I thought maybe you'd been to the bakery again."

He gritted his teeth against the urge to give the old cow the same treatment he'd given the cat. "I'm not feeling too good. I was wondering if you had some Tylenol or something for pain."

He'd successfully distracted her. "Oh, you poor dear." She grabbed a handful of the bottles off the TV tray and brought each in turn up for a closer look. "I'm sure I've got something you can use."

A news bulletin came on, and she paused in her search to glance at the screen. "This same thing has been on for two days," she complained. "Comes on right when I'm trying to watch my stories. They must not have found that man yet. They just keep showing . . ." Her voice tapered off. She reached up to press the glasses more squarely on her nose. Leaned closer to peer at the TV. And then looked at him.

His gaze was drawn to the sketch on the television screen. What the news anchor was saying blended with the background noise that filled his head most of the time. But the picture drew him.

Where had they gotten a picture of him? No, not a picture, he corrected himself, as he stood rooted in place. This was no photo. Someone had done a drawing of him. But when? Who had gotten close enough?

That cap he wore in the sketch hung on a peg just inside his kitchen door. It was one of his favorites. But try as he might, Sonny couldn't recall the last time he'd worn it.

He tore his attention away from the TV once the regular programming ensued. And found the old lady staring at him, fear in her eyes. The clamoring in his head grew louder. "Drawing looks like a couple dozen guys I know. Who could tell from a sketch like that?"

Moxley's voice was weak. "I'm sure you're right. When . . . How long have you had the beard?"

"Not long. You know, forget it. I'm starting to feel better." With false nonchalance Sonny turned and headed back to the kitchen. "Maybe after a nap I'll feel up to going to the store for some. If I do, I'll stop at the bakery. Maybe bring you brownies next time."

He looked over his shoulder expectantly. The old bat was still wearing the glasses. Still staring at him fixedly. And he knew what her expression meant. Cocking his head, he said, "Do you hear that? It sounds like Carleton."

Concern replaced the suspicion on her face. "It does? Is he in the kitchen?"

"No-o." Sonny pressed his ear against the door leading to the cellar. "It sounds like he might've gotten locked downstairs."

"That rascally cat." With the help of a cane, she heaved her heft out of the chair and waddled over. "No, don't you call him," she said as Sonny made as if to open the basement door. "He won't come for you. He must have slipped down there when I opened it for the broom this morning. Found a spider on the ceiling as big around as my thumbnail. But the broom put an end to him."

The old woman was out of breath as she reached the door and fumbled with the lock. "Carleton?" She flipped on the light switch, which only lightened the shadows below by a fraction. "You bad kitty. Carleton!"

In a flash Sonny moved behind her. Slipped his hands around her neck and squeezed. With his good leg, he kicked the cane away as Moxley's hands came up to claw at his, her big form putting up more of a struggle than he would have expected.

She was harder to strangle than the others had been. Her neck was as fat as the rest of her. He pressed harder and squeezed until her hands fell from his. Until her body slumped. And then he shoved her hard, watching with interest as her body bounced and rolled down the narrow stairway, getting caught near the bottom and lodging there at an odd angle.

Something furry sped by Sonny and through the door. Down the steps. The cat. *Perfect.* He laughed out loud as he swung the door shut and locked it again. A fitting ending if he'd ever seen one.

He'd always hated that cat.

o o o

"Want to talk about it?"

Cam spared Sophie a brief glance before returning his gaze to the traffic. Upon getting in the car he'd donned a pair of sunglasses, so she couldn't tell what he might be thinking. "What?"

"You've barely said two words since you left Gonzalez's office."

He grimaced. "She wasn't happy about the video going public. And she made damn sure to let me know that Miller was going to be even more pissed."

"I'm not sure what else you could have done besides contacting the kids. Jenna did that. The risk was always there."

"Result's the same. And I can't blame her. If the relatives of that victim see that scene . . . well, it'd be a PR nightmare." He slowed for the traffic light and looked over at her again. "Lucky for us that the video shows the offender more clearly than the victim, and it was dark. But I still want to get the woman ID'd ASAP."

"Hopefully sending her photo to law enforcement will spark something."

Luck. There had been a dearth of that in this case so far, and he didn't see circumstances changing that anytime soon. Gonzalez had made it clear that she expected results at warp speed. Amazing how quickly the SAC had forgotten the rhythm of an investigation once she'd been promoted. As an agent, Maria Gonzalez had been one of the best. Now with the pressure coming from on high, she was quickly becoming unreasonable.

He had a pang of guilt for the uncharitable thought. He'd worked long enough with Maria to know she hadn't lost her instincts about a case. But he wasn't so sure that pressure from the brass didn't, on occasion, make her ignore them. And that never boded well for the agents she managed.

Cam said nothing more until they pulled up in front of a modest brick single-story ranch in the Beaverdale neighborhood. Sophie watched as he gave the property a critical look as they exited the vehicle and walked up the drive.

The home, much like others on the tree-lined street, was dated, likely built in the 1940s or 1950s. But it was in good shape. The brown shutters had been freshly painted and the shrubs trimmed. The lawn didn't seem to have a blade of grass out of place.

"Sometimes I think I'd like a lawn to mow," he mentioned as they were climbing the front steps.

She looked at him askance. "I don't have much experience in the area, but I'd guess that most men don't share that dream."

He reached out a finger to drill the doorbell. "It might be relaxing. A way to unwind." Slanting her a sideways glance, he added, "And when a case keeps me too busy, I'd probably have a wife who shares my love of mowing who'd volunteer to take over."

She smirked. "It's your fantasy. But I have to tell you it's sounding more unlikely by the second."

They both sobered as a man comfortably settled in his seventies opened the front door. "Mr. Fedorowicz?" Cam produced his credentials. "DCI agent Cam Prescott. This is my associate . . . Mona Kilby." For a moment his mind had gone blank. Not a good sign when he was tasked with keeping Sophie's new identity secret. "I called earlier."

"Yes. Come in." The older man unlocked the screen door and held it open for them to step inside. He wore khaki shorts and a burgundy golf shirt. After he'd ushered them to seats, he closed the front door again. "It helps to keep the house cooler. Air-conditioning is expensive."

"I understand brick homes are easier to keep cool." Sophie offered the man a warm smile. "My childhood home was brick, and I remember my parents saying that."

"It is." The older man sat down on the couch to face them. His knees beneath the shorts looked like two shiny white doorknobs. He waved a gnarled hand at the picture window with its heavy curtains drawn. "Every little bit helps." His gaze shifted to Cam, his expression expectant. "I'm intrigued. What would bring the DCI to my door?"

"I'd like to talk to you about a cold case that occurred about fifteen years ago. A gun registered to you was used in the commission of a crime."

A pained expression crossed the other man's face. "My memory's not what it used to be, but something like that I can't forget. Yes, the gun was registered to me. My wife and I were foster parents for over ten years after our kids were grown. One of the teenage boys who lived with us for a few months stole the gun from my gun case. Robbed a convenience store. It was unloaded, of course. I keep the ammo locked up, too, but . . ."

He shook his head as if the memory pained him. "You get these kids—some of them are okay, just got born to the wrong people. They just need a chance, you know? But others, their future is set. Jamie Wallace was one of those kids. Bad to the bone. Stole everything that wasn't nailed down. Lied like an experienced con man. I knew after a week the kid was headed for prison. Heard a while back that he's there now."

"You got the gun back, I understand." Gently Cam steered the man back on track. "But then it was used four years ago in a possible home invasion."

Fedorowicz seemed to shrink into the couch. "I never even knew it was gone. Helluva thing, isn't it? My wife had just died. I'd been staying with my daughter in Ohio for a few months. Cops were able to contact me only by talking to the neighbors. They were the ones who discovered a basement window broken. Punks destroyed the gun case. Took every one of them, nothing else. Cops thought they knew what they were after."

Cam felt a flare of frustration. It'd been a long shot. The detective investigating the case at the time very likely had looked at all the possibilities. "Did any of your neighbors know you had guns?"

The older man nodded. "Oh, sure, a couple buddies and I went out to the shooting range frequently. The cops even made me give them their names." He chuckled ruefully. "As if they'd have any reason to steal mine. I'd had most of them for decades. They all had nicer weapons than I did."

"How about kids that lived in the neighborhood at the time?"

"Like I told the police, this is a settled neighborhood. There were plenty of kids when mine were growing up, but young people these days, they don't want houses like this." He stabbed a knobby finger to the east. "They buy brand-new homes in that new development a couple blocks from here. We get a few rentals with people in and out, but mostly folks are middle-aged and up."

"You mentioned a daughter." Sophie leaned in subtly. "Do you have more children? Grandchildren?"

"I have a son in Nevada. Three grandkids, ten, twelve, and fourteen." He nodded to the framed pictures scattered on top of the entertainment center, his dark eyes alight with pride. "Smart as a whip, all of them. And I don't give a damn that every grandparent says that, because it's true."

Sophie laughed. "Having met you, I'm sure you're right. Did the police by any chance ask for a copy of the names of the foster children who had stayed here?"

Cam smiled inwardly. Sophie could deny it all she wanted, but she had an investigative mind. She'd picked up some of the techniques naturally working side by side with law enforcement over the years. But a person couldn't acquire instincts. And hers were spot-on.

Fedorowicz pulled at his bottom lip. "Not that I can recall. By that time we'd been out of the foster care business for a while. I couldn't even name all the kids we housed, to tell you the truth. Some we took just for respite care, others just for a weekend until they got a permanent placement. There were probably forty or so in all. And my memory isn't good enough these days to name more than a handful of them."

"What about financial records?" Cam asked. Sophie had come up with a good line of questioning, and it was worth pursuing. "You received payment from the state as foster care parents, right? Did you keep the records from that time?"

The man looked abashed. "Clarice, my wife, would have told you that I'm a notorious pack rat. So I'm going to answer yes, probably. But the information would be in a box somewhere with old tax information in the basement. I can get the names to you later if you like."

"If it wouldn't be too much trouble." Cam got up and handed the man one of his cards. "You can call me with them, text, or email."

Fedorowicz chuckled. "I can guarantee I won't be texting. My grandkids are far more adept with technology than I am. But I have an email account. Go down to the library every Wednesday morning to check it. I'll get the names to you."

Cam stood. "I'd appreciate that." He and Sophie walked to the door. His hand on the knob, he turned, as if a thought had just occurred. "Would you mind telling me where you worked before you retired?"

"Forty years as a security guard for Wins-Go Freight." Cam had heard of the name. The trucking company operated out of Des Moines. "Had a couple second jobs here and there over the years to help make ends meet. Mostly night watchman for various places.

Same job, different employers." The older man shook his head. "Not like the kids these days. They hop from job to job. Maybe they're more ambitious. Sometimes, though, I think they just want to have immediately everything their parents had after thirty years."

"Did you ever take a second job with a funeral home?"

The man stared at Cam for a moment, before giving a bark of laughter that deepened the creases on his face. "Can't say I ever did. I'm not going to lie, a funeral home is the last place I'd ever want to be at night. Do they even hire night watchmen?"

"Do you keep up with any of the kids you fostered?" Sophie picked up the line of questioning seamlessly. "By any chance did any of them take jobs at a funeral home?"

The humor had vanished from his face. Fedorowicz aimed a shrewd look at her. "I have a feeling you have a very specific reason for asking that question." He looked from one of them to the other. Gave a little sigh. "And that you're not going to tell me what it is. Well, the answer is, I have no idea. We'd hear from a few of the kids for a while after they left us. Those that aged out of the system at the time they were staying here, usually. We haven't had contact with any of them for years, though. Lots of times we were just a stopping place in the revolving door of their lives. That's what Clarice used to say." There was a note of sadness in his voice. "Can't say I blame them. Most of them had tough roads ahead. The ones that made it probably wanted to leave their pasts behind."

Sophie touched his arm. "I'm sure you made a positive difference in their lives."

He patted her hand. "Thank you for saying that. I like to think so, but you just don't know." Shifting his attention to Cam, he said, "I'll get you that information you wanted."

After thanking him, Cam and Sophie walked to the vehicle.

"He was a nice man," she said, sliding into the car and buckling her seat belt. "And a bit lonely, I think."

Maybe it was the older man or maybe it was Sophie's observation, but for some reason Cam thought of his mother. Who was nowhere close to Fedorowicz's age, and probably not lonely since she'd been married for the last six years. But he hadn't talked to her in almost a week. He made a mental note to call when he had a chance.

"The visit was likely a bust." He put the car in gear and pulled away from the curb. "He didn't tell us anything that wasn't part of the police report Franks pulled from a few years back." He tossed a look at her. "Except for the foster kid route. That was a good thought."

"When he mentioned how long he'd had the guns, it occurred to me that he would have owned them while they provided foster care. Troubled kids in the house. It was a chance." She leaned forward and adjusted the radio. He restrained a wince when she settled on a classical station, but he refrained from remarking on it.

"Maybe. But it's more likely that he was targeted by one or more individuals looking for empty houses to rob." Which meant that this line of questioning had been a waste of time. Nevertheless, he'd check out the male names on the list the man came up with. Cross-reference them with the list of the state's violent sexual felons released in the last few years and the one of employees of funeral homes in the area. Sometime, one of these long shots was going to pay off.

And that time couldn't come soon enough.

He turned off Twana Drive onto Lower Beaver Road. Headed toward Urbandale. "I don't know about you, but I'm hoping to get something more substantial from Kevin Stallsmith."

o o o

Alfred Fedorowicz laboriously moved box after box, peering at the dates marked on the tops until he found the one he was seeking. He carried it over to the folding table he'd set up in the basement and started going through it for the information the agent had asked for.

It wasn't as if he had better plans for the day. And given his blasted memory lately, if he put the task off for long, he'd forget it completely. As he and Clarice had often remarked, getting old wasn't for sissies.

She'd never been a sissy, despite the excruciating agony she'd experienced at the end from the pancreatic cancer. He'd had three short months with her after she'd been diagnosed. Every day of her end had been approached with the grace she'd displayed each day of her life.

A drop fell on the folder he held. Followed by another. Alfred hadn't even been aware that he was crying. He took a handkerchief from the pocket of his shorts and wiped his eyes. Blew his nose noisily. Thoughts of his late wife could still ambush him, even after four years. Make him bawl like a baby, as though her death had been yesterday.

Determinedly he got back to work, welcoming the distraction. It took hours, as he'd known it would. There were so many children, and reading the names on the documents brought back memories that weren't always welcome. He'd liked the babies and toddlers best. It had been nice to have young kids in the house again after his own were grown. But most often they'd been chosen for kids ten and older. More boys than girls, he saw from the names on the ever-growing list at his elbow. Some names didn't even ring a bell. Alfred was ashamed of that. It only seemed right that each child would etch into his memory as they'd passed through his life. Seemed like he owed them at least that much.

Clarice would have remembered. He closed the tabs on one box and went for another. She'd know every name, recall a face for each, and be able to recite all of their sad stories. She'd had a soft spot for every one of the kids.

Heaving a sigh, he opened a new box and carefully went through the paperwork inside. He still recalled the ones that had been with them the longest. And others flashed through his memory as soon as he saw their names on a file folder. Like the name on the form in his hand.

Sonny Baxter.

Helluva a name to hang on a kid, Alfred had always thought, but it was the only one he'd had. And he was one Alfred remembered. One he'd never forget.

They'd had the teen for three months before the social worker had ever told him the reason for the therapist and heavy-duty medication. And the story of the kid's past hadn't been a pretty one. Knowing what the kid had been through, Alfred had even taken him shooting several times. The boy might have had no defense against what had been done to him in the past, but he'd damn well learn to defend himself for the future.

He'd been a quiet kid. Too quiet. Never any trouble and kept to himself. At least as much as he could with three other boys crammed into the house with him. An odd duck maybe, and who could blame him? Unlike some of the others, Sonny had never given them a moment's worry.

A dim memory rang, but Alfred couldn't lay his finger on the source. He dug farther in the box, for the file that Clarice had kept on each child. A list of their accomplishments. Another for her concerns about their behavior.

There it was then, in his hand, the thing that had been niggling at the back of his mind. Listed in Clarice's neat printing she'd noted the part-time job Sonny had gotten when he'd turned sixteen.

Cleaning up at Foster's Funeral Services.

Alfred dropped the sheet as if it had burned his fingers. Coincidence. It had to be, didn't it? Many of the teenagers that had been with them had gotten jobs at one time or another. For most it was the first time in their lives they'd had their own money to spend. At the time, he'd applauded their initiative.

Troubled, he replaced the sheet in the file and set it aside. But the information lodged in his head, burrowed in.

Should he call the agent with Sonny's name? Sic the law on him for who knows what the agent was investigating? The kid had lived enough misery for six lifetimes. Alfred had always felt sorry for Sonny Baxter, despite what he'd done to his mother when he was nine. The bitch, Alfred had once confided to his wife, had had it coming.

Of course, he wasn't a kid now. He'd be . . . Alfred squinted. Twenty-eight or so. He'd run off when he was seventeen, and he and Clarice hadn't heard a word about him since. He had no idea whether social services had ever caught up with him. Alfred wondered now if the kid had made something of himself.

Of if he'd done whatever it was that the agent had come here about.

Torn, Alfred struggled with his thoughts as he completed his task. Clarice would never forgive him if he brought more misery into that boy's life. On the other hand, they'd been a law-abiding couple. It would never have occurred to her to refuse to cooperate with the DCI.

In the end, he decided on a course of action. He'd include Sonny's name on the sheet of names and email it, as promised to Agent Prescott. But he wouldn't alert the agent to look at Sonny in particular.

It might be the last break he could offer that lost introverted teen that'd been through so much, while still complying with the law. As compromises went, it was one Alfred decided he could live with.

o o o

Kevin Stallsmith ushered them inside his split-foyer home, and seemed to barely listen to the introductions before demanding, "You have news? About Emily?"

"I'm sorry. We're here to ask you some questions about her disappearance."

Cam's answer seemed to deflate the man. "I thought . . . when your office called, I hoped there might be something new. I got permission to go in to work later." He rubbed a hand over his short sandy-colored hair, a dejected slump to his broad shoulders. "I talked to that detective a lot at the time. Timmons. He could give you all the information you need."

It didn't escape Cam's notice that Stallsmith didn't offer them a seat. "We have a copy of Detective Timmons's file. But I wanted to clarify a few things. Maybe we could sit down for a few minutes."

Stallsmith remained standing. "I should really get in to work."

"This won't take long."

With a show of reluctance, the taller man turned and walked up four stairs to a living area. He waved them halfheartedly to chairs but remained standing, arms folded.

His body language was more telling than a shout. Ignoring it for the moment, Cam said, "The ballistics on a weapon used in a case I'm investigating match the bullet found lodged in your wall when you reported your wife missing a few years ago."

Stallsmith looked at Cam and Sophie blankly for an instant. Then he threw back his head and gave a harsh laugh. "You guys are un-fuck-ing-believable, you know that?" Cam looked at him. Said nothing.

"The cops at the time were all over me. At first Timmons acted like I'd offed Emily and hid the body, for God's sake. Then got rid of the gun, because, hey, they couldn't find it anywhere. Now you waltz in and say, 'Wait, we think you kept the gun and four years later used it to commit another crime.'"

He walked toward the steps. Jerked a thumb. "Get the hell out of my house. I'm not answering any other questions without an attorney present."

"That's your right." Invoking it, however, had Cam's instincts quivering.

"You said, 'At first.'"

Stallsmith's attention jerked toward Sophie, his brow wrinkling.

"You said at first Detective Timmons thought maybe you had something to do with your wife's disappearance," she elucidated. "What changed his mind?"

The man snorted. "Maybe the fact that there was a bullet hole I couldn't explain in the garage ceiling but no blood. More likely because a couple dozen people swore that I'd put in sixteen hours straight on the job that day." His throat worked, and he looked away. "If I'd been home on time . . ."

Feeling Sophie's gaze on him, Cam said, "Mr. Stallsmith received a message from his wife postmarked the day she was last seen. A Dear John letter."

"Which she didn't write," Kevin said heatedly. "I told Timmons there was no way Em had left on her own, but he verified that it was her handwriting, so he just figured the letter meant she had reasons to split."

"Did she have reasons?"

Cam's quiet question had the other man flushing. "We had our ups and downs just like any other married couple. But things had been going pretty smooth. We were talking about starting a family. She wouldn't have left then. I still don't believe she did. Not willingly."

"She took clothes. A suitcase," Cam said for Sophie's benefit. He saw the way she was looking at the guy, sympathy in her expression.

Most likely the guy deserved some slack. But there was still the unexplained bullet hole in the garage that bothered him.

After reaching into his suit coat, he withdrew a copy of the sketch of the offender. Gave it a shake to unfold it and rose to hand it to Stallsmith. "You ever remember seeing this man around before your wife disappeared? Or since?"

When recognition flickered in the man's expression, Cam felt a flare of excitement. It was extinguished in the next moment when he said, "This has been all over the news. It says anyone who has seen him should call in." His gaze went from Cam to Sophie and back again. "He's the case you're investigating?"

"Take a good look," Sophie advised. "People change over the years. This sketch was done a few weeks ago."

Stallsmith studied it for several moments longer before shaking his head. "Doesn't look familiar." He handed it back to Cam. "Timmons thinks Emily left on her own. I've never believed it. Do you think . . ." He hesitated for a moment before barreling on. "Did this guy have anything to do with her leaving?"

There was nothing else here for them. Of that, Cam was certain. He rose. "All we know is the ballistics dug out of your garage ceiling match the weapon used recently in a murder attempt. But the weapon was stolen years ago. And illegal guns change hands."

"You say you got a letter from your wife." Sophie hadn't followed his lead. She was still seated. When Stallsmith looked at her, she went on. "Did she take anything else when she left? Was money missing out of your bank account?"

"We didn't have a lot of savings. But the credit cards were maxed out, the same day she disappeared. A few clothes, but mostly stuff Timmons said could be turned into cash. Said she might have used it to fund her disappearance."

Finally Sophie got to her feet. "And her family has never heard from her again? Her friends?"

"Not that they've told me." His mouth flattened. "I don't give a shit what Timmons thinks. People don't just disappear without a trace. Em was real close to her sisters. Whatever the detective thinks about Em and me, she wouldn't have run off and never contacted her sisters again."

"Would her sisters have told you if she'd been in contact?"

The man's hesitation was its own answer. "Maybe we weren't on the best of terms. More than once she'd go to one or the other of their houses after we had a fight."

"And when you'd call . . . they'd tell you what?"

Sophie's question seemed to make the man angry. "They'd tell me she didn't want to talk to me sometimes. Other times they'd say she wasn't there, even after I'd driven by and seen her car."

As if the ramifications of that admission hit him as he uttered it, he looked away. For a moment Cam actually felt sorry for the guy.

"Do you have a photo of Emily, Mr. Stallsmith?" Sophie sounded apologetic. "I realize there's probably one in Detective Timmons's file, but I haven't seen that. It would save time if you had one I could look at."

Clearly anxious to have them gone, the man shook his head. "I got rid of them after Timmons seemed so sure she'd just left. And that letter . . ." His shrug told the story. "I mean, if she didn't want me, I didn't want any reminders of her, you know?"

"But there was a chance she didn't leave you," Sophie reminded him softly. "There were times you believed she couldn't have. And for those times, I'd think you'd keep a picture around. To remind you of the possibility."

The man looked away. Then after a moment, he turned with a jerk and went through the tiny dining room down a hallway. Returned a moment later with a five-by-ten still in its frame.

It was a photo of both of them taken in one of the happier times in their stormy relationship. Their arms were hooked around each other's waists, and Emily's face was tipped up to her husband's.

A fist clenched all the muscles in Cam's stomach into one large hard knot. Emily Stallsmith was definitely not the woman that had been found two nights ago on the banks of the Raccoon River. But he'd seen her before.

He glanced at Sophie as her gaze sought his, immediately saw the recognition on her face.

The woman in the picture had just been excavated from the mass grave they'd found. With no identifying marks except for the number seven burned into her back.

Chapter 10

You're quiet." Cam turned off the exit ramp onto Interstate 80. "I've got copies of the case file from Timmons back at the office. It was solid enough police work."

Kevin Stallsmith's anguished expression as he made the identification of his dead wife in the morgue a half hour earlier was still vivid enough in her memory to lend her voice bite. "Solid? How can you say that when Emily Stallsmith was never reported as a missing person?"

"You can't blame the detective. The scene was obviously staged so people would think she'd left of her own accord." Cam shot a glare at a driver in a bright-red Camry in the lane next to theirs who was concerned more with her cell phone than with keeping her car from drifting over the line.

"Neighbors said the couple used to fight. A suitcase was packed. Her car was never found. A woman without the cash to take off and start over could use credit cards to buy easily disposed of items that can be turned into cash." He slowed and gave a honk of his horn when the Camry drifted their way again. The driver started, shot him a filthy look, and straightened the car, speeding away. If he had

had the time and inclination, he'd have her pulled over and arrested for driving while stupid.

"You said it yourself," Sophie said with some heat. "The scene was staged. Timmons should have seen that possibility. Especially with a bullet found in the ceiling of the garage."

"Which Stallsmith couldn't swear hadn't been there when he bought the place. Bad luck, Soph. Not bad police work. In Timmons's place I might have done the same thing."

"No." Her denial was certain. "You're much too suspicious not to have seen the possibilities."

He considered that for a moment. "Not sure that was meant as a compliment, but I'll take it."

She fell silent, and he was left to wonder in what direction her amazing mind had veered now. Regardless of the wig and dark makeup that could still throw him for a loop when he looked at her sometimes, she was the same Sophie. And he could hear the wheels turning.

"So Klaussen was Vance's first. Stallsmith was the seventh, although it's uncertain whether Vance, his accomplice, or both played a part in her murder. They could have still been evolving. What was the total of the credit card purchases after her disappearance?"

Cam searched his memory. "Six thousand or so. Another five hundred from their bank account. Not a fortune for sure, especially considering that fencing the goods or selling them on Craigslist or eBay would have resulted in less than the ticket price."

"Then there's the car. Which could have been sold to a chop shop for a thousand more. Not a bad haul. Nothing like what Vance was getting from the six victims found in the cemeteries," Sophie mused. She had her head turned toward the window, but he'd bet money she wasn't noticing the scenery. "Vance hatched that idea in prison, according to his cell mate. So it's hard to believe he spent the first few years that he was out selecting victims who yielded him so little cash."

"Okay, so we're back to your other idea. That the two were in a competition."

"Sixteen victims in four years is a heck of a competition," she said grimly. "And for the life of me I can't figure out their numbering system." Her voice turned musing. "Given the victim numbering, Vance would have had to come to Iowa almost immediately upon his release from prison in Nebraska and gotten started. We need to figure out when and how he hooked up with the UNSUB." She turned to face him again. And he didn't trust the speculative gleam in her eye. "How long will you be at the river scene?"

The reminder sobered him. "No telling." His last phone call had arrived while he was at the morgue with Stallsmith. The dig team had found a fourth body and was working to excavate it. The dive crew, according to Franks, still had found nothing. "Probably all day, or until the divers call it quits."

"Maybe I could take your car after dropping you there." The suggestion had his head whipping around to face her. "I really need to talk to Rhonda Klaussen."

"Are you kidding me? There's not a chance in hell of your going anywhere without protection."

She gave an incredulous laugh. "Even looking like this? My own mother wouldn't know me. As a matter of fact, if anyone I knew did recognize me in this mess, I'd be sorely offended."

"So be offended." His gaze returned to the road. "It's a wig and makeup, not a cloak of invisibility."

"And colored contacts," she reminded him. "As of this morning."

"Fine. Great. You turned your blue eyes brown. I think there's a country song title in there somewhere."

Now she was amused. "I believe that song is the other way around. 'Don't It Make My Brown Eyes Blue.'"

Impatience filtered through him. And this time he couldn't blame the red Camry. "Whatever. You still aren't going anywhere alone."

She settled in her seat with an air of satisfaction. And there was a note in her voice that he didn't quite trust. "That works for me."

o o o

Sophia stared at the 1940s-style white clapboard house tucked neatly between a newer ranch and a rambling Queen Anne. "When you said Sheldahl, Iowa, I honestly don't think I could have found it on a map."

"Lucky then that you didn't have to." From the clip in his tone, the force with which Cam put the car in park, Sophia could tell he was still smarting at the detour. And the reason for it.

"Don't be a sore loser," she said, trying to keep the amusement from her voice. "We drew cards to decide where to go first. A king beats a two every time. Had it been the other way around—"

"Had it been the other way around"—he opened the car door, aiming a meaningful look over his shoulder—"we'd be playing for something far different, and you'd be naked."

"At least then you'd be happier," she muttered as she unfastened her seat belt.

"Got that right."

Shock mingled with amusement. She clearly recalled the incident he was alluding to. There had been a time while they were together that they'd played cards for clothing. Strip Gin. As she recalled, she'd won then, too.

It was his reference to the memory that she found most surprising. Cam had been solicitous, protective, and, yes, bossy since she'd escaped from Vance. But barring that kiss outside Screwball's, he had kept things between them strictly professional.

If it could be considered professional to curl up beside her in bed and hold her until her demons faded.

Drawing a shaky breath, Sophia joined him on the walk before the tiny house. They'd never mentioned last night. And more telling, he hadn't used it today as a lever to convince Gonzalez that his fears about Sophia consulting on this new case were justified.

"This place . . ." he started. She stopped his words when she went up on tiptoe to brush her lips softly over his.

When she moved away, he blinked at her.

"It occurred to me that I owed you a thank-you for last night." Drawing the strap of her purse more securely over her shoulder, she walked by him toward the small wooden front stoop. Heard his surprised, "You're welcome," and smiled.

He'd joined her on the porch before the door was finally cracked open. A pair of wary hazel eyes peered around its edge. "Oh. It's you." The words were delivered with a decided lack of enthusiasm.

"Miss Klaussen. I have a few more questions."

The door opened more fully, framing the woman in it. "We already talked twice. I don't know what else I can tell you." But curiosity lit her expression as she surveyed Sophia. "Who's this?"

"Dr. Mona Kilby." Sophia smiled. "I've recently started consulting for the DCI on this case. I hope it's not a bother, but I'd like to speak to you about your ordeal."

"Doctor." The corners of her mouth went down, but she reached out to unlock the rickety front door. "Saw one of them, too. He said I was fine." She glared at Cam. "At least fine enough to sit in jail for two days."

"I'm sorry you were inconvenienced." They stepped into a postage-stamp-size living area. It boasted threadbare carpet and a sagging couch next to an end table and lamp that could have time traveled out of the 1960s.

"What the hell," she said finally. "Got three meals a day, and that wasn't always the case when I was with Mase." She waved them to the decidedly uninviting brown sofa. "May as well sit down."

The woman was lean but large-boned, heavily made up with bleached-blonde hair showing brown roots. Despite the lack of air-conditioning inside the house, she wore jeans, paired with a skimpy black cami and men's flip-flops. And her interest in Sophia was evident.

"What kind of work do you do for the DCI?"

"I'm a forensic psychologist, which means I ask a lot of questions." Cam remained standing while Sophia sat down on the sofa, hoping that the other woman would join her here.

With a sidelong glance at Cam, Klaussen sank to the edge of the opposite side of the sofa. "A head doctor, you mean."

"A thought doctor," Sophia corrected her with a smile. "I'm primarily concerned with the way people think. Why they do the things they do. How they feel." When Klaussen didn't answer, Sophia scanned the room. A miniscule kitchen could be seen through the next doorway with only ancient appliances and a counter and sink in it. The entire home was sparsely furnished, and it occurred to her that the woman wouldn't have been allowed to take many of her things—if she'd had any—from the home Vance had been living in.

"How'd you happen to end up in Sheldahl?"

The woman jerked a bare shoulder. "Victims' services arranged it. The lady that visited me gave me a choice of places to go. Never been here, but she said it was a small town . . ." She rubbed her arms with her hands, as if suddenly chilled. "It sounded safer. Like if people knew I was here, they'd notice if I was gone, you know? Maybe help if I needed it."

"The way you needed help in Alleman?" Sophia asked quietly.

The woman looked down. Gave a quick jerk of her head. "They didn't know I was there, I figure. When Mase . . . did stuff . . . I was usually gagged. He didn't like that as much, though. He liked to hear me in pain."

The memory of Courtney Van Wheton's screams careened across Sophia's mind then, on a sharp jagged wind that left trails of blood in its wake. It was hard—oh, so hard—to slam the door shut on the memory. To steel herself against the echoes that pulsed in her ears.

"Sometimes it's easier to feel visible in a small town."

Klaussen looked around. "It's not much, and it's mine for a only month. But they let me use that old Chrysler LeBaron out front for thirty days, too. It's enough to get me on my feet again. Next week I'm going to start applying for jobs. Had a pretty good job bartending once when I lived in Omaha. With tips and stuff, I did okay."

"Omaha." Sophia sent a surprised glance to Cam. "Is that where you first met Mason Vance?"

Rhonda hauled in a shuddering breath. Released it. She reached up and captured a strand of her hair. Wound it nervously around an index finger. "Yeah. About eleven or twelve years ago. We were hot and heavy for that first year until I got tired of his temper. Got out and took a different job across town. Took him six months to find me. Another six to make me pay for leaving."

A stab of sympathy speared through Sophia. The other woman's rough edges were apparent. According to her record, her past choices had been questionable. But no one deserved what she'd suffered at the hands of Mason Vance. None of his victims had.

"He'd taken to tying me up when he left the apartment." The strand of hair was unwound, then twined tightly again. Wind. Unwind. Nerves were apparent in the gesture. In the way her words started tumbling out. "He swore that he'd never let me leave him again. I got to where I prayed for him to take another of his trips and leave me alone. I'd half starve, but at least the torture would stop."

Cam had straightened his stance against the wall. Sophia circled around the new information. "He left you without food?" The sympathy in her voice was unfeigned. It wasn't hard to believe of Mason Vance. He was guilty of far worse.

Klaussen nodded. Dropped the strand of hair to set both large hands on her denim-clad knees. "At first it was just for a night or two. Then a weekend here and there. At the end he was leaving me for a week at a time. I don't know where he went." Her gaze lifted to Cam's. Became earnest. "I swear I don't. But I was always real glad. Just glad to be left alone."

"How'd you live when he left you for that long?"

The woman froze. Then she lunged from her seat with a suddenness that startled Sophia. "You don't understand. You can't possibly understand." She took a quick turn around the room, checking her pockets, coming up empty. "I need a cigarette." She tossed a look at Cam. "You got a cigarette?"

"You weren't tied during that time, were you? He didn't have to tie you anymore."

Something in Sophia's quiet voice got through to the woman. She came to a halt, clenching and unclenching one fist against her leg. "It's like that underground fencing for dogs, you know? And they wear this special collar to go outside and it zaps them when they get too close to it. So after a while, the dogs stay far away from the fence, even when they aren't wearing the collar, because they just don't want to get zapped no more."

"Because by then he was in your head."

Klaussen whirled to face her. "Exactly. And no one understands. No one who hasn't been there. He'd say, 'You stay put, girl. Don't make me come after you.' And you know what? I did. He'd stick me in the bathroom before leaving for days and tell me to stay there. And I'd stay. Even though there was food in the kitchen . . . help maybe outside the apartment . . . When he was arrested in Nebraska, it took me ten days to get the courage to leave the apartment. And then I ran. Got as far as Des Moines before I went to a library and looked for some newspapers online. Seen he got himself arrested." A small hard smile crossed the woman's lips. "I hoped he'd get exactly what he had coming in prison. Never expected to find him waiting in my van one night five years later when I got off work."

"How did he find you?" It was the first time Cam had spoken, and the sound of his voice had Klaussen shrinking a little.

"I don't know." She crossed her arms and dropped heavily on the sofa. "Maybe through my old boss. I'd used him as a reference when I got a new job at a convenience store. But once he showed up again, it all started over. Except now he wasn't just mean. Prison had made Mase vicious."

Slowly, painstakingly, Sophia drew out the rest of the story. After a few days spent "getting reacquainted" at her apartment, Vance had driven her to the house in Alleman, where she'd spent most of the time chained in the basement. She denied that she'd been left alone for long periods of time, although she admitted there'd be weeks at a time when he'd be at the gym all afternoon, then leave again at night. The only time she'd been freed was to drive him somewhere. Occasionally to fetch food and bring it back to him.

This was offered in a hushed voice that told Sophia better than words that Vance had quickly regained dominance over the woman. By that time, no psychological fencing had been needed.

After half an hour, Sophia still had questions but sensed the other woman was close to her limit. She opened the purse on her lap and searched inside it. "Have you been getting any help with all this, Rhonda?" She lifted her gaze to see the puzzlement on the other woman's face. "Emotionally, I mean. Recovering from a long-term ordeal can take a while. It's easier with professional assistance." It took effort not to look in Cam's direction. Sometimes help came in the shape of therapy. And other times comfort. It was going to take far more than a strong pair of arms, however, to help Rhonda Klaussen work through the shame, guilt, and emotional imprisonment that had resulted from her trauma.

"There's a church down the street." Klaussen pushed her long hair over her shoulders and looked a little embarrassed. "Not that I'm a churchy type, but the pastor's wife has been by a couple times. Brought me lunch." A note of wonder entered her voice. "Even said she was trying to get a benefit together for me, pairing with a bigger church in Boone. She said I could use the money to get on my feet again." She shook her head. "I don't know why she'd bother doing something like that for a person like me, but even if she don't follow through with it, it's a pretty nice thought. Guess I forgot there were people like that left in the world. People who help just because."

Empathy softening her voice, Sophia said, "That is kind of her. And you're more deserving of kindness than you believe." Having found what she was searching for in her purse, she handed it to the woman. Saw her frown as she looked down at the business card. "The names on that card are therapists in the area who deal with overcoming trauma. All of them work on a sliding-fee scale, so you can pick one you feel comfortable with. You won't have to pay anything until you can afford it."

"A head doctor?" But the words were less caustic than when she'd uttered them earlier. "Yeah. Well . . . maybe." She stood and tucked the card in her tight jeans. Then looked at Cam. "Do I get to ask a question now?"

He nodded, a bit guardedly Sophia thought.

Klaussen frowned. "You showed me a sketch that day in the jail. Asked me if I'd seen that man before. If he'd ever been in Vance's house. I hadn't. But the pastor's wife I was telling you about—her name is Tami—she gave me a coupon for a free meal at a restaurant here in town. Had breakfast there this morning. And I saw that same sketch on TV on the news. They said police were looking for him." Her gaze was direct. "Why are you looking for him? Is he a friend of Mase's?"

Obviously choosing his words carefully, Cam answered, "We don't know. That's what we're trying to find out."

The woman swayed a little. "Would he . . ." She moistened her lips before going on. "Do you think Mase would send him after me?" She included Sophia in the question, a note of panic in her voice. "Can he find out where I am?"

Sophia let Cam field the questions, mentally damning herself for not thinking of it before. Courtney Van Wheton's hospital room had a uniformed policeman at the door at all times. Sophia herself was in DCI protective custody. But the woman who Vance had allegedly abused for years—and lived to tell about it—was a sitting duck. Vulnerable. The guilt fueled by the realization was brutal.

"As you said, you're visible in a small town." Cam's voice was matter-of-fact but oddly reassuring. "The sheriff's department is keeping a close eye on your place. Before this guy ever got near you or your house, he'd be picked up."

Klaussen seemed only partially mollified, but she gave a jerky nod before walking to the front door again.

"Do you have a cell phone?"

In answer to Sophia's query, she pointed to an item next to the lamp on the table. "Victims' services gave me one. It only calls nine-one-one, but that's all I need, right?"

"That and the deputies who will be keeping an eye on you." She squeezed the taller woman's hand comfortingly. "You have nothing to worry about. Except for planning the rest of your life now that you're free."

A measure of tension eased from the woman's face. "Yeah, I'm free. Still sort of hard to grasp. Sometimes I just sit on the couch for hours before I realize I can get up if I want. Go outside. Go for a walk." Her gaze went past them to the tiny front yard. Beyond. "Maybe I'll do that. Later."

"It sounds like a start."

Sophia allowed Cam to usher her from the house to the vehicle. But once he pulled away from the house, she refused to let him leave town before she found the church Rhonda had mentioned. And then elicited a promise from Tami to go check on the other woman once they left.

Once he was finally allowed to leave the town, he slanted her a glance. "I would have liked to have heard more about the times Vance left her alone for days at a time before he went to prison."

"Me, too," she admitted, leaning forward to set her purse on the floor by her feet. "But I pushed as far as I dared this first time. She's been through hell—twice. She deserves some kid-glove handling."

He was silent for a moment, and she watched the cornfields and bean fields flash by the window. The plants seemed a bit taller than they had a few days ago when she and Van Wheton had escaped from the barn Vance had imprisoned them in. But the crops were still far too short to offer shelter for someone on the run from a madman. And again she was reminded of Klaussen's exposure.

"So you believe her then."

It took a moment for Sophia to follow his meaning. "Believe Klaussen's story? Certainly the psychological damage she described rang true. If she's not a woman who's experienced terrible abuse, her talents are wasted outside of Hollywood. More importantly, I have no reason to disbelieve her."

She shifted as far as she comfortably could in her seat to face him. "While we were hunting for Vance, I suspected there could be a team of killers. We know our UNSUB is an accomplice. More, Klaussen bears the burns, and, from what she described, she could well have been Vance's first victim. The one he practiced his fantasies on. So, yes, I believe her. Don't you?"

"She's clearly been victimized." There was little traffic on the county road. He flew by a pickup parked in a field where a few kids were picking up rocks. "I'm just saying that she wouldn't be the first victim who helped in the enactment of a crime because of psychological or physical force from her captor."

He was edging into territory that provided ample room for argument. "In the cases you describe, the women were still victims." Sophia had lent expert testimony at trials similar to the ones he was suggesting. In her estimation, a jury should never underestimate the extent of long-term emotional trauma and its effect on behavior. "Were you honest with her back there? Is she being offered protection, or is the law enforcement attention simply to make sure she doesn't take off before Vance can be brought to trial?"

He slowed for a stop sign to let a lone SUV pass. Accelerated again. "Does it matter? The result is the same. Call it hedging our bets. Beckett—that's Boone County sheriff Beckett Maxwell—was instrumental in our investigation into Vance. I trust him to keep an eye on Klaussen and to keep her safe from harm. It's a—"

"Win-win." She was familiar with his customary phrase. Broodingly, Sophia watched the rolling fields of green crops until they started to give way to strip malls and convenience stores. Maybe he was right. Perhaps it didn't matter at this point whether he found Klaussen entirely credible as long as the woman was kept safe. Sophia's concern might be better spent on the women in the morgue who were past protection. The others who still may be waiting, cold and silenced in a watery grave.

Klaussen's experience was beyond horrifying, and the emotional damage it had inflicted would take years to recover from. But she, like Courtney Van Wheton and Sophia, had a huge advantage over Vance's other victims.

All of them had survived.

o o o

His house was filled with static. Sonny could no longer quiet the noise by ignoring it or journaling about it. The jumble of sound had leaked into his head. Filled his brain. Until the noise was so strong he couldn't hear himself think.

Dropping the marker, he backed away from his journal and snatched up pillows to clap over his ears. But that only trapped the noise; it didn't muffle it.

Mommy's voice was an insistent buzz threading through the rest of the racket. He had pills in the medicine cupboard that could silence her voice for long periods of time. But the pills made him sleepy. Left him feeling drugged up and dopey. He took only one when he had to keep his mind clear and razor sharp. Even so, they slowed his reflexes. And they didn't stop him from seeing her. Standing in the doorway or sitting at the table. Sometimes he saw all of her. Other times it was just her face floating by, the eyes bugged out and the blue lips open.

With or without the pills, her voice always came back, inserting itself into his skull with needlelike precision. The medicine was little defense against her. It was his own fault, he knew, because he hadn't buried her body when he'd killed her. But what had he known? He'd been just a kid.

Escaping out the kitchen door to the porch had the inner noise quieting somewhat. He blinked in the weakening sunlight. It was easier to think here. Easier to pluck out the single thread running through his brain and make sense of it.

You can't stay here. Mommy's voice rang clear as a bell against the muted interior din. *You're not safe. You can't stay here.*

Relief filled him. *Of course.* Sonny laughed out loud, uncaring that the sound made the girl walking her dog on the sidewalk hurry past the house. Mommy was right. His photo had been on TV.

And although he looked different now, he needed to get away. He needed time to plan.

He needed quiet. The kind of quiet he'd had in Lucy Benally's house. Where he'd been safe and the silence had soothed the racket in his head to a dull murmur.

Sonny braced himself and then went back inside. He had to gather the things he'd need because he wasn't ever coming back. Some clothes and toiletries. His laptop. The equipment he used to move through the night unseen. To get in and out of places unsuspected. He still had some time, he knew. His name hadn't been on TV, only a sketch. He had time to gather what he wanted and place it in the trunk of old lady Moxley's car.

The plan of action soothed the noise the way nothing else could. Soon. Soon he'd go for Lucy.

She'd help him find the quiet.

Chapter 11

Cam and Sophie arrived at the river in time to see a soil-stained lifeless body lying on a sheet beside the open grave. It was, he thought, as he helped Sophie down the rocky ridge, a macabre sight that was becoming all too familiar. Franks saw them coming and approached.

"You want the good news or the bad news?"

"There's good news for a change?" He looked toward the cluster of people surrounding the body. "Let's hear it."

"This victim was wearing some sort of bracelet with writing on it. Maybe when it gets cleaned up, it'll point us in a new direction."

That was a big if, but at this point in the investigation Cam would take it. "Give me the rest."

Tommy had taken off his suit coat and rolled up the sleeves of his shirt. His tie was nowhere in sight. Cam didn't blame him. The day had been warm, and standing outside most of the afternoon would have been punishing. "The bad news is the dive team is ready to call it a day soon. They're getting into deeper water, and it's churning up pretty good. Makes for poor visibility."

Cam squinted into the distance. He could the see the skiffs on the water. Make out a tall lanky form a couple hundred yards away on the shore. A dog in a boat barked excitedly.

"Okay. Maybe there's nothing there to be found."

"You ready for worse news?"

Cam arrowed a look at the older man. "Sort of buried the headline, huh?"

Franks's smile was grim. "Dig crew thinks there's another body directly below the one they just took out."

"Fuck." Frustration roiled inside him at a seething boil. He placed his balled-up fists on his hips. "When the hell does this end?" He barely felt Sophie's hand on his arm.

"It ends here. Vance is in jail. His accomplice is on the run. This is just closure for their victims."

He clenched his jaw. He saw something else in Tommy's expression. "Don't tell me. There's a 'worser'?"

The other agent mopped the perspiration from the back of his neck with his palm, then wiped it on his pant leg. From the looks of his pants, it was an action that had been repeated frequently throughout the day. "Just that the media you must have passed on your way in showed up forty-five minutes ago, and it's just a matter of time . . ."

Cam got the message. Pulling out his cell, he put in a call to the Dallas County sheriff. After a terse conversation, they agreed the sheriff's office and DNR would supply additional manpower to keep gawkers away. Some of the officers would be in boats. Then he moved several feet away to call Gonzalez, steeling himself for her reaction. It wasn't long coming.

"This is a PR nightmare," she said heatedly. "We need to make this thing go away and fast. How close are you to an arrest?"

"Tips are still coming in on the door-to-door search." Cam shaded his eyes, looked out over the water. Someone in a boat was waving an arm. The handler on shore, Roberts, started jogging Cam's way, a radio lifted to his lips and dog at his side. "Something's breaking. I'll call you back. You should know that we've got media camped out here. Do you want a statement made?"

"Absolutely not." The woman's tone was emphatic. "Miller wants every announcement cleared through his office."

"Fine with me. I'll get back to you." Cam rounded the ridge that enclosed the cave and headed to meet Roberts. Sophie and Franks were at his side.

"Diver thinks he's seen something." George Roberts turned to point at one of the boats. "Sonar showed what he thought was a fallen tree, but once he touched it . . . might be some sort of bag."

o o o

Cam knelt alongside a criminalist in front of the long black bag resting on the grassy shore. George Roberts dug a handkerchief from his pocket and handed it to Sophia. Gratefully she took it and held it ready. The evidence team, which had been on-site at the dig, had finished photographing, measuring, and swabbing. The bag had been heavy and unwieldy. Cam and Franks had joined the search and rescue team to help lift the bag into the boat. It had taken four of them to unload it once they got to shore.

She still held out hope that the bag held . . . something else. Car parts. Illicit waste. Cam and the evidence tech were clad in Tyvek suits and headgear in case of just that eventuality.

But in her heart she knew what they'd find inside.

As Cam drew back the zipper with two glove-clad fingers, she pressed the handkerchief over her nose, gaze glued to the action. Despite half expecting it, the sight of a gleaming white skull was a shock to the system. The handkerchief didn't quite mask the horrendous odor of formaldehyde and decomposition that escaped as the bag was unzipped.

Sophie moved back a step, tried to breathe shallowly. The skeleton was not fully complete. And some of the bones were covered with a white waxy substance. Adipocere, she realized. Caused by the breakdown of soft tissue in the body. She wondered if the foundation bricks that had been put in the bag had jarred some of the bones loose over time, or whether the river's movement had accomplished that act on its own.

Cam rose and moved away as a criminalist leaned forward with a large set of tweezers and a magnifying glass. He took off his hood and unzipped the suit far enough to pull out his phone and started calling numbers. Sophia watched the criminalist work as Cam alerted the ME's office and the crime lab that a new rotation of personnel would be needed.

Something about the skull with its empty eye sockets seemed forlorn. Even sadder than the gut-wrenching site of the bodies extracted from the mass grave. Sophia decided it was because the watery burial was even more cavalier than the ground burial. Callous. Casual. Quickly disposed of, the victim simply ceased to exist for the offender.

Shaken, she moved away, gazed out over the river where other law enforcement personnel had collected in boats to keep onlookers away. Staring at the slow lazy current of the water, she wondered what other macabre secrets the Raccoon River had hidden in its depths.

o o o

"I can drop you at home." A muscle jumped in Cam's jaw. His voice was terse. "Micki Loring can meet us there. Gonzalez and Miller want some input before they hold a news conference about the river site." As much as he wasn't looking forward to the upcoming conversation, he didn't envy the two their PR task.

"I'll hang around if that's all right. I want to polish the offender profile and type up my observations from the Klaussen interview. And, if the opportunity arises, eat."

It occurred to him that neither of them had eaten since breakfast that morning. He turned into the next drive-through, ignoring Sophie's wrinkled-up nose, and ordered for both of them.

"Grease," she said unenthusiastically when he handed her a bag.

"Right off the food pyramid," Cam said solemnly. After peeling the wrapper off his burger, he drove and ate at the same time. "I'd give a lot to know how long that body has been in the water."

"We can't even be sure it's female yet." But her protest was half-hearted. They both knew the victim was associated with the crime they were investigating. Given the proximity to the grave, there was little doubt that a connection existed.

"Tony Bower, the criminalist, verified the sex." The man had done a couple of simple measurements of the pelvis and determined that much. But any further information would come from the ME's office. And Gavin Connerly, the consulting forensic anthropologist.

"It's the first of the bodies at the site to have completely skeletonized. It smelled as though it had been embalmed, though. I wonder if the offender—"

Sophie broke off as Cam's cell rang. With an apologetic look, he answered it.

Beachum's voice filled the line. "So we're checking out a call that came in on the tip line. Guy named Lou Vetter claims the sketch looks just like his next-door neighbor. Unfortunately he can't be sure what the neighbor's name is. Could be Scott. Sawyer. Maybe Steve." The agent mimicked the man's voice. "Definitely begins with an *S*. And the last name starts with a *B*, he thinks. Becker, Baxter, Banner. We've tried the neighbor's door. No luck. Tried the neighbor to the other side, who Vetter claims is an old lady who never goes anywhere. No answer there, either. I'd file this in the big-waste-of-time folder, but thought I should double-check on the name. I checked the list of former funeral home employees. Have a couple possibilities there. A Sean Becker and a Sonny Baxter. Vetter swears that's the name."

"Which one?"

"Either. Both. I think the guy fried a few too many brain cells somewhere along the line. The utility lead is out. According to Vetter, all the properties in the area are rentals and utilities are included. He knows this because he looked at the house next door before deciding on the castle he currently resides in."

"Landlord?"

"Got a name and number, but he's not answering his phone."

It was exactly the sort of circular information that wasn't actually a lead that gave tip lines a bad name. Cam timed the next light and cruised through right before it turned yellow. "I'm guessing there's some reason for this call. What's the address?"

The other agent read it off, adding unnecessarily, "That's River Bend neighborhood. Less than two miles from the Pinter's our guy was sighted at."

Interest flickered. Cam shot Sophie a look. From her expression she was following the conversation. "That better not be the same guy I chased down last night."

"Entirely possible. The justice system these days is a sad state of affairs."

Sophie pulled out her cell phone and checked a note stashed in her purse for a number. She quickly dialed it. He mouthed, "Fedorowicz?" She nodded. Spoke quietly into the phone.

"Give us a minute to check something. While we wait I can give you an update." Cam gave him a rapid rundown of the day's events.

"Holy shit. When we switch assignments tomorrow, that's the job I want. Pulling bodies out of graves, out of the river . . . Wait a minute. How do you smell?"

"You don't want to know," Cam responded wryly. Sophie ended her call, so he added, "Hang on," and looked at her expectantly.

"After Mr. Fedorowicz went through the files, he made a list for us. There's a Sonny Baxter on it."

A hard fist of satisfaction balled in Cam's chest. "Maybe. Maybe this is it."

"There's more. The man said he'd always had a soft spot for the boy because he'd been horribly abused. Even took him shooting several times so he'd know how to defend himself. And"—she paused a beat—"records his wife kept show he had a job cleaning up in Foster's Funeral Services."

"Worth checking out." His gaze met hers.

"Definitely worth checking out."

He spoke to Beachum again. "We're on our way. Keep trying the landlord. Talk to other neighbors on the street. I want verification of the occupant before I request a warrant. Preferably from someone in possession of all his brain cells."

"You got it."

At the first opportunity, Cam turned and headed toward the address Beachum had read off. There had been far too many twists in this case, but they were due for a break. He was hoping this was it. He reached for his phone again.

"Who are you calling now?"

His mouth quirked. "Gonzalez. She and Miller are going to have to work on that press conference without me."

o o o

Sonny peered interestedly between the slats of the blinds at Moxley's front window. The old bat always had them closed. None of the houses on the street had air-conditioning. The house felt closed up and stuffy. But the noise wasn't as bad here. The buzzing had subsided a little. Enough to hear Mommy's voice, as clear and sharp as if she were standing next to him. *You need to leave. You're not safe here.*

"I'm all right in here, Mommy," he murmured absently. "Moxley's dead. Just like you."

The two men in suits who had been on his porch, on *this* porch, ringing doorbells got out of their car again and started across the street. "Cops, Mommy." Sonny could tell. The way they dressed, the car they drove. He recognized it all. Knew there would be guns beneath the suit coats they wore in eighty-five-degree temperatures. He watched as they split up and started knocking at houses across the street. When a woman answered at one of the doors, Sonny felt a niggle of worry. Maybe he'd waited too long before leaving.

He brought the gun in his hand up to the window and pointed it at the man standing on the porch directly across the street from here. Nothing was going to keep him from Lucy.

Nothing.

o o o

"You sure about that, ma'am?"

"Positive. I don't know his name. Sorry." The young woman sent an apologetic look at Agent Beachum. "I really never talked to him. This isn't exactly that kind of neighborhood. But I saw him every once in a while." The drooling toddler she held yanked a strand of her dark hair, and she freed it from his grubby hands without missing a beat. "He drives this sort of grayish-blue sedan—"

Her mouth dropped when Cam pulled out his phone and brought up a picture of the car the offender had been seen getting into at Pinter's. "That's it! How did you . . ." Amazement was chased away by worry. "Why are you looking for him? Is he dangerous?" She gave a nervous laugh, but she hugged the toddler closer.

"You're not in any danger," Cam assured her. If she'd caught the UNSUB's eye before now, she probably wouldn't be standing here. "You never saw this sketch on TV before now?"

She looked at him blankly. "I only watch cable."

Cable. There was almost no furniture in the rooms he could glimpse inside, so she obviously had different priorities. He shook his head a little. "Okay. I want you to lock your doors and stay inside for the rest of the evening. All right?"

She looked from one agent to another. Paused when she got to Sophie's face. What she saw there seemed to convince her. The woman started swinging the door shut. "I will. Promise."

The four of them turned and descended her cracked concrete steps. "More believable than Vetter, right?" Beachum drawled.

"Much more believable than Vetter," Cam agreed. He strode back to his car at a fast pace. Unlocked it. Reached for his laptop in the backseat.

"So now we get our search warrant?"

"Now we get our search warrant."

o o o

Thirty minutes later Cam and Beachum climbed the side porch of the offender's house, checking the exits. Although the front door was locked, the side door was not. It would be their point of entry.

The properties on this side of the street were near replicas of one another. All had a smear of grass bordering the pocked sidewalk, with handkerchief-size backyards facing an alley. The detached garages were accessed from the alley. The one belonging to the offender boasted a new electric overhead door. The windows on both sides of the structure had been boarded over.

Cam had summoned a DMPD unit to assist with the search and had the squad car blocking the exit of the garage. If the UNSUB was hiding inside the structure, he'd be trapped.

With his attention on the house, Cam reached out to pull the screen open silently. He waited for the other agent to crowd inside it before turning the knob of the door.

"DCI!" They burst inside, sweeping the area around the door. Cleared the room. Approached the next, one on either side of the wide doorway. "Anyone inside, out here now, now! Hands in the air."

There wasn't a sound. It was quiet. Much too quiet. Cam caught the other agent's eye. Jerked his head toward the closed coat closet just inside the front door. Together they walked toward it. Paused.

Beachum yanked the door open. Cam covered the area. It was empty. Completely empty. No clothes hung inside it. No shoes were on the floor. He took the time to unlock the front entry for Samuels before heading toward the hallway. But instinct told him the effort was wasted. The emptiness almost echoed.

The tiny bathroom and two bedrooms were cleared. He sent Beachum to search the garage with the officers waiting outside it. Walking into the kitchen, Cam looked at the narrow door next to the stove. It had a latch and fresh padlock on it. He waved the other agent away and leveled his weapon. The bullet shattered the padlock and splintered the wood behind it. "Get my back."

He turned on the switch just inside the door and shouted again, "DCI! Hands in the air. Walk toward the stairway slowly."

Only silence greeted him. He'd expected no less. The wall at his back, he took the stairs sideways, weapon leveled.

The area was all one space, with a furnace in the center and a water heater tucked into the corner. It was empty save for plastic footlockers stacked neatly in one corner. That was another thing that struck Cam about the entire house. Neat. Tidy. With one exception.

He holstered his weapon. "He's not here. Let's get a look at the garage." He and Samuels headed back up the stairs.

When they reentered the kitchen, the other agent said, "You want me to have Dr. Channing come in and look at . . . this?" He gestured at the next room.

"I think she'll find it very interesting." With a sense of déjà vu, Cam pulled out his phone and called the lab.

They were going to need another crime scene team.

○ ○ ○

Sophia moved slowly through the UNSUB's living room, taking in every detail. She'd suspected the offender might have a mental illness. This place all but shouted it.

The walls were covered with writings in black marker. Sometimes the words were in print, others in big loopy cursive letters. Most was legible. In some places, though, the words were scrawled with large angry letters that all but dripped venom. And the messages varied very little.

Fuck you mommy your dead your dead now you see can you see?

Fascinated, Sophia brought out her phone. Snapped a picture. Then several more.

The noise its loud too loud very loud too much noise I need quiet more quiet.

See what I do for you what you make me do its never enough theres always more and more and more.

"Jesus." She started at the sound of Cam's voice. So engrossed in the scrawls, she'd hardly been aware of him coming up beside her. "It's like being trapped in this guy's mind. Freaky."

"More like watching it unravel," she murmured, her gaze shifting to another wall. The writings stretched almost to the ceiling behind the couch. Lower in other spots, but none below waist high. It was so textbook that she initially questioned whether the scene had been staged to throw them off track.

But in some places the marker was fresh and black against the pale wall. In others it grew fainter, as if it was running out of ink. There were spots that looked as if someone had tried painting over the words before writing over them. If this had been staged, the offender had taken a long time to do it.

You should have stayed dead why arent you dead you should never came back Ill kill you again and again and bury you this time deep very deep.

Silently she walked by Cam to turn toward the short hallway.

"Where you going?"

"To check the medicine cabinet."

The bathroom was barely large enough to turn around in. It was spotless. Even the door to the shower that, she knew from experience, was almost impossible to keep clear of water spots. After taking a tissue from her purse, she used it to open the metal-framed cabinet above the sink. Stared at the crammed shelves. If the offender had fled, he hadn't taken his medication with him.

One by one Sophia used the tissue to carefully turn the pill bottles so she could read the prescriptions. Haldol. Trilafon. Mellaril. Clozaril. The number of labels was dizzying. She sensed Cam's presence before he spoke.

"What's the name on the bottles?"

"Sonny Baxter." She looked at him. "The guy next door got the initials right at least."

He snorted. "Probably as right as he's been in a couple decades. Is Baxter a hypochondriac or really sick?"

"These meds are all prescribed for heavy-duty psychosis. Schizophrenia, possibly, although the diagnosis may be unspecified. There are half-full bottles here dated eight years ago. None are more recent than three years ago." She brought one container up for Cam to read. She wasn't familiar with the doctor on the label, but the prescription had been filled at the nearby Pinter's.

Cam was matter-of-fact. "Three years is a long time. What with staff turnover and the number of people they see in a day . . . not that surprising they didn't recognize him as a past customer. So." He peered closer to read some of the markings. "Is this guy crazy?"

She grimaced. "You know I hate that word." His grin told her that was why he had used it. "Certainly these medications indicate he has a significant mental illness."

"Which you guessed early on," he interjected.

"Several of these drugs are used to treat hallucinations and delusions. It's common for patients to feel there's no need for them to take medication, or to quit when they're feeling better. Or because of the side effects. They can be rather intense." She felt a flare of impatience. The medications indicated a vast trove of information on the offender that would offer a great deal of insight into his needs and motivations. "We have to get a warrant for his medical records. Now."

"We'll get them."

"The zinc tablets might be significant, as well," she said slowly. She felt Cam's gaze drilling into her but couldn't look away from the row of boxes on the top shelf. Four of them. All nearly empty.

"How so?"

"FDA issued a warning about them last year. Long-term use of them as cold remedies has been linked to permanent loss of smell."

Cam blew out a breath, his hands on his hips. "I'll be damned. You ever get tired of being right?"

She shook her head. Not in answer to his question, but in silent wonder. The UNSUB's medicine cabinet alone was a wealth of information about the offender. The wall of his living room was like a peek into the frenzied state of his mind.

"Prescott! You're going to want to see this!"

Cam responded immediately. Sophia was right behind him. The basement door was standing open, and John was calling from a cramped cellar that had a strong odor of mildew. They descended the stairs to join the two agents, and Sophia was struck by how clean the area was. As tidy as the upstairs. There were no cobwebs, no dust on the floor. A broom was propped in one corner, as if waiting to be utilized again.

John Samuels was kneeling in front of the plastic footlockers. Beachum stood next to him with a camera.

"Got the photos before we opened them," Beachum assured Cam. "Take a look."

Sophia leaned closer to peer into each container. All held neatly folded women's clothes. Shoes in one. Tops and bottoms in another. Undergarments in the third. Her stomach tightened.

"At first I thought maybe the guy was a trannie. But they're all different sizes."

"How many sets?" Cam's voice seemed to come from a distance.

The agent flipped through the middle container with a gloved hand. "Fourteen bottoms."

The floor lurched a bit beneath her feet. Sophia grasped Cam's arm to right herself. *Fourteen.* It didn't match the number on the back of the corpse Baxter had been assaulting. But it represented a sickening loss of life. How many had died at the hands of Vance and how many to Baxter?

She had to look away. Had to, to keep the nausea circling in her stomach from worsening. It wasn't all that unusual for serial killers to take trophies. An article of clothing or an item of jewelry. A finger from the victim. She'd consulted on a case last fall where the killer had carefully cut off all his victims' hair and braided it into an intricate scarf, which he'd then dyed and worn out in public.

There was absolutely no reason for the sight of those clothes to hit so hard. Not when she'd seen far worse.

"You okay?" Cam asked her in an undertone.

"These aren't souvenirs." She hugged herself, suddenly chilled. "He was just tidying up."

Arrested, Cam stared at her. "How do you know that? Why didn't he get rid of them?"

"In case they come back."

"What . . . ?"

But Sophia was already walking away. Back up the creaking narrow stairs. Through the kitchen. To stop in the front room. The scrawling on the walls pressed in on her, the chaotic thoughts they represented a silent psychotic episode.

I taught her to be quiet so quiet so sweet and quiet my darling my sweet one good-bye my darling.

She spied a black marker on the floor along the baseboard. Crossing to it, Sophia crouched down in front of it. Then lifted her gaze.

The words jumped off the wall.

Get out of my head out of my head out of my head get out get out get out get out.

"There's takeout in the garbage with a receipt stamped yester-day." She heard Cam in the kitchen. "He hasn't been gone long."

Then he walked into the room and to Sophia's side. "Where would he go?" He asked quietly. His face was damp with perspiration. The heavy armored vest he wore had to be like an oven. "He's a creature of routine, you said. Uncomfortable outside his familiar surroundings."

She forced herself to focus. "Somewhere else he knows well. Where he feels safe. Now that we have a name, how difficult would it be to get his Department of Human Services file unsealed? A list of his foster homes might be helpful."

Cam nodded. "That's a good thought. You think he might go back to one of them?"

"Maybe." Her gaze returned to the wall in front of her again. "One of them might have meant something to him."

He stood there for a moment, reading more of the graffiti. "This time you'll die you'll die you wont come back not this time not again dead is dead your dead stay dead Mommy stay dead stay dead." He glanced at Sophia. "You think he's fantasizing about killing his mother? Is that what this is all about?"

A wave of exhaustion hit her then. "I think he *has* killed her. At least fourteen times. With every victim he kills her over and over again."

o o o

"You hiding dead fish in here?" Seth Dietz walked in outfitted in Tyvek and a wiseass attitude. "Or is that Prescott I smell, fresh from his stint at the river?"

"Bite me," Cam invited mildly. He was pulling out kitchen drawers and opening cupboards, while the other two agents were pawing through the rest of the trash they'd dumped on a towel they'd found in the bathroom. "I haven't had the luxury of eight hours to enjoy a full night's sleep and a bubble bath."

Dietz set his hard-cased wheeled suitcase on the floor and knelt to open it. "Can't beat Mr. Bubble. Maybe you ought to pick some up. Although the smell isn't as bad in here. But in the driveway—"

Cam turned, his interest sharpening. "The driveway?"

"Yeah, between the houses. But maybe it's coming from the house next door . . ."

The agents were out the kitchen door before he finished his statement.

"You knock at that house?" Cam asked.

Alex Beachum nodded. "Hit all the homes on the street, both sides. Went to the front door. No answer."

Cam pulled out his phone. Texted Samuels to join them. Then stared at the door on the next house again. It was almost directly across from Baxter's and stood partially open. Cam didn't get more than four feet toward it before the smell hit him.

When the third agent arrived, they crossed to the house. Cam and Beachum went to the door and Samuels stood to the side, his weapon leveled. Reaching out to pound on the door, Cam shouted, "DCI. We need to talk to the occupant." He stopped, listened. There was no sound from the interior of the house.

The odor was stronger this close to the structure. Alex Beachum took an exaggerated sniff. "Know what that smells like?"

"Like probable cause." Cam tried the knob of the screen door. Found it open.

He and Alex drew their weapons. They crept into the kitchen, fanned out. Cam was first into the small living room. An easy chair with a heavily creased cushion sat empty. Next to it was a cluttered TV stand with several pill bottles lying on their sides. A few had dropped to the floor.

The two other agents checked the tiny coat closet and found it stuffed with clothes. Cam's gaze was fixed on the drawn slatted blinds on the front window. One slat was wedged downward, leaving an opening. As if someone had been peering out at the street. Maybe an inquisitive old woman.

Or perhaps someone else was watching the agents' progress as they canvassed the area.

Cam gestured to the others, and they walked down a hallway that was eerily similar to Baxter's. Like the house next door, there were two bedrooms and a bath. Each of them took one of the rooms to clear.

They, too, were empty. But at least one of them hadn't been for long.

"Someone went out the window." The lone window in the second bedroom had been opened, and the screen was lying on the ground below. "I'll check the garage out back," he said over his shoulder as he climbed through the window. "Clear the cellar."

"On it."

Cam jumped lightly to the ground and ran toward the leaning garage on the alley. Rounding the corner, he saw the old wooden door raised and the stall empty. He jogged to the black-and-white blocking the entrance of Baxter's garage. "Has anyone left from the garage next door since you've been here?"

"About ten minutes ago." A fresh-faced patrolmen who looked all of sixteen pointed north. "Before your agent came back here. Old woman with a walker got in the car and headed that north."

Lead sank in his gut. "An old woman? You sure?"

"Pretty sure. Couldn't really see her face, but she was wearing a dress and scarf on her head. Had on those heavy support hose like my grandma wears, with orthopedic shoes. Carrying a big handbag."

Cam radioed Beachum. "Any chance the owner of the house took her car out a few minutes ago?"

"Not likely," came the agent's voice. "Found her on the cellar steps a minute ago. She's in no shape to go for a drive. She's been strangled."

Chapter 12

You can't possibly know all that yet." Lucy checked the clock on her office wall. "You haven't had enough time to conduct a thorough investigation."

"What part of preliminary findings didn't you understand?" Gavin Connerly covered a yawn as he ambled through her office doorway and leaned his narrow hips against her desk. He made up for the minor annoyance by offering his Mountain Dew, which Lucy accepted guiltily. Caffeine was a vice of hers. She'd given it up because it made her jittery. But sometimes, she thought as she took a deep drink, it helped calm nerves, too. And she'd had plenty to get jittery over the last few days. Not the least of which was the reappearance of the man standing next to her.

She screwed the lid back on the bottle and handed it back to him. "I've never been big on preliminary. We can't afford to get any of the details wrong. This case is too important for any snap judg—" The rest of her warning was lost when his lips covered hers. The man was sneaky that way. His mouth moved on hers for a moment. Tempting and warmly seductive.

He straightened again. Folded his arms over his chest. "Believe it or not, at Berkeley I'm something of a big deal." His wry tone stripped the words of ego. "I actually get called on fairly regularly to consult on high-profile investigations nationally. My goal before I leave is to get you to admit that I might—just might, mind you—know what I'm talking about."

"I wasn't second-guessing—"

He threw his head back and laughed with real amusement. "That's exactly what you were doing, and the fact that you don't even realize it is actually sort of adorable."

Her eyes narrowed. *Adorable* had never been a word easily applied to her. "Fine. Tell me again." She pushed away from her laptop to give him her undivided attention.

It didn't seem to faze him. He paused to take a drink from the soda before answering. "It was pretty easy to reassemble the skeleton. Most of it was intact. I'm guessing the beating it took while in the river jarred some of the bones loose. That river flooded five years ago. Regardless of when the body was dumped, the bag could have moved quite a way from its original dump site, and come into contact with logs and all sort of debris."

He paused to reach over and push a strand of hair away from her face. The intimacy of the act had her jerking away, an involuntary reaction.

His eyes glinting, he continued. "Preliminary examination indicates that the skeleton found today is female. The measurements of the pelvis and examination of the skull made that an easy call. Almost certainly Caucasian. She was likely between the ages of twenty-eight and thirty-five at death, because her collarbone is completely fused, but the sagittal suture on the cranium isn't. I did the measurements and X-rays necessary to submit the dental findings to an odontologist. Is there one the DCI uses?"

Lucy nodded. "Dr. Harvey Lind at the U of I College of Dentistry."

"He'd be able to verify my estimate of age when I send him the information I put together. And the submission of the data for matching dental records might make this victim a relatively simple ID."

"If she was from in-state," murmured Lucy. Some of the six victims that had been found in fresh graves atop burial vaults had been kidnapped from outside Iowa.

He reached into his back jeans pocket and withdrew a badly mangled bag of M&M's. "I examined the auricular surface of the ilium, the sternal ends of the right ribs three through five and pubic symphysis, and did a comparison against a database of standard markers."

Ripping open the bag, he poured some into his palm as he spoke. "Hyoid bone was fractured, indicating a possibility the victim had been strangled. Can't rule out the possibility that the damage occurred from the impact of the bag coming in contact with something in the river. But the spiral fracture of the ulna was definitely perimortem."

Lucy eyed him as he popped the candy into his mouth. Chewed. She had an ongoing feud with the office vending machine. Working late as often as she did, she didn't always get regular meals. The machine inhaled her money but steadfastly refused to return the items she selected. It had a particularly suspicious habit of providing stale peanuts whenever she desperately craved chocolate.

It went to figure that Connerly could coax the recalcitrant machine to part with the sweets when she couldn't. He seemed to have the touch, with women and machines alike. Discomfited by the thought, she belatedly tuned in to his words again.

"Perimortem? You found signs of healing before death?"

He nodded. Swallowed. "Barely. You can double-check, but I'd estimate that the injury occurred at least two weeks before her death. Oh, and these remains aren't the source of the finger bone found in the cave. Once I reassembled it, the skeleton was complete." He took a last helping of candy before offering the rest of the bag to her. Lucy snatched it up with a desperation she was too hungry to be embarrassed by.

"Not bad for a few hours' work," she allowed. Sharing his chocolate had her feeling equally generous.

"I'd like to get that DCI agent in here—the redhead—to help do a facial reconstruction. I gotta get permission from the ME, though. She can be real testy about things like that."

Lucy smirked. "Really? I hear the ME is a saint. Maybe if you ask real nice, she'll okay it."

For a man who rarely walked above a stroll, he could move remarkably fast. He took her hand and tugged her from her seat to his arms with dizzying speed. "I am capable of much more than nice," he assured her with a smile, his arms wrapping around her waist.

Lucy could blame it on the chocolate. Or her lack of sleep. But against her better judgment, she smiled back. "I remember exactly what you're capable of." He had the ability to strip her of a life's worth of defenses armed with nothing but a lazy smile and a sharp sense of humor. He was capable of tempting her, a woman not known for indulgences, to forget duty long enough to be wicked with him.

And the buffer of the miles between their occupations made indulging in Gavin Connerly safe enough to soothe even Lucy's hypercautious nature. She went up on tiptoe to catch his bottom lip between her teeth. Nipped lightly. "Exactly how many miles is it to your hotel?" And was gratified when she felt his body shudder.

He drew back a little to survey her. "I've never been inside your place. Maybe we can pick up some takeout and head to Bondurant. It'd give us time to talk."

Something in his tone had her beating an emotional retreat. Having sex with Gavin was far enough out of character. The thought of allowing him into her home, into her life, had mental walls springing up.

"Tell you what, Connerly." Although her voice was conversational, her hands were anything but. "We can talk. Or we can . . ." She rose up to whisper a suggestion in his ear, and his gaze went a little unfocused.

"We'll talk later." He shepherded her out of the office, barely allowing her time to grab her purse and lock up. "But we *are* going to talk, Luce."

"If you still have the strength to talk later," she murmured sultrily, "then I'm horribly out of practice."

o o o

"We got the license number, color, make, and model of Moxley's car from DMV. There's a BOLO out on it now. We've also alerted surrounding counties. Someone will see him."

They were walking up the drive at Cam's house. Sophia was nearly staggering with exhaustion, but Cam's voice was alert as he discussed strategy with the SAC. Stars studded the sky, but the moon was slivered, as if its fullness had been carved away with one brutal slice. She felt the same. As if each new event of the day had pared away another layer of skin until her nerves lay raw, exposed, and vulnerable.

"Well, the garage gave us a lot of information. That's where he embalmed them. The supplies and equipment for it are stored there. He also had a walk-in freezer. We'll need lab results, but I think he might have kept victims in it while waiting to dispose of them. Like Dr. Channing guessed, he also had a small boat and trailer there." He listened for a moment as he fit his key into the dead bolt and unlocked the door to allow them inside before resetting the security system and securing the door again. "We've got feelers out with all the banks in the area, but we found no trace of bills or bank books. Pinter's clerk said he was a cash customer. Dr. Channing thinks he would have been far more likely to shun banks."

He listened for a moment, then slanted Sophia a glance. "Yeah. She said organized offenders can descend into disorganization. She says he's unraveling as a result of an untreated psychosis, triggered by an emotional event. You should have seen the prescriptions. Hard to say where Baxter came into contact with Vance. He doesn't have a record."

It was impossible to say which beckoned more insistently—a bath or sleep. Sophia decided she'd get rid of the wig and contacts first and go from there.

Cam draped his suit coat over the back of the couch, then remembered to take the tie he'd wadded up out of his pocket. "Yeah, the warrant came through okay on Baxter's juvie DHS records, but accessing them is slow. The foster father's files showed he was placed by Polk County, and we've got a query out. Hopefully we'll have a response midmorning." He started walking toward his office, still talking. "Yeah, search on the river begins again tomorrow morning, too. Briefing's at eight so . . ."

Instead of trailing after him Sophia headed for her bedroom to grab her robe. From the sound of things, she had less than seven hours to clean up and get some sleep. Right now both seemed equally pressing.

But for some reason after taking her customary brief shower and combing her hair, the thought of crawling into bed had become suddenly unappealing. Details of the day crowded in, and her thoughts couldn't turn in any direction without bumping into one of them. They weren't exactly musings guaranteed to summon slumber.

She gathered up her things and took them back to her bedroom. The light was still on in Cam's office, but she could no longer hear the sound of his voice. The phone call with Gonzalez must have finally ended. She busied herself putting her things away and then turned, her gaze falling on the neatly made bed.

Last night's scene flickered across her mind. Cam had offered comfort after her PTSD flashback. In his arms she'd felt safe enough to finally shut her eyes.

Safe. The word had her mentally squirming. She had a doctorate in psychology. Trauma-induced reactions were, clinically at least, familiar territory. But she was self-aware enough to recognize that safety and caution had guided her life choices for most of her years. The only time she'd ever veered from the familiar—the safe—was when she'd chosen to go into forensics rather than solely clinical psychology. And even then she'd hedged her bets for far too long, trying to balance the two sides of her occupation with a career in academia and a forensic consulting firm.

Teaching had, she could admit now, completely and utterly bored her. She walked to the dresser and laid her comb down on the surface. She'd done it to please her parents and husband, all academics. But the routine of following a predetermined course outline, grading papers, and the petty university politics had never truly appealed. She wondered now how long she would have continued fooling herself that her life completely satisfied if she hadn't walked into her husband's department office to find him enthusiastically banging a young coed on his desk.

It had, she thought wryly, been a life-altering wake-up call. And so had her brief fling with Cam Prescott last month, in a totally different sort of way.

In just twelve short days, she'd felt more alive with the man than she had throughout her entire marriage. Even before. The relationship had been totally out of character for her. The selection of the man even more so. Cam wasn't safe. He wasn't risk-free. And he definitely wasn't boring.

She turned and walked slowly to the windows, drawing the curtains over the blinds. It wasn't especially comfortable to admit that she'd pulled away from him because her feelings for the man were too raw, too unfamiliar. She hadn't been equipped for a no-strings relationship. She, a woman who valued guarantees in life, had realized there was no guarantee of a future with Cam Prescott. No assurance that he would ever reciprocate anything close to the welter of emotion he incited in her.

Mason Vance had showed her the folly of living her life afraid to take risks. Thoughts of the man made her skin prickle. If things had turned out differently, she'd have died at Vance's hands, never having taken a chance on anything other than the somewhat tepid relationship she'd had with her ex-husband. And that made her rather ashamed of herself.

There was lingering emotional damage from her time spent in captivity. Sophia was the first to admit it. But it didn't impact her ability to do her job on this investigation. And it didn't factor into her realization that she'd almost let something infinitely precious slip through her fingers, because she'd been so busy protecting her heart.

The thought shook her. After she'd escaped from Mason Vance, Cam had told her over and over how brave she'd been. But he'd never realized that it had been sheer cowardice that had sent her running from *him*.

Sophia was done running.

She walked through the bedroom door on feet that faltered a little when she found his office dark. Taking a deep breath, she continued to his bedroom and peeked inside. Empty.

Just then she heard the shower in the adjoining bath turn on. The sound nearly sent her fleeing. She actually turned toward the bedroom door.

And then had a mental flash of how she'd left him the first time, fueled by the same cowardly fear. Her purpose solidified. She walked to the bath, pulled the door open. She could see Cam's form through the glass shower stall, and a tendril of heat unfurled, curling through her system. She saw the exact moment he noticed her. He froze in the act of sluicing the water from his face. Stared for a moment, then opened the door of the stall.

"You okay, Soph?" He gave her a quick once-over as if to answer his own question. "I'll be done here in a minute."

"Yes." Untying the robe, she gave a slight shrug and let it slip down her arms to pool on the floor. "I really am okay." She walked to the shower stall and stepped inside, brushing by him to do so.

Her hands immediately went to his chest. Her fingers flexed. His came up to cover them. Swallowing hard, he rasped, "Listen, God knows this isn't easy for me to say. But this probably isn't a good idea right now for you. I don't think—"

The concern mingled with desire on his face told her everything she needed to know. "It's all right." She closed the distance between them and went up on tiptoe to nip lightly at the corner of his mouth. "I've done enough thinking for both of us." Sliding her arms around his neck, she pressed her mouth against his and sank into pleasure.

The kiss in the car at Screwball's had been too unexpected and much too brief. It had been over before her defenses were sufficiently lowered to enjoy it. But Sophia was done erecting defenses around this man. The thought was frightening. Exhilarating. Liberating.

His arms came around her then and pulled her closer. His lips opened, and his tongue went in search of hers. He knew how to kiss a woman—hot, deep, and devastating. With a single-minded intensity that had the rest of the world fading. Inner fires flaring. She pushed aside a persistent niggling doubt and dove into the flames.

His flavor was dark temptation, lethal to her senses. Her hands played over the muscles of his shoulders, her fingers stroking in remembered pleasure. She'd always loved the contrasts between them when they'd lain naked and entwined, his sinewy strength against her softness. And she'd enjoyed stripping him of that strength, torching his control until desperation turned his breathing ragged, his hands hard and frantic.

The warm water cocooned them in its spray, and the moment spun out, wrapping them in a dark intimate heat.

When he lifted his mouth, it took an instant for Sophia to remember to breathe. Her bones were lax, hot molten wax, and she leaned heavily against him. Nor did her strength return when she opened her eyes and saw him watching her, his gaze narrowed. His eyes were antique gold when washed with desire, and that's what she saw in them now. But it was what she noted in his face that had her heart turning over.

There was passion there, yes, but also the signs of exhaustion he had successfully kept at bay for almost eighteen hours. He was a protector to the core, a cop, that ex–Army Ranger toughness as much a part of him as his eye color. Perhaps that was why his unexpected tenderness could be so devastating.

It was that gentleness as much as his passion that had been responsible for tripping up her normally safe decisions. Caused her to want too much. Feel too deeply. She'd walked away from him then. Run actually, from him and from her own feelings. For all intents and purposes, Sophia had lived her life between the lines. And Cam was so far outside the lines he shouldn't have even been in the picture.

But he was. He *was* the picture, and although he'd let her flee, she hadn't been as successful leaving behind the feelings he'd elicited from her. She allowed herself the indulgence of studying him. His dark-brown hair was painted a shade darker by the water, and he kept it a shorter length than favored by most of the agents. She'd seen a picture of him last month in which his hair had been longer, sporting what he'd called an unmanly wave. She'd decided on the spot that she preferred it grown out but doubted she'd ever see it that way.

His jaw was stubbled, his eyes shadowed, and she felt a sudden ache of tenderness. He'd push on until he dropped, or until he put Baxter behind bars. And he'd do so without considering the physical cost to himself.

But it was what she saw in his golden-brown eyes that had her pulse stuttering and conscious thought draining away. Unvarnished desire. Smoky tendrils of heat suffused her. She'd spent her life neatly compartmentalizing her life, weighing risks, skirting threats to her equilibrium. To her heart. He represented the biggest risk she'd ever taken. And she was through running from the possibility of heartbreak.

Their gazes tangled. He stroked a lazy path up her spine, and she shuddered in response. An alarm shrilled in the distant recesses of her mind. She'd heeded it once and regretted her cowardice. If there was one thing a brush with death had taught her, it was that moments were meant to be seized.

His head dipped, and his teeth closed over the cord of her neck, testing not quite painfully. The uncertainty of their future had once frightened her until she'd learned what true fear was. But this. *This* was worth taking a chance.

Thoughts grew foggy. Reason clouded. She dragged her lips across his jaw, felt his whiskers lightly abrade her mouth, and the sensation cemented her decision. He was the only one who could make her believe that these feelings, wild and primitive, were more important than a relationship of shared interests. He shattered her safe risk-averse world and all too easily became the center of it.

It wasn't the frankly carnal passion between them that had frightened her so much. It was finding herself wanting more. His lips moved over hers then, and there was a flare in her belly, hot and immediate.

He cupped her face in his palms, and his mouth devoured hers, their tongues tangling, breath mingling, teeth clashing. He walked her backward a few steps until she felt the shower wall at her shoulders, and still he didn't lift his mouth from hers. She softened against him. Here was the hunger she craved. The hint of savagery that called forth an answering wildness she would have once denied existed.

He urged her legs apart with his knee, then stepped between them. His erection pressed against her belly, and she squirmed against him, wanting to feel him where she was empty and aching. As if aware of her frustration, his hands went to her butt, and he lifted her. With her legs wrapped around his hips, she rocked against his hardness, feeling his reaction even if she couldn't drag her eyes open to watch it.

Her head lolled against the wall, fingers on a tactile journey, dancing over the hard planes of his chest, the hollows beneath his ribs. The ridges of sinew and bone.

There was something exquisitely sensuous about focusing on touch alone. She mapped a journey along his biceps, across his shoulders, while he followed the streams of water along her skin with his tongue. He sipped at the drops collected in the hollow beneath her neck. She shivered each time his mouth found a new inch of skin to taste. To savor.

This rollicking of her pulse was familiar but no less heady for it. Every brush of his lips, every teasing slide of his tongue, was a dark promise of things to come. It fueled a quiet desperation in her system. He was pressed close. She wanted him closer. Seamed against her. Buried deep inside her. So close even the pulsing water couldn't dribble between them. And then closer yet. And she wanted him quaking, too. Wanted to release the primitive nature that he kept so tightly harnessed. She wanted, quite frankly, to strip him of every defense as easily as he'd crumbled hers.

To that end, she relaxed her fingers and went on a quest designed to unleash his control. Her senses scattered when his tongue circled one nipple, teasing it tauter, and then took it in his mouth, drawing strongly from her. It took all the strength she could muster to concentrate on the places that made him shudder. The soft velvety skin beneath his arm. A fingernail scraping over one male nipple. Her fingers lowered. Over taut muscles in his belly that jumped and bunched at her touch.

He raised his head; the sound of his hissed breath was its own reward. Her reach was constrained by the closeness of their position, but she was thorough in her investigation. She brushed her fingers over his back, feeling the flesh punctuated by vertebrae. The muscles beneath her fingers quivered under her touch like an impatient stallion's.

Sophia felt seared by his gaze. It painted her face, her breasts, causing her nipples to tighten even more. She knew from experience that he'd take pleasure and return it tenfold, and the knowledge sparked comets of heat through her veins.

Eyes locked on him, she arched her back, a carnal invitation, and watched the color slash over his cheekbones. His jaw tightened, and she knew intuitively he was battling against the urge to rush the ending, an urge she wouldn't protest. She saw the moment he won the battle, saw the slight curve to his lips as he reached out a finger to brush it across her swollen and tender nipples.

She jerked against him in involuntary response, and her reaction seemed to ignite something inside him. He slid a hand up to cup one of her breasts, capturing the taut bud between thumb and forefinger before lowering his mouth to take the other nipple between his lips.

Kaleidoscopic colors wheeled behind her eyelids. Sophia leaned back while pressing closer to his lips, and he responded to her unspoken demand by suckling strongly from her. The whisper of teeth against her flesh had hunger leaping forth, an uncaged beast. Her earlier plan to make him ache, make him need, was forgotten. Her fingers twisted in his wet hair, urging him to take more.

He lifted his mouth, and the cooling water tightened her nipples almost painfully. She met his lips with hers, all pretense stripped away. She felt alive in his arms, color returning to a world that violence had washed gray and sepia. And the heat careening through her veins warmed a place left icy and cold from her time at Vance's mercy.

A more logical part of her wanted to backpedal. There was danger here. Of feeling too much. Offering more, much more than Cam could ever return. But to live was to risk. A heart intact was also one that hadn't felt the depth and breadth of emotion.

Sensation heightened unbearably everywhere they touched. Pulse points were sharpened to razor-edged keenness. Everything else dimmed. Her flesh came alive under the stroking of his healing palms, hot and demanding over her curves, gentle on her injured wrist. The contrast kept her off-kilter, swinging from lust to tenderness and back again. Cam trailed a finger along her thigh, circling teasingly around the heat centered between her thighs, and the inner warnings were silenced.

He leaned in for a kiss. Hot. Wet. Rawly carnal. His palm covered her mound, which was damp and aching. His tongue searched out hers even as he parted her slick folds and entered her with one exploring finger.

Her hips arched and bucked against him at the dual assault. Her blood was churning in her veins, frothing and crashing like white water. There was primitive demand in his kiss. In his touch. In a demand that she reciprocated.

Sophia's hands streaked over his body, tempting, teasing, reveling in the sensual warmth of skin covering bone and muscle. He eased another finger inside her, increasing the sensual assault. Then he found the tight cluster of nerves and started a rhythmic circling designed to send her a little crazy.

One of her hands found his rigid erection, tightening her grasp when she heard the raw guttural sound he made. He was strength sheathed in satin, and he leaped in her palm with an urgency that was telling in light of his outer control.

There was a demand in his touch, a promise. And while she could fight the sensual assault, the conclusion couldn't be denied.

He removed his fingers and repositioned her. Sophia twined her arms around his shoulders. He was inside her in one barely restrained lunge that brought a moan from both of them. She met his demand with her own, her hips bucking against his in a frenzied need for fulfillment. He clutched her hips in hard desperate fingers, urging her to an even faster pace. Her blood began to pulse, scorching rivers beneath her skin. Need coiled in her belly.

He was muttering something in her ear, his voice raw and urgent, but she couldn't hear, couldn't think. The sound slipped away as evasively as wisps of fog. Nerve endings spiraled to concentrate where they were fused so intimately. The rhythm quickened. Breaths shortened.

The climax shattered her first, intense and tumultuous. The eddies continued, stealing her breath, her awareness. Her response snapped Cam's control, and he gave one last surge before following her headlong into a pleasure too long denied.

o o o

Sneaky little flickers of guilt marred what should have been a perfectly relaxing late-night drive home. Lucy had insisted on driving separately to Gavin's hotel room. The hours she'd spent stretched out naked over him, under him still had nerve endings quivering in memory.

Ravenous, they'd ordered pizza and devoured it like a couple of feral dogs. Afterward, she'd seen the change in his expression, forewarning her that he hadn't forgotten his promise—or threat—to talk.

It was telling that the idea of a looming discussion about their relationship would strike terror into her heart. Lucy was morally fastidious, dictated by the demand of her job and personal choice. It was just her luck that she'd chosen the one man in the world who seemingly wasn't satisfied with a no-strings-attached hookup.

She'd successfully managed to divert Gavin of his intentions, and they'd spent another hour engaged in languorous sex. And when he'd fallen asleep, she'd taken the opportunity to . . . not *sneak*. That word was imbued with a negative connotation. She'd left quietly. Lucy didn't spend a complete night with a man. Not ever. Doing so would mean sleeping, eventually. And then she'd be vulnerable. Defenseless.

The way her mother had been twenty years ago when she'd passed out drunk with her newest "boyfriend." Leaving him to set the bed on fire, with her in it.

Lucy shoved that memory back into the vault where she usually kept all recollections of her childhood. She didn't need to consider where her lack of trust emanated from. It was the way she'd operated most of her life. And she didn't know a man on earth who could understand it, much less accept it.

She certainly hadn't wanted to try explaining it to Gavin.

It was with a degree of relief that she turned into the long drive next to her home. The privacy offered by the property had appealed to her, as had the space. But she hadn't yet spent a winter here. Lucy had a feeling she would be less satisfied with the detached garage at the back of the place once the snow began to fly. Iowa winters weren't for wimps. But for now the garage was fine, and the walk to the back deck was lined with solar lights that provided a welcoming glow against the nearly black night.

Except . . . She squinted at the light showing in her attic window. Her nape prickled. Had she left the light on there? Slowing her pace, she tried to think. She'd been up there yesterday to look through a box for more summer clothes. But she hadn't turned on the light to do so, had she?

She reached the deck. Turning, she scanned the shadowy yard. The security lights on the outside of her garage were still on. Others were glowing from their mount above the back deck. She saw nothing to alarm her. Nerves quieting, she mounted the steps and crossed to the back door, her keys in hand.

When her cell shrilled, she made a grab for it, thinking at once of the case. Of work. But when she read the screen of the phone, a tendril of shame curled through her. *Gavin.*

She hesitated for a moment, torn. Then dropped the phone back into her purse. It was better this way. Better that he learn to accept what she could offer him.

And what she couldn't.

But the abrupt silencing of the phone as it went to voice mail had the muscles in her stomach tightening. It was easier to be irritated with the man than it was to grapple with her trickle of unfamiliar remorse. What was his problem, anyway? They'd met exactly twice—both times this month. Hardly the basis of a fairy-tale romance. Better that he realize now. Lucy Benally didn't do fairy tales. At least not the romantic ones. Based on her experience, it was far easier to believe in the monsters that populated the somewhat gruesome children's stories.

She stepped inside her kitchen, flicking on the light, and set her purse on the table. As she turned back toward the door, a sound caught her attention. She stopped. Listened. A floorboard somewhere in the recesses of the house creaked.

Lucy strained but heard nothing further. She'd traded the constant city noises for the relative silence of the country, but that meant that random sounds could be startling. The creaks and groans of an older home settling. Crickets chirping from some as of yet undetermined location in the cellar. The sound of a mouse that had had the misfortune to come inside looking for food and had instead met its end.

Directly above the kitchen were the bathroom and the attic stairs. And it was a little ridiculous to think that a burglar had entered her locked home and then snuggled in for a bubble bath.

The idea lightened a little of her tension. But just in case, she headed for the front hallway closet to get the baseball bat she kept there. She'd feel better with it in her hand while she did a room-to-room search. It was the only hope she had of relaxing enough to sleep tonight. Her cell rang again behind her, and she was reminded she hadn't locked the door. *Damn Connerly*. Her brain was mush after their hours together. She wasn't thinking clearly.

He appeared from nowhere. Just rose from the shadows to block her way. She stifled a yelp of shock, one hand flying to her chest. The light spilling into the room behind her afforded enough illumination to make out his features. Scruffy bearded face, a shapeless cardigan sweater several sizes too large for him. A wrinkled skirt, from which legs encased in orthopedic hose and shoes extended. But despite the bizarre overall effect, she recognized the man immediately. His sketch had been all over the news.

In the next instant she turned to run. Not for the back door but for the stairway that would take her upstairs. To the gun she kept there.

"You don't want to do that." A single shot punctuated his words, the bullet embedding in the wall next to her. It was close enough for Lucy to feel the sprinkle of dislodged plaster. She froze, her whole body quivering, caught in suspended animation between survival and flight. She had a single moment to regret ever leaving Gavin's bed before the man spoke again. "I've been waiting for you, Lucy."

o o o

It was the absence of Cam's warmth that woke her. Sophia opened her eyes. Found herself alone in the bed. The adjoining bath was dark. Without considering, she rolled out of bed, then hesitated for a moment when she remembered she was naked. The last time she'd seen her robe, it had been a wet crumpled pile on the bathroom floor.

She went to Cam's closet and took a shirt off the hanger, buttoning it as she crossed to the door, and rolled up the too-long sleeves. If she found him working, she'd simply bully him back to bed. He was already sleep deprived. He needed more than an hour of rest to replenish him.

There was also the possibility that he'd suffered another flashback from his time on that interagency drug task force. He'd known exactly what she was going through last night when he'd come into her room. Cam still occasionally suffered trauma-induced reactions himself.

There were no lights on in the condo. But as she padded through the living room, she could hear the low murmur of his voice. And gave an inner sigh. She flipped on the light switch. "Seriously, you have to give the case a rest." He looked at her, clearly startled, his cell pressed to his ear. He hadn't paused for clothes. He was completely and gloriously nude.

She felt herself blush, a completely ridiculous response given the last few hours, but the involuntary reaction had long been the bane of her existence. The look he raked her with had tendrils of heat igniting beneath her skin.

"Yeah. Thanks for the update. I'll keep you posted." Unceremoniously he ended the call. Sent her a long slow smile. "I think that just became my favorite shirt." He stalked deliberately toward her. "In fact, I think I want it back. Immediately."

She rounded the desk to put it between them. "Was that call about the case?"

"Yeah." The answer was immediate. And so was her recognition of the lie. That easily, the inner warmth was doused with a cold reminder of the other time he'd lied to her. And how that fact had weighed heavily on her decision to break off their relationship.

"New rules, Cam." Her voice was steady. Her hands weren't, so she wrapped her arms around her waist. "If there's something you don't want to talk about, tell me. Something you can't discuss, just let me know. But do me the courtesy of not lying to me. I haven't earned your distrust. And that's what you're telling me right now. You don't trust me enough not to lie."

The corner of his mouth curled up wryly. "Out of all the women to fall for, I had to pick a shrink."

Sophia didn't return the smile. She couldn't. His words echoed and reverberated inside her. *Of all the women to fall for . . .* Her knees went abruptly weak.

He propped his palms on the desk. Leaned toward her slightly. "No." His voice was quiet. His gaze direct. "That wasn't about the case. At least not this one. It was federal agent Del Harlow. My FBI contact during my time on the interagency task force."

Confused, she said, "That was a year ago, wasn't it? And what's the matter with the man? Doesn't he know how to tell time?"

His expression went grim. "What's wrong with him? Other than being a lying son of a bitch, nothing that I know of. In his defense, he's heading for LAX from Southern California. Couple hours earlier there."

The information had her mind working. "You were in Southern Cal on that task force," she said slowly. "What did he lie to you about? And why is he still in contact? I thought that case ended in a big bust of that Mexican cartel." Another thought occurred. "Does this have anything to do with the picture I found in your desk drawer a few weeks ago? Of you with that other man you said was your cousin?"

His look was arrested. "Jesus, that mind of yours . . . Why would you even ask that?"

"Because that was the last time you lied to me," she said simply. Still cold, her arms tightened around her waist. "You didn't want to answer questions about him."

"You're something." His expression was caught somewhere between chagrin and amusement. "Prior to being sent down to infiltrate the Sinaloa cartel, I spent a week at Quantico, where I learned, among other things, how to beat a lie detector, which was intriguing, and how to withstand the effects of physical interrogation, which was less so. And you . . . you just look at me and know when I'm not being honest. How's that work?"

"I see you differently than anyone else does." The words, while true, revealed too much for her to be comfortable with. No longer able to meet his gaze, she paced to the corner of the room. Pretended great interest in the canvas print of a fan-filled Kinnick Stadium at night, the crowd outfitted in alternating sections of black and gold. It was paired with a large sepia-toned historic shot of Wrigley. "It's all right. I don't need to know the rest."

"Well you deserve to." When she looked at him over her shoulder, a mask of weariness had slipped over his expression. "God knows you're all wrapped up in this now."

"In what?"

"My place is under twenty-four-hour surveillance by the FBI," he answered starkly. "Physical and digital, although the cameras are all on the outside, at my insistence."

Her eyes widened in shock. "Why? I thought that task force was long over with."

"It was," he agreed grimly. "Until a packet arrived slipped in the folds of the Sunday newspaper one day. It was the morning you wanted to go to the art festival. I begged off because I had to call Harlow. Tell him someone from the cartel had traced me back to Des Moines. There were pictures included in the envelope of DCI headquarters. The license plate on my car. The address number on my house. A picture of me . . ."

"And a copy of the one of you and the man who isn't your cousin." She turned more completely to face him. "Is he threatening you in some way?"

Cam rose to jam a hand through his hair. "We don't know. The man . . . his name is Matthew Baldwin. We got close while we were down there." Something must have shown on her face, because he added, "He wasn't a total scumbag. He was just a guy. Got tangled up with the cartel because his wife is the niece of Pablo Moreno, its head. And when the Sinaloa cartel decides you're going to work for them, people have two choices—do it or die. So Matt did it. Gabriela, his wife, didn't realize what her uncle did for a living."

"But the bust you orchestrated down there was said to have gutted the cartel. To cripple it."

He gave a jerk of his shoulder. "It helped. But it was like chopping off the snake's tail while leaving the head. The cartel is rebuilding. And Moreno is vicious. Anyone left standing was bound to get looked at hard for being the traitor."

She frowned. "As far as they knew, you were arrested with the others in the bust. So how did that lead them to you?"

His smile was terrible. "That's the million-dollar question, isn't it? The cartel has the money to get their hands on all kinds of information. Harlow figures they've been tracing all the arrestees through the justice system and making sure they really ended up in prison. Anyone spared would be suspected of turning on the cartel and marked for execution."

Ice encased her. "They . . . they know you're a cop?"

"Someone does." He looked as if he was regretting the entire conversation. "I don't want you to worry. I would never have allowed you to be brought here for protective custody if I wasn't certain it was safe. I figured it was the most secure place to bring you. Not only would you have round-the-clock protection; you'd have the feds watching the place, as well. I have someone tailing me at all times."

Sophia mulled the onslaught of information over. "They're using you as bait." The realization had her stomach doing a slow roll. "Does Gonzalez know?"

Again Cam shrugged. "Couldn't say. The decision to enlighten my superiors is made much further up the chain of command. I'd guess no. Harlow flew out to California to meet with some informants, so that's how I know as much as I do."

"Can you trust him?" Sophia demanded. Alarm, fueled by concern for him, was making its way through her system. "You said yourself that he's a lying son of a bitch."

"He is that." Cam straightened. Folded his arms across his chest. "My mom had a heart attack while I was down there. Harlow was supposed to be my connection to home. Supposed to communicate messages back and forth between the family. He never told me about her illness. Not a word." His expression was terrible. "Told my stepfather he wasn't able to get in touch with me while she was in the hospital, which was total bullshit. She'd been recovered for six months when I got home and that bastard never mentioned a thing about it."

Concern for him morphed to indignation on his behalf. Her fingers balled into fists. "You're right. He is a bastard. Which makes it less comforting to think of you leaving your welfare in his hands."

He smiled a little at her tone. "Not his, the agents on surveillance detail. Otherwise, yeah, I'd be worried. Harlow's just the info guy on this. He got a list of names of those who might have been put on my trail. I had a cover, of course, but it wouldn't last long against the cartel's money. I have a pretty good idea now who sent those photos. I guess I always suspected."

An awful sense of comprehension filled her. "You mean . . . the man in the picture with you?"

"Matthew Baldwin." He gave a slow nod. "Which serves me right for ignoring my training, everything I've ever been taught, and saving the son of a bitch's life."

Chapter 13

C am scrubbed a hand over his face. Turned half away. "Long-term undercover operations have risks associated with them. Everyone knows that going in. But what most don't realize is the natural human reaction you have when you're with the same people day in and day out. Some of the members of the cartel were just lowlife scumbags, especially the enforcers. They liked the killing, the violence. They were no better than Vance, in a different way. They fed off people's fear. Others . . ."

He rolled a shoulder. "It's a job, one that pays well. The rampant poverty in Mexico makes it easy to get recruits. But Baldwin . . . he was a decent guy. Got tangled up in it by marrying Gabriela. And then stayed in to protect his family. Moreno would kill his own niece and great-niece in a heartbeat if Matt betrayed him."

"You're saying Baldwin wasn't arrested in the bust."

He smiled humorlessly. "Because I made sure he wouldn't be. Sent him off on an errand as a ruse fifteen minutes before the bust went down. Figured once he heard about it, he'd take advantage of the chaos to get his wife and daughter and leave the country. Apparently he didn't. And the fact that he was spared would have made Moreno mighty suspicious since Matt was supposed to be at that meeting."

It was the first time he'd admitted aloud what he'd done for Baldwin. No one knew. Not his FBI contact. Not the DEA agent who had infiltrated the cartel a year after him. It hadn't been a decision that he'd come to lightly, nor had he borne it in the time since without guilt.

But few could understand deep cover. Black and white melded into murky shades of gray. The constant threat of exposure warped perspective. A scene flashed across his mind of one of Moreno's intermittent "loyalty tests." Cam would be dragged to an abandoned building, or to one of the underground tunnels the cartel used as their drug route into the United States. Then the barrel of a gun would be placed at his temple while the enforcer played a perverted game of Russian roulette while questioning everything about his story. His cover. His background.

In that kind of environment, where trust was at a premium and human life utterly devoid of worth, he'd come to value the friendship that had sprung up between him and Matt.

Maybe he'd always known he'd pay for that lapse.

Lost in his thoughts, he hadn't even realized she'd moved until he felt her against his back, her arms twining around his waist. "That task force was a horrible risk," she said fiercely. "And it's still costing you. Whether you'd spared Baldwin or not, Moreno was going to follow up on everyone arrested. There was always a chance it would end like this."

Cam let out a deep breath. Her words were true enough. But chances were that Matt had been the best equipped to trace him. They'd spent a lot of time together. He'd know Cam better than any of the rest of them could. "Moreno is still weakened. Several of his lieutenants were scooped up in that bust, and a couple talked." He didn't tell her that one of those men had been executed while in federal custody. That wasn't exactly the sort of news guaranteed to allay her fears. "A lot of his money and energy is going toward rebuilding. New routes, new officials to bribe . . . The hits to his operation have been substantial." At least according to Harlow, more immediate pressure on the man was being brought to bear. If the agent was right, Moreno's long reach might be hampered for a while.

He loosened her hands and turned to scoop her up in his arms, enjoying the moment when surprise chased away the worry in her expression. He'd told her far more than he'd meant to. Which was something he had in common with all the offenders Sophie had interviewed over the years. She had a way of listening that extracted information not willingly offered. The realization was a little discomfiting.

"We're losing sleep discussing something we can't change." He strode with her to the doorway, paused. Obligingly she turned off the light. Then he continued with her back to the bedroom. "This deal with Moreno is being handled by the feds." Which made him feel marginally better about Sophie's safety while at his side.

Dropping her on the rumpled bed, he followed her down on it and pulled a sheet over them. Then he snaked an arm around her waist and pulled her close. "Oh, and Dr. Channing?" He rested his forehead against hers and let his eyes droop. "When this thing is over I'm having the shirt bronzed."

o o o

"This is a nice place. Quiet. I recognized that the last time I came. Come over here. Now."

Her legs had gone leaden. Lucy had to force them to obey while her mind scrambled to comprehend his words.

The last time he'd been here? And how had he arrived this time? There had been no sign of a vehicle on the property.

"It's not safe for you here." Her voice was remarkably steady as she moved to obey him. "The police are looking for you. You need to go far away so they can't find you." Gaze darting around the room, she looked for anything she could use as a weapon. Saw nothing more lethal than a lamp. She stifled a wild laugh. A lamp against a gun, being wielded by a man who had killed numerous times already. She didn't like her odds.

"It feels safe." His mouth curled, the expression in his eyes a little dreamy. "The last time I came, that's exactly what I thought. How safe it felt. Of course, it's safer since I disposed of the gun I found in your bedroom."

The words dashed a single thread of hope she hadn't even realized she'd been clinging to. "You should go. I have money that will help. And you can take my car, my phone. It will be hours before anyone knows you were . . ." Her words tapered off as she saw for the first time the wall over her couch. Everything she'd had hanging on it had been taken off and piled neatly on the floor. Black writing was scrawled on the beige paint. Reading it, she went cold.

safe with lucy lovely lovely lucy so quiet its so quiet here she knows how to be quiet.

"You were quite late," he said matter-of-factly, following the direction of her gaze. "It calms me to journal. I waited for you, though. I'm very good at waiting. I wait for just the right woman."

Chills skated over her skin. He'd stalked Courtney Van Wheton, she recalled sickly. An eyewitness had helped Agent Turner draw the sketch of this man in the park watching the woman days before her kidnapping. Maybe he was the one Vance had sent out to scout the next victim.

Victim. The word returned a little strength to her limbs. She'd be damned if she was going to allow herself to be victimized by this sick freak. "I can help you get away." She took a tiny step toward the kitchen. Involuntarily her gaze landed on the defaced wall again.

quiet so quiet were soul mates lucy and me I'll teach her to be quiet so very very quiet.

Her stomach lurched. Suddenly she was certain that whatever role Vance had played in the kidnappings and tortures, this man was the one who had killed the women at the end.

"I picked you out. The first time I saw you at the river with Janice. I knew you were the one when I watched how gentle you were with her. How tender." He approached her deliberately, the gun still leveled.

"You . . . you watched us?" Immediately she realized how easy it would have been. The spot was surrounded on two sides with woods. He could have been anywhere in those dense trees and at night no one would have seen him.

"I was glad it was you." Another step toward her. Lucy took another away. "I knew then that you and I were alike. We both love the dead."

There were knives in the kitchen. A butcher block full of them that may be no match against a gun but certainly evened the odds. "The victims at the river were embalmed. That was you?" A tiny step away. Keep him talking. And maybe he wouldn't notice that she was moving infinitesimally across the room.

He nodded, a pleased expression on his face. For the first time, she noticed the marker in the sagging pocket of his sweater. She recognized it as one he must have taken out of her kitchen drawer. "They can love me longer when they're embalmed. I knew you'd see that. I knew you'd understand."

"Oh, I do," she assured him grimly. Her muscles bunched as she prepared to flee. "I understand exactly."

"Benally!"

Every ounce of blood in Lucy's veins did an abrupt freeze. She recognized Gavin's voice at the back door, although she'd never heard it before raised to a bellow. Gone was his normally affable tone. The fury in his tone was palpable.

It seemed to ignite the fury of the man standing in front of her.

A house-rattling knock followed Gavin's shout and melted her stupor. Taking advantage of her captor's distraction, she raced for the lamp across the room. Grazed it with her fingertips before being hit from behind with a flying tackle that knocked her to the floor, the breath driven from her lungs.

"Not one sound," the man murmured. The gun's barrel was pressed beneath her ear.

"You think you can call all the shots between us? I'm not going to be brushed off by mind-blowing sex, sharp words, and a snotty attitude. Although you're masterful at all three."

Gavin's words made it even more difficult to draw a breath. It was the very real danger he was in at that moment that kept her utterly still, rather than the cool metal pressed against her. Once he realized she wasn't coming to the door he'd give up. Go away. And then the only one she'd have to worry about was herself.

That thought actually provided a thread of hope. *Go away, Gavin.* The words careened through her mind, a demand. A plea. *Please, please go away.*

The slender hope shattered in the next instant when a tiny sound was heard. The knob of the kitchen door was turning.

She opened her mouth to scream a warning. A hand clapped over her lips, muffling the attempt. She could feel her captor motionless above her. Knew that despite the weapon he still held on her, all his attention was focused on the approaching threat. Lucy writhed beneath him in an attempt to recapture his attention. A footstep sounded in the kitchen. She tried to free a hand to peel his from over her mouth. When that failed, she managed to wrestle a foot away long enough to bring it down twice in two soft thumps of warning before the intruder trapped her leg with one of his.

"You use whatever tools you have at your disposal to keep people at a distance." The anger in Gavin's voice was threaded with a softness that brought a sting of tears to her eyes. "I know you, Luce. Doesn't matter a damn how long it's been since we met, I *know* you. And we're . . ."

It was hard, so hard to watch him reach the doorway. To take in the scene in a split second. And to wait, barely daring to breathe, for the instant her attacker would shift the weapon to aim it instead at Gavin. Everything inside her coiled in readiness for that moment.

"My keys are right here." After meeting Lucy's gaze for one terrible second, Gavin looked at the offender, raising his arm slowly to allow his keys to dangle from his fingers. "Rental plates on the car, so highway cops aren't going to think twice about it heading west. Lots of places for a person to lose himself in the west. Yellowstone. Oregon's Willamette Forest. Or LA." He gave that lopsided smile that too frequently made Lucy's resolve weaken. "It can be as easy to lose yourself among three million people as it can be in the wilderness. You've got a lot of options. All you have to do is walk out of here and choose one."

She sensed the intruder's response the instant she felt the gun leave her throat. Lurching violently beneath him, she struggled with all her might to disrupt his aim while Gavin dove for cover toward the kitchen door.

The sound of the shot was deafening. The first bullet caught Gavin in the shoulder before he hit the floor and rolled away. Her attacker rose, yanking Lucy to her feet as he dragged her with one arm around her neck a few feet toward the doorway. Gavin was at the counter, drawing a knife from the butcher block.

She threw her weight against her attacker, knocking him off balance. But not before he squeezed the trigger again.

Time freeze-framed to a slow reel of horror-filled milliseconds. The shot shattered the silence. Blood spread on Gavin's white shirt. He looked shocked. Grabbed for the counter. Lucy gave a powerful lunge to free herself. To go to him. She was held fast. Powerlessly she watched his grip slip from the counter. He fell to his knees, his expression dazed. When their eyes met, the helplessness she saw in his was a vise to her heart. He fell to his knees, still clutching the knife.

Then the weapon clattered to the floor. Followed by Gavin's body.

Lucy looked at her captor. Saw the intent on his face as his focus remained on Gavin. "I understand now. Look at me. Look at me." The insistence in her tone finally diverted his attention. He eased the pressure on the trigger to glance at her.

"His spirit is gone." Gavin might be dying. The crushing pressure in her chest that came from that knowledge made it difficult to speak. But another bullet would make his death certain. "There's nothing stopping us now. We can go somewhere. Get to know each other better."

The things the freak had said to her earlier made it difficult to speak. Relentlessly she pushed the memory aside. Focused on getting him away from the man bleeding on her kitchen floor. "I have a place we can go. We can be alone and spend as much time as we need to learn about each other." She had his attention now, and Lucy forced her mind to function.

"My grandparents have a hogan on Navajo Nation lands. It's been empty for years, but it's isolated. The land around it is breathtaking." She hadn't been in her grandmother's hogan since she was eight. Had no idea if it still existed. Her mother had frittered away the money from the sale of the land before Lucy's tenth birthday.

"We can be alone there. No one would question my presence on my family's land."

Suspicion was stamped on the man's face. "You're lying. Women do that sometimes. You tried to trick me earlier. Why should I believe you?"

A barely inaudible sound reached her. It might have been a groan from Gavin. Or it could have been her imagination. She spoke louder to cover the noise, and faster, her eyes fastened on the offender. "The man you just killed was a threat to me. Now I'm free. Free to do whatever I want." She saw Gavin's foot twitch. Just a fraction of a movement, but the sight of it had her going weak with relief. She laid a hand on the stranger's arm to keep his focus on her. The small intimacy made her flesh crawl. "This is what I want. A new start. With a man I can trust. Can I trust you?"

He stared hard at her for a moment. Two. It took every bit of her will not to look away, despite the loathing she felt. Despite everything this man was believed to have done, she didn't see evil in his eyes.

She saw crazy. And that scared her even more.

"Navajo Mountain can be seen in the distance behind the hogan. Dawn paints it pink and gray, and when one looks at it during those early morning hours you're filled with a kind of inner peace that most people spend their whole lives seeking. It's a very special place."

"I took Janice and the others to my special place," he said slowly. "I could hear the sound of the river nearby telling me everything was all right. No one could hurt us there."

She swallowed hard. Lucy couldn't forget for a moment that the reason no one could hurt those women by the river was because this man had already killed them. She reminded herself that crazy didn't mean less dangerous. Just the opposite.

"I've been to your special place. Now I'd like to show you mine." She had no specific plan in mind other than getting him out of here. But a road trip would offer a lot of opportunities for escape. Right now she had to get him out of the house. Away from Gavin.

It seemed an eternity before his free hand came up to touch hers fleetingly. "I'd like that, too. But first we have a job to do. If you don't bury the dead, either in the ground or in the water, they'll come back. That's what Mommy did. Do you have a shovel? We could do it behind the house before we leave."

"It's all right." Subtly she leaned her weight toward the doorway. "I work with the dead on a daily basis. His spirit has left him. We need to go before someone comes looking for him."

The slight pressure she was exerting seemed to work. The stranger loosened his arm around her throat, to settle it around her shoulders. "We can be alone at the hogan?"

"The last time I was there the nearest neighbor was miles away." Of course she had no idea what the area looked like now, but it didn't matter. Not right now. "It will just be the two of us. Is that what you want?"

"It's exactly what I want." He moved forward, bending her down with him when he scooped up Gavin's keys. They walked through the kitchen toward the door. From the corner of her eye Lucy noted the knife block. And for the space of a second she considered following Gavin's lead and lunging for a weapon.

The next step took them past it. The stranger still held the gun. She couldn't predict if he'd use it on her right now, but she could be reasonably certain he'd use it on Gavin if he were given any indication that the other man was still alive. Connerly's only chance of survival was to remove the threat from her house.

So she walked through the open door with a man suspected of killing at least four women, hoping with every fiber of her being that doing so gave Gavin a chance at survival.

It was a slender hope. But it was all she had.

They walked across the deck. Down the steps. With each stride she wondered about the man she was leaving behind. How much blood had he lost? After that first horror-filled moment, she hadn't dared chance a look to see. Lucy had an inner strength that had helped her overcome life-altering events. But she knew her strength was no match for that image.

They stopped at Gavin's car. "I'm sorry, Lucy, but I have to do this." He pulled out a pair of zip ties from the back pocket of his jeans. Held them out before her.

A cold knot of dread settled in the pit of her belly. Lucy searched her captor's face, striving for an earnest expression. "That's not the way to build trust."

"Trust will come later. First I have to get you out of the state." He brought up the gun in one fluid move, made a little motion with it. "Put these on and you'll be showing me I can trust you. If I can't . . ."

The threat in the unspoken words was implicit. Wordlessly she thrust her wrists through the loop, gritting her teeth as he leaned forward and pulled the cord tight with his teeth. The nylon bit into her wrists. Then he fumbled with the key fob until he found the button that opened the trunk.

Lucy looked at the rising lid with horror. Even with her hands tied she could defeat a seat belt and car lock. But this . . . She looked at the dark confined place. Looked back at her captor. "I'll be good—I promise." The lies tumbled from her lips. "But don't make me go in there. I'm claustrophobic. I can't do it. Please, please don't make me."

His shove was ungentle. "Get in."

With a sense of impending doom, she did as she was told. Maybe she could get her wrists loose on the road. Then when he opened the trunk, she could launch a blitz attack.

That small hope died when he pulled another zip tie from his pocket and expertly bound her feet. When he was done, he gave her a small smile. "There you go. You'll be fine, my love. I promise. Soon we'll be able to start our new life together."

As the trunk lid lowered, she felt a flare of panic. She wasn't really claustrophobic of course, but she'd never been locked in a trunk before. Bound. Headed out of state with a known killer.

She'd never left the only man she'd ever cared about to die on her kitchen floor.

The engine started. The vehicle began to move. Lucy's religious beliefs were unorthodox, to say the least. A mixture of the traditional Navajo teachings of her grandmother and smatterings picked up through life experiences. But right now she was praying to any god that would listen that Gavin was conscious. That somehow, someone would come to help him.

Gravel crunched as they headed down her driveway. Lucy was a realist. She knew exactly how grim the outlook was. She realized that the chance of help arriving in time was a slender one.

It was equally possible that she'd left Gavin to bleed out on her kitchen floor. That her act meant to save him had only sentenced him to die alone.

That possibility was far more torturous than being imprisoned by a madman.

○ ○ ○

He wasn't dead. Gavin was almost certain of it. He had only the haziest of notions about what the afterlife might entail, but he was fairly certain it didn't include cool tile beneath his cheek that still held the faintest aroma of lemon-scented cleanser.

He'd heard Lucy talking the killer into leaving the house. Heard the car leave. Conscious thought was getting fuzzy. But panic filled him at the thought of her on the road with the zombie lover.

She didn't have a landline, but his cell was in his pocket. All he had to do was get up. Take it out. Dial 9-1-1.

Gavin willed his body to move. Nothing happened. Not a twitch of muscle obeyed him. He could feel the fire in his arm and side. Feel the warm sensation of blood leaving his body. He tried again, commanding his legs to move. Again they failed him.

He was lying on his injured arm. Bleeding from the opposite side. He sent a mental command to his body again. Felt his fingers on his good arm curl in response. Then lift a fraction of an inch from the floor before going lax again.

Shifting tactics he summoned a mental image of Lucy walking out that door with a man who had murdered and buried at least four women. Maybe more. And this time he was able to bend his arm toward his hip.

Slowly, excruciatingly, he inched his fingers toward the cell tucked in his back jeans pocket. When he managed to free it, only to have it clatter to the floor beside him, Gavin went weak with exhaustion. There was a reason. An urgent one, to make a call. But the logic was slippery and unconsciousness was becoming increasingly difficult to battle.

It was Lucy. Something about Lucy.

Clenching his jaw, he struggled against the fog crowding his mind and demanded his fingers to work. Moved the phone inch by inch. Stopped, battling to remember how to use it.

The command for speed dial was all he could manage before sliding it closer to his mouth. A cloud of mental fog enveloped him, threatened to suck him in. Suck him under.

A vaguely familiar voice answered. "Prescott."

Gavin's remaining strength had been sapped. His eyes slid closed. And no amount of commands could make them open again.

"Connerly? Is that you?"

"Lucy," Gavin mumbled. "My car. He . . . took . . . her. West. Need ambulance. At Luc . . ." That was odd. The thoughts were there. Ready to speak. But his tongue was too thick to talk. The words he wanted to force out remained unuttered.

He had a single thought of startling clarity that this must be what dying felt like. Then the dike of his resistance crumbled and unconsciousness rushed in, dragging him to blackness.

∘ ∘ ∘

"Connerly? Connerly?"

Groggily, Sophia sat up in bed. Blinking at the bare-chested man beside her, she struggled for lucidity. Of course. Cam always had his phone on the bedside table. She did the same.

A moment later understanding replaced the fog of sleep. Trepidation filled her. "What's wrong?"

"Not sure." His voice was terse. He was already swinging his legs out of the bed. "Where's your phone?"

The urgency in his manner had her grabbing her cell from the opposite bedside table to hand to him wordlessly. "Something's wrong. It was Connerly's number that called, but he isn't talking anymore. I don't want to disconnect." She bounded out of the bed after him, hesitating for a moment when she realized she was naked. After snatching up his crumpled shirt from the floor, she drew it on and half ran after him to the office.

"Here." He thrust the phone at her. "I can't get at my contacts list without hanging up. Keep the line open. Try to get him talking again."

Sophia followed Cam to his office. "Where's Benally live?"

"Uh . . ." It took a moment to remember. "Bondurant. Not in the town. She bought something rural. She likes her privacy. Did something happen to Lucy? Or Gavin?" There was no sound from the cell she held to her ear.

Cam sat down at the computer and swiftly brought up a list of contacts. "Not really sure. But Connerly didn't sound great. I think he was trying to say the offender has Lucy. And that they're heading west."

Her stomach plummeted at the thought of brave, solitary Lucy at the hands of the perverted UNSUB she'd profiled. Lucy, who used an abrasive manner for the same reason others erected privacy fences. Lucy, the woman of contradictions who had left behind her ancestral Navajo aversion to dead bodies and dedicated her life to working with the same.

Cam dialed a number on her phone. She listened with one ear as she tried to summon the man on the other end of the phone she still held. "Gavin, are you there? It's Sophia. Are you hurt? Is Lucy?" Cam was biting out commands about sending an ambulance to the residence of Lucy Benally in rural Bondurant, Iowa. And he wasn't being pleasant about it.

"How the hell would I know the address? You have a listing of your residents, don't you? Find it. Fast." Disconnecting, he consulted his computer screen again and punched in another number.

"Gavin, if you're there, talk to me." Sophia's voice was low and soothing. She strained to hear a sound from the cell, but there was none. Not even breathing, which had her heart seizing. "Are you hurt? Is Lucy?" She kept up a running one-sided conversation in the hopes that if the man was there, if he was conscious he'd hear a familiar voice, at least.

But a cold fear was taking hold that he was unconscious. Or worse.

"Sorry about the hour, Dusten, but I've got an ambulance dispatched to Lucy Benally's place in Bondurant. Not sure of the address, so the service might need some help. We have reason to believe the UNSUB we're after might have been there. Sonny Baxter. And he may have taken Lucy when he left." Cam fell silent as the other man talked. "Yeah, whichever deputy you've got located closest would be fine. Give him this number." He reeled off Sophia's cell number from memory. "No, I'm staying here. Calling to mobilize my team. I need an update as soon as one's available. Thanks."

He spared a glance in Sophia's direction before turning to consult the computer screen again. "Anything from Connerly?"

She shook her head, her throat full, then belatedly became aware that he couldn't see the gesture. "No. I can't hear the sound of his breathing, either. But the line is still open."

Waiting for the phone to connect, his gaze met hers again. "Keep talking. If he's there, it might help to hear a voice."

If he's there. The words ricocheted in her head, even as she continued her monologue on the cell phone. She couldn't summon a reasonable explanation for the silence on the phone. Unless he was hurt. Unable to talk.

Or if he was . . . Her mind skittered away from the other idea that occurred. The one she didn't want to consider. "Everything's going to be all right, Gavin. Help is coming. Help will be there soon." More silence. Sophia wondered exactly what the medics would see when they entered Lucy's house.

The minutes ticked by with excruciating slowness. Cam called Franks and updated him, tasking the man with calling the rest of the team to tell them to stand by. He was currently on the phone with SAC Gonzalez. Sophia headed for the kitchen for a bottle of water. Her voice was growing hoarse with the endless talking.

"Gavin, tell me about Lucy. Did he take her? Where are they going?" She reached in the fridge for the water, but her hand froze in the act of retrieving one.

"Luce . . ."

The word was so faint that at first Sophia thought she'd imagined it. "That's right, Gavin. Lucy. Where's Lucy?"

"Rez . . ." His voice was stronger now, but slurred. "West. Luce. Give 'em . . . hell."

Sophia covered the phone with one hand as she raced back to Cam's office. "He's still alive! He's talking."

"Just a minute." Abruptly he cut off the person on the other phone to look at her. "Ask him if it was Sonny Baxter. If Lucy is still . . ." He stopped to amend his words. "If she's okay."

Sophia did as directed but was met by silence again. "I think he's in and out of consciousness." She snuck a look at the clock on Cam's computer screen. Eleven minutes since Cam had called for an ambulance. "But he did say Rez. And west." The words were puzzling. "Lucy grew up on the Navajo reservation. Utah, I think she might have said. Why would he take her there?"

A feral smile crossed Cam's lips even as he spoke into the phone he was holding. "Yeah, I'm still here." To Sophia he said, "It's like you've said before. Everyone has an anchor. Maybe that's Lucy's. Could be she figures to get him away from Connerly to a place where she has the advantage." He returned to his conversation on the cell. "I'm on it. I'll keep you updated."

Disconnecting, he rubbed his jaw. He'd shaved after showering, but already his face was stubbled. Just noticing it summoned a brief memory of the feel of its former smoothness against her naked thighs.

With a jerk, Sophia slammed the mental door on that memory and focused on what Cam was saying. "If he's heading to the reservation, it can only be because Lucy convinced him. That takes him away from the familiar, away from his anchor. That doesn't make sense, does it?"

"Unless he no longer has an anchor here." Sophia thought for a moment, flipping through mental files. "He has to know his house isn't safe anymore. He could have learned from the news that you discovered Martha Moxley's body. Vance's home is under surveillance, but Klaussen said she was never aware of anyone else visiting the house while she was imprisoned there. And none of the neighbors ID'd him from the sketches your agent showed them." She fell silent, her mind racing.

Cam surged to his feet. Glared at her silent cell while he paced the room.

"We know he's smart enough to stay off well-traveled roads," she mused. The offender had avoided traffic cameras by doing just that after he'd kidnapped Van Wheton. "So if he does head west, that's likely what he'll do. And he may travel close to a cemetery where the first six victims were buried."

He jerked around. Shot her a surprised look. "How do you know?"

She gave a slight shrug. "Those areas are familiar to him. You might want to check with Fedorowicz, see if Baxter ever mentioned traveling out of the Des Moines area. If Baxter doesn't think Moxley's vehicle is safe, he could have taken Lucy's or Gavin's." She broke off suddenly, listening hard at the cell she still had to her ear.

A powerful wave of relief surged through her. "It sounds like the medics are there."

As if summoned by her words, the cell Cam was holding sounded. Sophia listened, barely daring to breathe as he spoke tersely to whoever was on the line. She trailed behind him as he strode out of the room toward his bedroom, trying to glean a sense of what was happening at Lucy's house. Cam pulled a pair of pants out of his closet, sat on the edge of the bed, and drew them on with one hand. Then he strode to the dresser and pulled a pair of socks from his drawer. "Thanks for the update. Keep me posted if there are any other developments."

He tossed the cell on the bed and sat down again to drag on socks. "It's okay to disconnect. We'll trade."

With an odd sense of reluctance Sophia hung up and crossed to hand the phone to Cam, picking up her own. "Well?"

"Connerly's in rough shape." He stood, went back to the closet to choose a shirt. "At least two GSWs. Lost a lot of blood, but breathing. Only vehicle in the vicinity is Benally's, from the description."

"So Baxter has Gavin's or Moxley's," Sophia surmised.

"Moxley's car was over twenty years old. If he's smart, he ditched it close to Lucy's. He'll have taken Gavin's." Cam buttoned up a wine-colored shirt and jammed the tails into his gray pants before fastening them and going back to the closet for a suit coat.

"That makes sense. He'd suspect we'd know about Moxley. He'd realize it wasn't safe to keep it on the road too long. Unless . . ." When her voice tapered off, his gaze sharpened.

"Unless?"

"Unless he's suffered a complete mental break." Which, of course made him even more unpredictable.

Cam shrugged into the suit coat and shoved his feet into a pair of black dress shoes. He went to the dresser to pick up his credentials and then snagged the phone off the bed, placing a hand on Sophia's back as he moved toward the door, guiding her out of the room. "While you get dressed I'm putting out BOLOs on Moxley's and Connerly's cars and having roadblocks set up on westbound roads in a four-county area. It's a lot of miles to cover, and he's got a head start."

"So you'll alert state police in Nebraska. Possibly South Dakota."

His hand left her back and swept under the shirt to give her butt a pat. "I'll make a cop out of you yet. We're leaving in five."

That put a hurry in her step. His sense of urgency was contagious. The thought of Lucy trapped with a known murderer had the blood congealing in her veins. "You barely got dressed in that amount of time," she called over her shoulder, but the protest was automatic.

Lucy was in danger. Gavin was critically injured. The real concern wasn't how long it took her to get dressed.

It was whether it was already too late.

Chapter 14

The trunk of a car was no place for self-recriminations. But they were uppermost in Lucy's mind while she twisted and squirmed, trying to free herself.

If it hadn't been for her, Gavin would never have been at her place. Would never have encountered the deranged killer who seemed to think he and Lucy were soul mates. The truth of the observation seared through her. If she'd had the courage to have that talk he'd wanted at the office, it would have been over. He'd have gone back to his hotel room, perhaps with a bruised ego but alone. Safe.

Something inside her scoffed at the thought. Connerly was about as easy to get rid of as a burr on a shaggy mutt. And spending last night with the man had only made him more determined. The only way to have avoided his following her home was if she'd stayed all night at his hotel.

And that thought was as agonizing as the memory of leaving him bleeding in her kitchen.

Lucy didn't put much faith in hope. Hope was believing her mother's empty promises that things were going to change. That the newest job was going to bring them riches. That the latest boyfriend was going to be their ticket off the reservation, which her mother had despised.

Her little brother and sister had clung to false hope long past the age at which Lucy had stopped believing. But they could do that. Lucy had gone to work by that time to bring in enough money to put food on the table. She'd made sure there was a Christmas tree every year with a small present for each. Hope was useless. Determination was always the solution.

Until now. Because she had no logical reason to believe Gavin was alive. She'd gone to medical school. She knew what that amount of blood loss meant. But she stubbornly clung to the hope that she was wrong.

Believing otherwise made it almost impossible to gather the courage to plot her escape.

The zip ties seemed to grow tighter the more she struggled against them. Lucy had seen a YouTube video once showing how to break loose from the bonds. After several minutes in which she managed only to cut off her circulation even more, she was ready to track down the person in that video and beat an apology from him.

The trunk in her sensible midsize sedan would have allowed room to turn over. To move around in a search for anything in the area that could help her escape. But Gavin's small sports rental barely had room for her. An amenity that had likely escaped him when he signed the agreement. And she hadn't felt any objects rolling around. In all likelihood, the space was empty save for her.

She stopped her struggles for a moment to consider. At some point the offender was going to have to stop the vehicle, if only to relieve himself. At that point it was likely he'd allow her out to do the same. When he did so, she had to be ready. The way to inflict real damage would be to swing her legs up and out to kick him in the face. If her ankles weren't free, her success would be improbable.

And running away with her ankles bound would be impossible.

The tight confines of the trunk had her curled in an almost fetal position. With only a little more maneuvering, she could bring her knees closer to her chest and reach her ankles with her bound hands. Trying to break free of the binds might not have worked, but having two hands to work at them could be more successful.

The memory flashed through her mind then, in sudden, vivid Technicolor.

Gavin had badgered her unmercifully to tell him what the initial for her middle name stood for. She'd steadfastly refused to tell him so he'd resorted to guesses. Silly outlandish guesses.

"Is it Yamaha?"

"Idiot." Her slur was punished with a quick pinch on her ass. *"That's Japanese, not Navajo."*

"Yasmin? Yolanda? Yankee? Yancy? Yapany?"

"No, no, no, no, and eww."

He fell silent for an instant, his hand running over her spine almost absently. "I'll tell you mine if you tell me yours."

"But I don't care what your middle name is."

He rolled her over in the bed. Settled himself over her with his weight on his forearms. "But if you tell me, I'll shut up."

"Finally," she teased. *"An offer I can't refuse."* But it had taken a few more moments to tell him. Not from any reason to keep it secret, but because sharing the detail was a small intimacy that made her a bit uncomfortable.

Which, in light of their position was ridiculous. "It's Yanaha. It means brave."

"Yanaha." Gavin drew the word out as if savoring it. "It suits you." He pushed her hair away from her face in a motion that seemed almost caressing. *"Because something tells me you're the bravest woman I've ever met."*

The memory had her eyes blurring. She blinked away the tears, infuriated by the weakness. She didn't feel brave. She felt vulnerable and weak and terrified for Gavin. She told herself that he wasn't weak, either. But she'd autopsied victims with gunshot wounds. Knew the damage bullets did as they tore through a body.

The thought of what they'd done to Gavin's had the vise in her chest tightening.

The car came to a stop, and she stilled. When it pulled forward a moment later, the anticipation streamed out of her body. The pause hadn't been long enough for a traffic light, so it had only been a stop sign. And not one on a highly traveled road. If the man had a brain, he'd avoid the interstate. Iowa was crisscrossed with county and gravel roads that were lightly traveled and even more lightly patrolled.

The thought only made her resolve harden. In this instance, as in most of life, she had only herself to rely on. When the car stopped, as it would have to at some point, she was going to be ready.

But it wasn't only escape she was after. She was going to make this man pay for what he'd done to Gavin Connerly.

o o o

"Iowa State Patrol is out in force on major highways and county roads," Cam addressed his team by radio, on a channel reserved for their use. "Sheriff departments in neighboring counties have called in all available personnel to help patrol some of the lesser traveled blacktops." He shot a look at Sophie as he drove. "Dr. Channing thinks there's a good chance Baxter is familiar with the gravel roads and rural blacktops, especially around the town cemeteries where the first six bodies were discovered. She believes he may be drawn to travel those areas."

If Baxter knew they were after him, he'd travel north or south before heading west. But the man had no way of knowing that

Gavin had lived to warn them. They were banking everything on the accuracy of Connerly's information. Cam had a feeling this was their last shot at catching Baxter. And Lucy Benally's life depended on their success.

He finished by giving the agents their assignments. Cam was putting a lot of stock in Sophie's prediction and had placed his people in each of the counties where the first six victims had been buried. He himself was heading toward Dallas County. Sophie wanted to run by the small home housing Klaussen. According to Feinstein's office, the woman had left to go job hunting that morning, with the stated intention of having dinner with a friend. She hadn't returned before the callout.

When he was done, Cam looked at Sophie. Found her regarding him. "Patrol on the western sides of the counties will have roadblocks on every major road and highway. And we also have blocks set up every possible place he could cross the Raccoon River. Unless he plans to swim, there's no way for him to cross without detection." His assurance didn't chase the worry from her face.

"Klaussen's disappearance worries me." Her hands were tightly folded in her lap. "It seems likely that if Vance ordered Baxter to kill me, he'd also want to get rid of Van Wheton and Klaussen. All of us can provide evidence linking him to several crimes."

"Even if Baxter had known where Klaussen was being held, she was fine when she left Sheldahl this morning. It's unlikely that he would happen upon her while she was out searching for jobs."

"Unless he lured her somehow. Maybe he was the dinner date she mentioned."

Dawn was breaking behind them, lightening the sky a fraction at a time. "She said she'd never seen him. And we know she saw the sketch, so she'd be forewarned."

"I'd feel better if you added her car to the descriptor the patrol is looking for."

After a moment he reached out and did that. Set the radio down again and said, "Satisfied?"

"Not really." She gave a shake of her head under the drab wig. Cam found himself anxious for the day she got rid of it for good. And not just because it would mean that she was finally out of danger. A memory of her long, blonde hair spread out over his belly and thighs had him warming for an instant, before he firmly yanked his attention back to the matter before them. "Klaussen is a loose end. And Vance isn't the type to leave loose ends."

He scanned the upcoming intersection carefully, flipping on his LED dashboard strobe and going through it without breaking speed. Debating whether to share his next thought, he finally said, "She might have taken off. We didn't have cause to restrict her movements, but the fact that she didn't come home last night suggests that as a possibility."

"I hope you're right." Sophie shifted into a more comfortable spot. "Certainly it beats my fears. That we're going to find her dead and abandoned the same way you found Martha Moxley."

The words had barely left her lips when his cell rang again. It might be time, Cam thought wryly, to just glue the damn thing to his ear. But the unfamiliar voice on the other end of the call quickly caught his attention. "Department of Human Services," he murmured to Sophie and saw her straighten expectantly. But it was several more minutes before he was able to answer the questions that were clearly written on her face.

"Fedorowicz was right." Cam finally ended the call. He slowed for a tractor pulling out of a farmyard. Passed it. "Baxter had plenty of reason to be screwed up. His mom loaned him out to pedophiles for cash. Beat him. Burned him. When he was nine, her boyfriend had gotten a little too rough with her and left her tied up in the apartment. She tried to get the kid to untie her, and he attempted to strangle her instead."

"My God." Sophie's voice was faint. "That kind of abuse . . . the damage it'd inflict would take years of intensive therapy."

"Given the numbers of bottles in his medicine cabinet, therapy wasn't all he needed." He reached for his sunglasses to block the glare of the early morning sun. "Way it sounds, she never regained custody. But once Baxter ran from his last foster home, DHS lost track of him."

"So he stewed in his psychosis long enough to reenact that scene from his childhood. Strangling his mother over and over with every victim."

Cam reached forward to turn the LED light on again and blew through a deserted intersection on the blacktop. He hoped like hell that the sympathy in Sophie's tone was for the victims. Because despite Baxter's sad story, it was the man's actions as an adult that mattered.

And there would be no mercy shown when he was finally caught.

o o o

"Not good, Mommy. Not good at all." Sonny peered through the windshield at the line of cars stopped in the road. He buzzed down his window and craned his head out the window to see what was going on. Traffic had been almost nonexistent when he first started out. But over the course of forty minutes or so it had picked up steadily. He'd alternated gravel with rural blacktops, favoring the ones he knew best.

He'd once worked for Schwan's for a couple of years, delivering frozen goods to residences. He'd taken the rural routes that no one else wanted, because they involved more driving and fewer sales. But Sonny had liked it. He'd enjoyed the scenery. The quiet. He'd spent a lot of time exploring the area along the river. The wooded spots had always soothed the racket in his brain. Those times had been the happiest in his memory. Even if they had eventually led to him losing his job for not staying on his route.

But today he hadn't been able to take the roads he'd mapped out in his head. He'd hit a detour where a road was under construction and gotten off track. Right now he figured he was south of Perry only a mile or so, which he figured would be less traveled than the northern route. So unless there'd been an accident, there was no reason for the police presence.

A line of three cars was ahead of him. He could see a deputy leaning down to talk to the driver up front. Ahead of the deputy were two patrol cars blocking the intersection.

They're after you, Sonny. Get away now. Get away fast.

He ignored the voice in his head, watching the deputy wave the first car on. He wanted to see what would happen. The two squad cars parted to allow the vehicle through. Gauging the distance, he realized he'd never make it without having all three uniforms shooting to stop him.

He preferred better odds.

There was a steady thumping coming from the trunk. Lucy. Definitely not quiet. He could feel a headache coming, which ignited his temper. He had to be patient with her. It would take lessons, but she'd learn fast. They always did. The thumping came again. Louder. Continuous. Sonny could feel the burst of static in the back of his brain. A low constant buzz. But it'd get worse. Much worse.

He couldn't drive for days with that noise in the trunk. Lucy's lesson would have to come long before they reached their new home.

The deputy was still busy with the front car. A woman had gotten out of it and was yelling in the man's face. The argument had the drivers ahead of Sonny sticking their heads out of their windows to watch. Glancing in his rearview mirror, Sonny saw a pickup approaching. Now was the time to make his move, while the deputy was distracted and before he got boxed in.

Lucy began yelling. Yelling and thumping in a way that would go unnoticed as they drove. But it would definitely be heard if there was anyone nearby. The static in his head increased a notch.

He did a U-turn in the middle of the road and zoomed off the way he'd come. He checked his mirror again. The deputy wasn't paying attention to the woman anymore. He had a radio to his mouth. Sonny knew what that meant.

He pressed on the accelerator. He wasn't worried. Not really. The deputy was at a disadvantage. Sonny had a head start and he knew exactly where he was going.

And the first thing he'd do when he got there was deal with Lucy Benally.

o o o

Sheriff Feinstein had been right. There'd been no one home at the house where Rhonda Klaussen had been staying. The car she was using wasn't in sight. Cam and Sophia had tried looking in the windows, but with the shades drawn there was nothing to see, even with Cam's Maglite.

He hadn't mentioned the wasted trip as he drove east through Dallas County, and Sophia knew she should feel grateful for that. But what she felt instead was trepidation. Despite what they'd found—or hadn't found—her earlier concern for the woman refused to dissipate. Mason Vance wasn't one to leave witnesses. No one knew the man better than Klaussen had reason to. Sophia was beginning to hope that the woman *had* run. It might be safer for her than if Baxter found her and took care of one last item for his partner.

At Cam's direction she'd used her iPad to find online county plat maps. She'd systematically opened one site after another, until each of the counties that had roadblocks set up had a digital map open and available. Sophia hadn't even realized the maps existed. They might have come in handy navigating the gravel roads that crisscrossed the state in the era before GPS.

The radio crackled. Her muscles tensed, even though he'd been in constant contact with his team, the troopers, and sheriff offices since they'd left Des Moines.

"Cam, it's Jenna. I'm at the roadblock south of Perry on P58. We think we spotted a vehicle resembling Gavin's turning around rather than waiting its turn at the block."

Hope streaked up Sophia's spine. Bondurant was almost directly east of Ankeny, which was east of Perry. She leaned forward to speak into the radio Cam held. "Any sign of Lucy in it?"

"Negative." Cam took a right at the next corner and barreled toward Jenna's location. "We weren't even close enough for a license plate. But we're in pursuit."

Sophia took a moment to bring up the correct county plat map and held the screen up for Cam to consult.

"P58. If he's in that area, there are only a few other places he can cross the river. North of Perry on 144 or west of Minburn on F31. Do you have him in sight?"

"Not exactly. We're following the plume of dust. He went south on the first gravel. Holy shit." The radio went dead.

"Turner! Jenna!"

Sophia traced the route Jenna had indicated with her fingertip on the screen. "Gets pretty curvy and zigzaggy on that road," she murmured.

Jenna's voice came back on the radio. "Sorry about that. Almost missed a curve. Had two wheels off the road. Thought I was going to have to pull Deputy Koblaski out of the ditch."

"Stay in pursuit. Report back." Cam passed the radio to Sophia, and she did a silent exchange, handing him his cell. A moment later he had the Dallas County sheriff on the phone.

"I'm standing in front of the county plat wall map and directory," Sheriff Mort Feinstein said without preamble when he answered. It was obvious he'd been in close contact with his deputies. "We've got his only way over the river blocked, so he either has to head back east—"

"In which case he'll hit the Polk or Story County roadblocks," Cam inserted.

"Or he'll try for the next road over the river, which would be F31."

"The way I figure it we've got him boxed in on about a five-section area between US Highway 169 where he turned around, F25, US169, and F31."

"Wouldn't make sense for him to try to go north at this point," the other man agreed.

"I'll keep the roadblocks in place. I'm pulling my agents in to comb those sections. Do you have a digital plat directory you can email to me?"

The sheriff's voice sounded surprised. "Sure. You think he's going to hide out somewhere in the area?"

Cam slowed and pulled into a short farm drive that ran from the road over the ditch to the bordering field fence line. "He's trapped, even if he doesn't know it yet. He can try to blow through a roadblock, in which case I don't like his chances, or he can go to ground. Wait us out. That'd be a whole lot easier if he knows the area."

There was a pause for a minute. Then the sheriff came back on the line. "I just emailed the map to you. It has all the residences in the county with owners, occupants, and addresses. Although it sounds like you just need to focus on the one township if you're planning a door-to-door search. Call for backup if you need it."

After finishing that call, Cam immediately made another, ordering a State Patrol Air Wing pilot to divert to the five-section area.

That would give them eyes in the air and on the ground, Sophia realized. The noose was tightening around Sonny Baxter.

She waited for Cam to complete the call before saying, "He could try for a wooded area along the river, much like the one he chose for his dump site. Someplace he's been before, somewhere he's comfortable. I don't think it would occur to him to go to one of the rural homes if he didn't know it already. This isn't a social offender. Although capable of organization when given time to plan, we saw at his house how close he is to coming completely unwrapped. He's going to want safe. He's going to want familiar. He'll know he needs a different vehicle to escape detection."

"You don't think he'll just steal a car?"

"Maybe." She smiled a little when she saw Cam's frustrated expression. "But it will be from the place he goes where he feels some measure of security." She sobered at the next thought. "As the stress he's under increases, he'll become more erratic. Difficult to predict. But one thing for certain. The more pressure that's brought to bear on him, the greater the danger Lucy is in."

o o o

The darkness in the trunk reflected Lucy's thoughts. She'd known that when the car had stopped it meant her best chance to attract attention. But then the driver had turned around. Sped away.

She could spend all day spinning rosy scenarios about the reasons for the offender's abrupt change of direction. But she didn't hear any sirens in the distance, so she didn't kid herself that help was anywhere in the vicinity. And they were on gravel again. She could tell by the steady ping of rocks hitting the undercarriage of the car. By the dust that filtered in the cracks of the trunk and caused her to wheeze. Gravel roads in the state were like a rabbit warren. Obviously plotted according to some grand design evident only to county engineers and the farmers that traversed them regularly. And he was driving fast. The roads weren't maintained with the regularity of blacktop. She was bounced and jostled as he hit potholes and ruts, one time banging her head on the top of the trunk with enough force to see stars.

Lucy gritted her teeth. Squeezed her eyes shut to keep out the dust. Yet another thing the freak would pay for. His debt was mounting.

She wondered about Gavin then, and a vise clutched her heart. The image of him lying on her kitchen floor with the lifeblood leaking from him was too vivid. Branded on her mind. So instead she deliberately sought another mental picture of him. One that evoked better memories. Of Connerly, lazily leaning against her desk or the stainless steel counter in the autopsy suite. Of her running her fingers through his straight, blond hair that he kept only inches shorter than hers, once he released it from the thong he usually pulled it back with. Of the way his pale-green eyes could light with amusement. Narrow with annoyance.

And he'd been annoyed the last time she'd seen him. He must have wakened shortly after she'd dressed and slipped out of his room. And then, true to form, chased her through the night, unwilling to let her circumvent their conversation so easily. A more stubborn man she may never have met.

And that stubbornness just might have gotten him killed.

The vehicle slowed, turned sharply. Lucy was thrown to the side. Righted herself with effort. Her back was sore from its constant contact with the imperfections in the roads. But she forgot the aches when another realization occurred.

They were coming to a stop again.

Immediately she tried to yell, but her voice was dry and raspy with the dust she'd swallowed. Instead she began to kick her feet as hard as she could against the sides of the trunk. She'd managed to get the zip ties off them prior to the first stop, so her feet were free.

She only hoped she'd have a chance to use them.

There was the sound of gravel crunching. Then the lid of the trunk popped open with a suddenness that had her ducking away from the bright sunlight. "You've been very bad." The man reached in and hooked his hand in the bonds securing her hands and yanked her out of the trunk.

Before she could get her legs under her, he dealt her a ringing slap that made her ears ring. She ducked his next blow so it caught her in the shoulder instead. "I'm sorry. I'm sorry. I was just trying to get your attention." She kept her head down in what she hoped looked like a cowed position. All the while surreptitiously studying the area where they'd stopped with her peripheral vision. "I have to go to the bathroom. I'm sorry. I can't help it."

She started to struggle to her feet, thought better of it. If he hadn't yet noticed that her ankles were no longer bound, there was no reason to bring it to his attention. "I understand." The hand in her hair, on her throat seemed almost caressing. Recalling that each victim they'd found had suffered a broken neck, she shuddered in revulsion.

"Lessons can be hard. But the sooner you learn to be quiet, the happier both of us will be." Because her head was still bowed, she didn't see his fist coming until it was too late. The blow caught her in the side of the jaw and sent her sprawling.

She was still disoriented when he dragged her to her feet again. "See what you made me do? I don't like violence. I really don't. But believe me, these lessons are a lot easier than the ones my mommy used to teach me."

His mommy? What brand of crazy was this twisted pervert? "I understand now. I really do."

"Do you?" His hand came down to brush the hair away from her face. "Do you really?"

"Better than you think." She surged to her feet, driving both bound fists upward as she rose. Caught him in the crotch hidden behind the baggy skirt. His fingers tightened in her hair as he doubled over. She aimed a vicious kick at his thigh. When he gave a high-pitched keening scream she followed up by driving her fists upward toward his nose.

Blood spurted, but she was still caught securely. "Fuck you fuck you little bitch little fucking cunt. I'll kill you now I'll fucking kill you." His right hand was twisted in her hair. She saw the gun in the right pocket of the sagging sweater and grabbed at it as he was trying to disentangle his fingers to draw out the weapon.

Her fingers were numb from the tightness of the bonds. She touched the grip of the weapon before her hands were knocked away. She threw herself from one side to the other, kicking and fighting, wincing in pain as strands of hair were ripped from her head during her struggles. He tried to push her away so he could draw the gun. She went for it again. Got it out of his pocket. Dropped it.

Giving her a violent shove, he bent awkwardly to pick up the weapon. Lucy sprang to her feet and ran toward him, kicking the weapon out of his reach and then used the heel of her foot to kick at the thigh he seemed to be favoring. The man screamed again, dropped to one knee. And then she kept on running.

Stumbling as she weaved and dodged, she traced a zigzag pattern that only a fool would believe could thwart a bullet. At any second she expected to hear one whiz past her ear. Feel it spear through her body.

She sprinted across the farmyard, behind a rusty machine shed. Nearly wept when she saw that the field fencing didn't border the farm property. Likely the farmer had left it open for easy access of the equipment.

Now it just meant freedom.

Lucy didn't look back. She didn't want to know if the offender was gaining on her. She didn't want to see the weapon aimed in her direction, knowing that any moment a bullet was going to slam into her body the way it had Gavin's. Fear lent her feet wings, and she curved and angled back and forth across the uneven soil, trampling the beans growing there without compunction.

And while she mentally prepared to die, she thought of the man she'd left bleeding out on her kitchen floor.

o o o

"We're doing a grid search of the properties in the five-section area where we think he might be holed up. Got lucky, and found the owners home on all of them so far. I've got the team spread out, poring over every acre." Cam spoke tersely into the phone as he retraced his steps to the vehicle. Gonzalez necessarily wanted to be updated, but right now her call was a distraction he could ill afford. He'd had nothing to report on the four places he'd checked so far. And he could feel time rapidly running out.

But apprising the SAC of every development was necessary to keep the resources flowing. The massive manhunt under way represented a substantial financial cost to the state. The Air Wing support alone was a major ticket item. So he'd play by the rules even while he chafed at the need for them.

"Nothing to report from the road team." He'd opened his email on Sophie's iPad and now studied the plat directory Feinstein had sent him. "He hasn't tried to cross the river again. Doesn't mean he doesn't plan to." He listened for a moment and made a sound of agreement. "If he's here, we'll find him. I'll keep you updated."

When he hung up Sophie was using an app tool to highlight spots on the roads and properties delineated on the screen. "We've cleared these homesteads," she said, tracing four highlighted areas. "These other spots I've colored indicate those checked by your agents so far."

Cam bent closer to study the map. The agents were spread out and working inward. Pressing in on Baxter, hopefully, unless he'd somehow managed to slip by them again. Franks and Robbins had been given the wooded spots closer to the river. Although it would be impossible to cover the dense woods, all they had to do was find the vehicle for the direction of the manhunt to change.

"We have two other homesteads on this road before we hit this gravel intersection." Sophie traced her finger on the road delineated on the screen. "We'll have to decide then whether to continue on this road or start on the east–west one."

Cam started the vehicle. By then it would be time for another update from his team, and they'd reassess. He was heading out of the farm driveway when he received another radio call. He stopped again. Picked up the receiver.

"Prescott."

He could hear the roar of the Air Wing pilot's motor in the background. "I've got a visual of someone running through a field, headed north. I'm going to circle the property, drop down a bit closer. I'll let you know if I sight a vehicle."

Sophie clutched his arm. Even without her reaction, a burst of adrenaline surged through his veins. "What are your coordinates?"

The man quoted his longitude and latitude positioning, and Sophie used the tool to mark an X on the screen to delineate the spot. Cam stared hard at it. "That's about four miles from here. I'll head over that way."

"Sounds good."

Gravel spewed behind him as he turned out of the drive. Threw a hard grin at Sophie. "I guess we decided to go west at the intersection."

Her gaze met his. She'd forgotten to put in the brown contacts this morning, he realized. Maybe, just maybe, the need for the disguise was soon coming to an end. "If it's Lucy the pilot saw, it means she got away. She's still standing," she said.

"If it's Lucy," he cautioned. He barely slowed at the next corner before taking it wide and picking up speed. "But it still leaves a big question. What the hell happened to Baxter?"

Chapter 15

Sonny doubled over, pressing his hands to his ears. A million angry bees were droning in his head, the din making it impossible to think. Only one voice could be heard. The same one that always cut through the noise with bladelike precision. *You fuckup. What a disappointment. Can't you fucking do anything right?*

"I'll kill you again," he mumbled to the voice. "I'll bury you this time, too. You'll never come back. Not ever." But when his gaze raised to the direction Lucy had run, the voice faded away, replaced with rage.

This was the police's fault. Fucking roadblocks. Lucy had been fine, just fine in the trunk. Another few lessons and she would have learned to be so sweet. So understanding. They could have explored death together, and she'd begin to see, Sonny knew she would, exactly what drew him to the dead. They would have made a perfect combination.

And now he had nothing.

He picked up the weapon and struggled to his feet. The little bitch had landed a hard kick at his wounded thigh. He could feel wetness clinging to the jeans he had rolled up under the skirt and knew the injury had reopened. He had to tend to it. Get patched up and think about what to do next.

Turning to look at the property, he was struck by how much it had changed since he'd first seen it. Gone were the apple trees the owner, Gladys Stewart, had been so proud of. No more apple pie to offer Sonny when he stopped here on his route. No more chatting over coffee later, which she'd insisted he needed to thaw out from the cold delivery truck.

Unconsciously he headed toward the back door of the tidy single-story ranch. It had been years since he'd seen Gladys. He hadn't known how much he missed her until this moment. He crossed the yard. Climbed the two concrete steps to the door and opened the screen. The bump key was still in his pocket. He used it now and walked into the back entry.

Past melded with present in a disjointed abstract. He wiped his feet on the mat that was still there. Gladys always had insisted on that, in that kind way of hers. Sonny walked past the mudroom and laundry area, took a right through the kitchen, and stopped when he saw her.

"What the fuck are you doing here?"

He frowned. It wasn't Gladys at all. It was Mommy standing in the living room, belting a robe around her waist. Gladys never had that mean in her voice. Gladys was always sweet and kind.

"Did you hear me? Why didn't you call? You know you're not supposed to be here."

Sonny stayed very still. It helped manage the noise in his head. Mommy approached him. Circling like an irritated jungle cat.

"I'm in trouble. My Lucy . . ." A sudden sense of loss hit him then, and he stifled a sob. Brought his free hand up to wipe at tears that suddenly blinded him.

"What's loose? What the hell is wrong with you?" Mommy gave him a hard shove on the shoulder. "You need to man up before you ruin everything. I've told you a million times not to come here for a while. I'll call you with your instructions. Or come to your place."

"I don't like you in my house," he muttered. Her image planted there, popping up when he least expected it, superimposed on the counter while he poured a glass of water. On the ceiling before he closed his eyes to sleep. "Stay out of my house."

She gave a bark of laughter. "Same goes, asswipe. Listen, you need money? I'll give you more. But you have to go home, lay low until I contact you again. Police are all over the place after finding those bodies you ditched."

Desolation howled through him. His special place. Gone. Like Janice was gone. Lucy. Everything he'd worked for, everything that had been *his* . . . all gone. And the reason, the reason for everything bad in his life was standing right in front of him.

"That's not my fault." He raised his hand, pointed the gun at her. "It's yours. I've lost everything and it's *your fault*! You should never have come back, Mommy. You should never have made me kill you again."

o o o

"I've got a visual on the vehicle matching the description you gave." The pilot's voice was calm as he read off the coordinates.

"Almost there. Thanks."

"Let me know if you need anything else. Out."

Cam immediately put a call out to his team. "All vehicles to the following address." He read off the road address and the coordinates. "We've got a positive ID on Connerly's vehicle there."

The radio burst with voices of the other agents as they gave their current location and approximate arrival times. They'd been close to the center of the grid they'd been working, so no one should be more than a few miles away.

Jenna's voice sounded. "Cam, I've got eyes on the woman the pilot saw. It's Lucy. We're picking her up."

Sophia made a soft sound beside him. Cam glanced over to see her hands clasped at her lips. And wondered if she was thinking of her own harrowing escape from Vance only days earlier. "Good." He gave her the coordinates of the property a half mile up the road. "I'm calling all vehicles in. Connerly's car has been ID'd in the drive. If Baxter isn't there now, he hasn't been gone long."

"Don't start without me."

Now that the endgame was about to begin, Cam could feel a cold calm descending over him. "I'm not making any promises."

o o o

Mommy threw her hands up. "Whoa, calm down. Have you been taking your meds? We both need to keep a clear head." She kept circling, circling. Sonny had to turn, too, to keep her in his sights. "You've been such good help." Her voice went low and soothing. Not like Mommy's at all. "You've done everything I asked. You take good care of Mommy. Best boy in the world—that's you."

"I'm tired," he whispered. He felt bone weary. Sad. Defeated. "I can't cross the river. We were going to Lucy's special place, but I can't get by the roadblocks. How am I going to get west if I can't pass the roadblocks?"

"Roadblocks?" Mommy's voice had sharpened again. "Are they looking for you? And you brought them to me? What the fuck were you thinking?"

He ducked, as if dodging the expected blow that would have accompanied the words in his childhood. Disappointing Mommy meant he always had to pay. And pay and pay and pay.

"I want to see Gladys. I miss Gladys."

"Jesus, you freak." She yanked him to a stop with a hand bunched in his sweater when he would have gone in search of his friend. "This was your gig. You set it up, and, man, it was a beauty.

Gladys might not be around anymore, but the cash rent payments on her four hundred acres will continue to keep us comfortable as long as we want. You see what land prices are doing around here? I'm trying to figure a way to sell the whole property, but it'll be a whole lot trickier than accessing her rent payments. Why don't you go home now and think about how we can pull that off?" She smiled real big. Her face wavered, then morphed into a skull. Two empty eye sockets and a jaw of grinning teeth.

"You should have stayed dead." He trailed her movements with the gun. "This time I'll bury you. They always stay dead when I bury them." Sonny frowned. "I think. I don't know about Channing. She might come back. She didn't get buried."

"How sad and lonely were you when I came back, huh? When you were living in that crappy little foster home and I found you and let you come and stay with me?"

Mommy kept moving around him. It made him dizzy following her. "I took care of you. I helped you make something of yourself."

He shook his head, winced at the pain. "No. You made me find the women. Help you hurt them and use their money. You're not a good mommy. You brought the bad men home. You've never been a good mommy!"

She launched herself at him then and knocked him to his knees. She wanted the gun, and he let her have it. Guns wouldn't stop Mommy. There was only way to stop her. He reached up and wrapped his fingers around her throat. Squeezed. She gasped, brought fingers up to tear at his grip. But he was strong. Much stronger than when he'd killed her before. "This time you'll stay dead."

The shot hurt his ears. Sonny looked down. His fingers were loose on Mommy's throat. Odd. The second shot drove him up and back, and he felt the pain now, the searing agony. Worse than when she'd let the men use him. Even worse than that. The third shot had him slumping to the floor next to her. The buzzing in his head ceased.

He never felt the next two bullets.

"Fuck. Fuck. Fuck!" The woman known as Rhonda Klaussen screamed the words as she rose. "You've ruined everything, you stupid little prick. Everything!" She kicked Sonny's lifeless body, over and over again until the exertion calmed her. Then remorse filtered through. Her little Sonny. Her baby boy. Someone was going to pay for this.

She ran to the TV and turned it to the local channel. A female anchor's somber face filled the screen. ". . . county manhunt for the man many have coined the Zombie Lover. He's believed to be an accomplice of Mason Vance, who's awaiting trial for the alleged murders of—"

Not waiting to hear more, Rhonda hurried to the spare bedroom. If her idiot son was on the run, the cops wouldn't be far behind him. And by coming here, he'd ruined a smooth little operation that had netted them nearly a couple hundred thousand a year, and that was aside from what the women had brought in. *Fuck.* She grabbed a bag and started stuffing in bankbooks, cash, records, and receipts . . . anything that would give the bastards a place to start.

She ran through the house and out the door, sprinting for the detached garage that held the brand-new four-wheel-drive pickup that Mase had just had to have. Liked to spend it, that guy did. Throwing the bag into the second seat, she climbed into the truck and revved it to life.

When the cops got here—and she had no doubt they were on their way—they'd find the kid. Sonny. Probably eventually find old Gladys Stewart, too, if they happened to search that abandoned cistern behind the barn.

Rhonda pulled out of the drive and headed down the road, the back of the truck skidding a bit when she hit a patch of loose gravel.

That agent, Prescott . . . she had a feeling he'd never completely bought her story. It was only a matter of time until he discovered that the real Rhonda Klaussen had been dead for almost eight years. Time to ditch that identity.

And go back to being Vickie Baxter.

o o o

The farmhouse was cleared much too quickly for the offender to be hiding inside it. With a flicker of surprise Sophia saw Cam come to the back door and wave her inside only minutes after the team had swarmed the home. Agents Beachum, Robbins, and Patrick headed out the door and fanned out on the property.

"UNSUB's dead inside," Alex Beachum said as he passed her.

The relief was overpowering. Sophia stood still, drawing several deep breaths until the strength returned to her knees. It was over. The words reverberated through her mind, rippling and eddying, making them hard to hang on to. There would be no new victims. More bodies, she grimaced, remembering the call Cam had taken right before he and his team had surrounded the house. But no new ones. Lucy was alive.

She winged a silent prayer for Courtney Van Wheton as she climbed the two back steps to the house. The only thing that would make this ending perfect would be to get word that the woman had come out of the coma she'd been in since shortly after her escape.

Baxter's body was in the living room. Sophia recoiled just a little at the bizarre sight. Still dressed in Moxley's clothes, he was sprawled on his side in pools of blood that hadn't yet congealed.

"Suicide?"

Cam, not surprisingly, was on the phone. He covered the mouthpiece to say, "Homicide. I'm guessing no more than fifteen minutes ago. Maybe less." While he resumed his conversation, Sophia looked through the house, careful not to touch anything before the crime scene team arrived.

The decor was dated. In one bedroom she found a double bed with an afghan coverlet neatly folded at its foot. On the walls were wedding pictures that had to be at least fifty years old, judging by the hairstyles. She used the sleeve of her jacket to cover the knob of the closet door so she could open it. Women's clothing hung from rods inside. Sophia checked the dress sizes. Fourteen. Nothing that looked to have been in fashion for years.

When she rejoined Cam in the library, he was off the phone. Squatted next to the body. "According to the plat directory, this residence belongs to Gladys Stewart."

"Is she . . ." Sophia hated to put the thought into words. "Still alive?"

His mouth flattened. "Guess we'll find out. That was the lab on the phone. They cleaned up that bracelet found on one of the victims. Just a cheap mass-market-produced rubber bracelet, but they were able to recover enough of the message to be fairly certain of it. 'Prayers for Ivan.'"

From the expression on his face, that information was obviously supposed to mean something to her. It didn't. "What's the significance of that?"

"According to the lab, Ivan Krensky was a five-year-old boy from Norwalk fighting a rare form of leukemia. The bracelets were sold as a fund-raiser to help his parents seek experimental medical treatment for him. He died six years ago."

"Six . . . but . . . Vance was in jail six years ago."

"Sort of puts a whole new light on things doesn't it?" He squatted down, pulled out a pair of scissors he must have taken from the kitchen. Began cutting the sweater and underlying shirt off Baxter's body, slicing it down the back into two neat halves.

"What are you doing?" His actions were as baffling as his words had been moments earlier. Dead bodies were the jurisdiction of the ME. Period, end of story.

"Checking out a hunch. DHS said that when Baxter was a kid his mother beat him. Burned him. I started thinking about Klaussen. And how the picture changes if you ignore the story she told us about being Vance's first victim." He dropped the scissors back in his suit pocket and carefully pulled aside the two halves of material. Unconsciously, Sophia stepped closer to look at what he bared. Found her stomach hollowing out.

The scars on Baxter's skin were old. Faded. But the number they formed was unmistakable. Two.

"Oh, my God," she breathed. Mental puzzle pieces snapped into place, but the picture still wasn't clear. "Klaussen lied about not knowing him. She had to have. Maybe the three of them were connected someway even before Vance went to prison in Nebraska." She shook her head. The pieces still didn't make sense. "Fedorowicz pegged Baxter's age as twenty-eight. He'd have still been a teen when Vance went inside . . ."

"Vance isn't responsible for the four, no, make it five bullet holes in Baxter." Their gazes met in mingled comprehension.

"Klaussen did this?"

"No honor among thieves. Or serial killers, as the case may be." He got to his feet. "I'm guessing one of the agents out there is going to find the old wreck of a vehicle Klaussen was given to drive hidden in one of the outbuildings."

Sophia didn't answer. She couldn't. Because the details of the evidence found on the property wasn't her primary concern right now.

It was the inescapable fact that this case wasn't over at all. Not even close.

o o o

Cam looked around as they were led to their table on the outdoor patio of Mickey's. "The significance of this place doesn't escape me. I've grown increasingly fond of it in the last few weeks."

She smiled sedately. The first night they'd gone home together last month Cam had happened upon her sitting at this very table, not entirely sober and brooding over a margarita. The news that her ex was going to be a father, coupled with his wedding announcement, had held enough bite to send her out to drown her sorrows. She smiled wryly. Amazing what being kidnapped, beaten, nearly raped, and almost assassinated would do to realign a woman's priorities.

But that was giving Mason Vance much too much credit. The man sitting across from her was the cause of her uncharacteristic change from a woman who kept her feet firmly on the ground to the one who now, emotionally at least, was on the high-wire working without a net.

The waitress brought the drinks Sophia had preordered. A glass of wine for her and a Blue Moon for Cam. He took a drink of the beer and set it down again, a satisfied expression on his face. "Feels good to relax for a little while. Think about the things that have gone right lately."

Sophia raised her glass, toasted him. "Lucy is alive. Gavin will be okay." Although not, she felt a pang, without a second surgery and some grueling rehab. "Agent Boggs is recovering nicely at home, according to his wife. Plenty to be thankful for."

He drank, set his bottle down. "I received a new batch of lab results that I need to go through. And the ME's office called about the autopsy tomorrow on victim—"

"Just an hour away from the case." Sophia reached over to touch his hand. "Sixty minutes or the length of the meal, whichever is longer. We deserve that much, don't you think?"

"You do." In a smooth motion, he had her hand in his. "You deserve far more. You can't deny the case is taking a toll." His fingers stroked the back of her hand.

"And no talking about the case while we're here."

"Wow," he said mildly, reaching to tip his bottle to his lips again. "You're strict. That's kind of hot. It'd be more so if you were dressed in leather, issuing commands, but still."

"Incorrigible." She didn't try to hide her amusement. "And it's not a command, it's . . . a suggestion."

"Well, as it happens"—he curled her hand in his—"I'm in the mood to be easily swayed by suggestion. Especially yours."

Seeing her opening, she took a deep breath. "That's good. Because I have another. It concerns the two of us."

She told herself that she was prepared for the immediate mask of wariness that descended over his expression. But judging from the kick in her chest, she'd been lying to herself. It took a measure of courage to continue meeting his gaze. "I know you think my joining you in the shower the other night was an aberration."

He moved his shoulders uncomfortably. The shadows turned his eyes dark. Unfathomable. "Not the phrase I'd use, but yeah. Something like that."

Sophia leaned forward. "It wasn't. I knew exactly what I wanted then, and I do now. My thinking has actually cleared over the last few weeks."

This time the pull he took from his beer was longer, as if he required fortitude. When he put the bottle down, he seemed to choose his words carefully. "You're a professional, Soph. You've worked with people who have gone through traumatic experiences, and I'm guessing one of the things you'd tell them would be not to make life-altering decisions until their emotions settle down. I have it on good authority that relationships that get their start under intense circumstances never last."

She pulled away and sat back, torn between hurt and humor. "Even I know that's a movie quote. And I rarely watch movies."

He lifted a hand. "Sandra Bullock and Keanu Reeves, *Speed*. But it's still true. Trauma affects the way we think. That's why the agency made damn sure the PTSD I suffered from after the task force was under control before I was cleared for active duty again."

"You're forgetting one thing." She waited for his gaze to meet hers. "Our relationship started before this case ever began."

"I'm not forgetting anything. Actually it was over before the case started, and I'm certain you had your reasons. Didn't tell me what they were, but you had them."

"They seemed to make sense at the time." Thinking of the awkward breakup, she winced a little. "I'd spent my entire life doing what was safe. What was smart. Getting involved with you was neither." She stroked the stem of her wineglass as she spoke. The rhythmic movement calmed her jittery nerves a little. "But guess what? Playing it safe doesn't guarantee safety. Being smart doesn't guarantee happiness. So I'm through playing it safe."

She met his eyes. He barely seemed to be breathing. "I had sex with you the other night because I wanted to. Because I'm through running away from my feelings. I plan to do it again. Frequently. So consider this fair warning."

Sophia took her time rising, rounding the table to bend down and kiss him lingeringly before straightening. "And now I'm going to the ladies room to give you the opportunity to miss me a little."

Before she could leave, he pulled her back down for a more thorough kiss. Both of them were breathing heavily when their lips parted. "I miss you already."

Sophia smiled slowly. "That was the plan."

Cam watched her wend her way through the tables to enter the building. Stop to throw him a glance over her shoulder before continuing through the doors. He sat back and blew out a breath, feeling like he'd just been pole-axed. There wasn't a man with a pulse who wouldn't react to that kind of invitation from Sophia Channing. With or without the wig and makeup she was still Sophie. Still fascinating. Complex. Gut-wrenchingly sexy.

And if he was being perfectly honest, he was probably more susceptible than most. It'd be easy to pass off his feelings for her as protectiveness. Concern. But like she'd said, they'd started before the case ever began. And when she'd walked away, his feelings hadn't dimmed.

He ran his thumbnail around the label of the bottle. Chances were, there'd come a time, probably not in the far-off future, when she'd come to her senses again. When she'd recognize that every reason she'd had for walking away the first time was still valid. He let the certainty of that thought sink over him, knotting the muscles in his gut. She wasn't a risk taker. She hadn't needed to tell him that.

But he was. And if ever there was a risk worth taking, it was Sophie Channing. He rose, withdrawing his wallet to extract a couple bills to throw on the table. He headed for the doors she'd disappeared through in search of her.

There were far more pleasurable ways to spend sixty minutes than having dinner.

o o o

Sophia smiled at her reflection in the mirror after touching up her lipstick. The woman looking back at her was still a stranger, but it wasn't the disguise that mattered. It was the act of bravery—and it had required more emotional courage than it should have—to tell Cam how she felt. He didn't quite believe it, not yet, but if he were given a chance, he would.

She snapped her purse shut and left the restroom, ridiculously eager to return to their table. A man brushed against her, muttered an apology. "It's fine," she started to say. Until he turned and said loudly, "Mona Kilby, is that you? My God, how long has it been?" He pulled her close for a hug, murmuring in her ear, "I have a gun pointed at your gut. Messy cleanup. Do what I say."

Her organs froze in reaction. She tried to shove him away, at least to wedge enough distance between them that she could get a better look at his face. And when she succeeded her heart stuttered in her chest.

Matthew Baldwin.

The man who Cam had risked his career to save. The same one who might well be in Iowa to kill Cam for his part in crippling the Sinaloa cartel.

She thought fast. "My car is parked out front. Why don't we continue this . . . reunion out there?"

The man's teeth flashed. "You're a cool one." One hand was in his jacket pocket. A jacket, though it was still eighty degrees out. Her gaze lingered on the bulge there. "I happen to know there's a very bored federal agent parked close to your car. So I'm going to take a pass on that."

"What do you want?"

"I want a conversation with Cam." He propped a hand on the wall close to her face, leaning in like an old friend catching up. People passed them without a glance. "I figure in another few minutes he'll come looking for you. Until then, you're not going to scream. You're not going to make a scene or do any one of the things running through your head right now. Or when he walks up to us I'll put a bullet in his skull. Got it?"

She moistened her lips. "I understand." There wasn't a doubt in her mind that he'd follow through on his threat. And she was equally certain that she'd do everything she could to prevent it. She gasped suddenly, then began wheezing, feigning an asthma attack. "I . . . it's my asthma. Please." She fumbled with her purse. The small can of pepper spray was still on her key ring, courtesy of Agent Micki Loring. Sophia had her hand in the purse searching for it when it was snatched away from her.

"Looking for a nebulizer? Or . . . this?" He brought out her keys, the spray cupped in his palm and grinned at her. Sophia's fists curled into balls. The next person that happened by, she'd shove the man, run to warn Cam. He wouldn't shoot her in view of a witness. She was almost certain of it.

"Well. Someone's impatient." Following the direction of his gaze, Sophia's heart plummeted. Cam was approaching the back of the restaurant. And she recognized the exact moment when he noticed them together.

His face went hard. Expressionless. And as he closed the distance between them Sophia seized on the fact that he, too, was armed. It didn't diminish her concern. But it helped even the odds.

"Old buddy. How 'bout those Cubbies?"

Cam surveyed the man unflinchingly. "Matt. Came a long way to talk baseball."

"Well, it's my passion." He gave Cam a once-over. "Prison suits you. But then again, you didn't go to prison after that bust, did you?"

"Neither did you."

The undercurrents to their words were rife with meaning. Cam stared at him a minute longer then said, "We'll discuss it one-on-one. She doesn't need to be here."

Baldwin shook his head. "Can't take the chance that she'll alert your federal friends out front. She stays. I'm not carrying." He took his hand out of his pocket and held both arms away from his body. Cam did a brisk, thorough frisk. Nodded.

"Okay. But we're not going out the back. Not that I don't trust you, old *pal*, but I don't want to run into any buddies you might have waiting in the alley."

"Fair enough." The man turned around, spied an open booth, walked toward it. Feeling a bit surreal, Sophia slid in next to Cam.

"Moreno has Gabriela and Zoe." The man wasted no time. "They're staying at his estate. He pretends it's to provide care for Zoe after she was so sick a while ago, but they're not free to leave. Gabriela realizes that. She's scared for the baby." Matt swallowed hard. "I'm scared for both of them."

Cam was silent for a moment. "Why didn't you leave when you heard the bust was going down? Moreno didn't have them then. You had the opportunity."

"Think I didn't know?" The blond man leaned forward. "I was two blocks away from returning to the meeting when I saw the place swarming with federal agents. I got in my car and headed home, fully intending on scooping up Gabby and the baby and heading to an airport. Didn't matter where we went, at least not at first. I could worry about laying a false trail later. Once they were safe."

He rapped the table lightly with his knuckles. "But when I got home, Gabriela was rushing Zoe to the hospital. Her cold had turned to pneumonia. She was there for eight days, four in critical care." His smile was terrible. "Gave me a reason for missing the bust, so my little girl almost dying is the only reason Moreno let me live."

The explanation was close enough to what Harlow had told him the other night to ring true. Or Harlow could have been fed faulty information to make what Cam was hearing right now *sound* like the truth. He rubbed his jaw.

"You understand the credibility issue here, right?"

"I do." The man gave a slow nod. "Especially since I was given the task of finding you and killing you if you weren't in prison."

When Sophie gave a little gasp, Cam found her hand under the table. Squeezed it reassuringly.

"But here's the thing." Baldwin looked from one of them to the other. "I'll go right out that front door with you. Turn myself over to the feds. I wasn't exactly promoted after the whole thing went down, but Moreno is having a hard time rebuilding with the pressure they're still putting on his operation. I know things. His new routes. The schedule of shipments. I'll give the feds everything I've got, but first they have to come up with a workable plan for getting my family away from Moreno." He sat back. "I don't care about prison. All I want is safety for my wife and child."

Cam glanced at Sophie. Saw the understanding on her face. "We're sort of in the middle of a case. I've still got a killer to catch."

Baldwin nodded. "I have a little while. But only a little. I've been following your case. When it's over . . . I want your word that you'll help me find a way through this."

There was an easy decision to make here. All Cam had to do was alert the agent in the car out front. Let them haul Baldwin off and get the information he seemed so desperate to give.

That would be the safe thing. The smart thing. There was no reason for Cam to be involved. Unless he remembered the times he'd sat at Matt and Gabriela's kitchen table, sharing a meal with them. Recalled being asked to act as Zoe's godfather at her baptism.

He could pretend the man sitting across from him was no different from the other drug runners who had been on Moreno's payroll.

But that would be a lie.

Feeling as if he were stepping off the edge of a very steep precipice, Cam nodded.

"You have my word."

Acknowledgments

Writing can be a very solitary pursuit. Until, that is, the author needs some expertise with research. As it happens, *this* author tends to veer in directions I know very little about, so I'm always grateful for people who spring to my rescue when I send out a frantic email ☺.

Special thanks once again to John Graham, ex-narc extraordinaire, for all things DCI-related—the details are always a tremendous help; to Jim Peters, founder, STAR 1 Search and Rescue (1993), Ames, Iowa, and his German shepherd, Rocky—a special note of appreciation for the fascinating information regarding cadaver dogs; and to Chris Herndon, death investigation consultant for the intriguing details for my corpse-riddled plot. I am in your debt.

As always, any errors were mine alone.

About the Author

Photo © Lee Isbel of Studio 16

Kylie Brant is the author of thirty-five romantic suspense novels. A three-time RITA Award nominee, a four-time Romantic Times award finalist, a two-time Daphne du Maurier Award winner, and a 2008 Romantic Times Career Achievement Award winner (as well as a two-time nominee), Brant has written books that have been published in twenty-nine countries and eighteen languages. Her novel *Undercover Bride* is listed by *Romantic Times* magazine as one of the best romances in the last twenty-five years. She is a member of Romance Writers of America, its Kiss of Death Mystery and Suspense chapter; Novelists, Inc.; and International Thriller Writers. When asked how an elementary special education teacher and mother of five comes up with such twisted plots, her answer is always the same: "I have a dark side." Visit her online at kyliebrant.com.